THE LEGION OF THE LIVING DEAD:
THE COMPLETE CASES OF
MR. STRANG, VOLUME 2

THE LEGION OF
THE LIVING DEAD
THE COMPLETE CASES OF MR.
STRANG, VOLUME 2

CARROLL JOHN DALY

ILLUSTRATRATIONS BY
JOSEPH A. FARREN

POPULAR PUBLICATIONS · 2025

THE LEGION OF THE LIVING DEAD

Mr. Strang—Terror of the Underworld—
Fears No Odds and Asks No Quarter!

1

STRANG STRIKES

EXCEPT FOR THE cone of light over the desk, the room was shrouded in thick darkness. Shadows loomed there, shapeless and somehow ominous. The appearance of the man at the desk did little toward dispelling the curious tension in the air.

He was rather strange-looking—attractive and almost repulsive at the same time. Some persons—women especially—were intrigued by his stern features, severely cut black hair, thin, rather cruel lips. On the other hand, men most often noticed his eyes—the eyes of a dreamer, a poet, and an executioner—all combined.

At first glance, then, one would recognize him for a man with strong conflicting characteristics, a dual personality. And that was exactly the case. Even as he sat at the desk, busily writing in a large, black ledger—his handwriting was small and neat and shaded, almost perfect enough to be script type—the duality of his nature was apparent.

The ivory penholder in his hand was carved by some long-dead artist into a feathery filigree. The paper-knife at the edge of the desk blotter was smooth, ancient jade, fashioned by slim Oriental fingers holding a sliver of Damascus steel—when China was a young and robust nation! Those two treasures, and the priceless *objets d'art* in the

*With a shrill scream,
he leaped!*

showrooms beyond the black blot of the doorway identified Mr. Strang Cummings, merchant in works of art so
rare and so precious and so famous that only wealthy men
could buy his wares....

But the sharp overhead light also revealed the other facet
of this amazing man. At his left elbow, gleaming and ready,
lay two heavy, deadly automatic pistols of large caliber. And
the words which went marching in orderly rows across the
pages of the big ledger read:

> Edgar "Spike" Galucci. *Killed his cousin Giovanni for forty
> dollars. Nov. 8, 1935.*
>
> Samuel Sternheimer. *Extorted $130 from the widow O'Kelly,
> threatening to publicize her daughter's scandal.*

For this man who sat in a dark room chronicling crimes

Death was stalking into
that dank, dark cellar

which were unknown, for the most part, even to the police
of the city, was Mr. Strang. Mr. Strang, who had shaken
the under world of a metropolis and of a great state, until
the very mention of his name—the knowledge that he was
stalking his prey in the night—brought quaking terror
to the hearts of the huge criminal organizations. He had
bribed, threatened and killed to obtain his vast knowledge
of the half-world. He was turning that knowledge into a
powerful weapon with which to beat crime into the dust—
to eliminate it....

Slowly, deliberately, Mr. Strang laid the mellowed ivory
penholder on a jet pen rack which was a gift to Mr. Strang
Cummings from a famous Persian art collector. He blotted
his last lines of writing carefully, closed the ledger.

At the door of the room, there came a low knock. Mr.
Strang moved with the lithe grace of a panther. The cone
of light disappeared, leaving the room in utter darkness
now. There was the rustle of swift footsteps in the high-

piled Bokhara carpet, some indefinable, unidentifiable noise. Then the light returned, this time a soft, indirect lighting which flooded the entire room with warm, bright luminescence.

The ledger had disappeared from the desk. The two shiny automatics had vanished likewise. Mr. Strang Cummings, suave and placid, was standing in the center of the room. "What is it?" he called. And then, without waiting for an answer: "Come in, Jergens."

The door opened and a small, thin, elderly man stood there. He peered at Strang through thick-lensed glasses, said: "I'm frightfully sorry to disturb you, Mr. Cummings, but you said—"

Mr. Strang cut through the apology in such a way that the man could feel no offense. "Then Commissioner Barton has come? And his daughter?"

"Yes, sir."

Strang turned, slid aside a cunningly concealed panel in the wainscot, revealing a clothes locker there. He withdrew hat, coat, gloves and stick. "I will be with the Commissioner and his daughter immediately, Jergens."

"WE'VE GOT THIS parole racket licked—almost, Strang," Commissioner Barton was saying as the car weaved through traffic. "Licked, by thunder—or we will have it licked in a week. With your help, of course. With your help, especially."

He leaned back in the cushions, glanced past his daughter, Sheila, toward Strang. "Not that I approve of your methods. In fact, the less I hear about them, the better I like it."

Sheila looked seriously from Strang to her father. "What

do you mean? What's wrong with Mr. Cummings' methods?"

"I don't know a thing about them," the commissioner blustered. "Not a thing. But they might be extra-legal. Might be outside the law. Not that I'm saying so, understand?"

Strang was wearing an odd tight smile on his lips. "And being a strict old-time policeman, you're horrified if anyone steps an inch outside the law?"

"I'm not talking inches. Neither are you." Barton barked.

"In the old days, Commissioner," Strang drawled, "when you were a rookie—didn't you ever take a tough down into a stationhouse basement and use your night stick to beat some of the fight out of him?"

Barton's face flushed, but the honesty which had made him famous forced him to answer: "Yes, I guess I did."

"And it was pretty effective?"

"Damned effective," Barton agreed.

"But I daresay it wasn't in the Rules and Regulations of the Department, even then. It was outside the law, Commissioner. Just as now—"

"I don't want to hear a confession!" Barton yelled.

"Just as now," Strang went on calmly, "in a hypothetical case—in the case of our war against the vicious parole system, for instance—it might be barely possible that we should have to go outside the law."

"But I think Mr. Cummings is right, Daddy," Sheila said. "Fight fire with fire. Fight hot lead with more hot lead. You can't turn the other cheek when your opponent has no moral sense—no ethics."

"Hmmph!" snorted Barton. "Don't be getting crazy

ideas, Sheila." And then, with a sigh of relief that he could change the subject gracefully: "Well, here's the prison. We can send the crooks here, Strang, and be sure they won't get any mollycoddling. If there were only some way to keep them here—! Maybe when we get your bill through the legislature—!"

But Strang was not listening. He was staring through the window on his side of the car, staring toward the gaunt stone entrance to the prison. A sleek black limousine was parked at the curb, ahead of the Commissioner's car crossing from the door to the car, swaggering vaingloriously as he went, was a large fellow, too well tailored, too well barbered.

Commissioner Barton had seen the fellow too. "Damn!" he said. "That's Slick Larry Markus. Nine arrests—two homicide. Four convictions. Four paroles. This is the fourth. Why? Great Scott, *why?*"

A bitter smile had formed on Strang's lips. "Probably his grandmother is dying—or something."

Markus had swung into the limousine. It glided away. "Did you notice the chap at the wheel, Commissioner?" Strang asked.

"No. Who was it?"

"Looked very much like Mason's man Rudolph to me."

"Mason? That can mean only one thing!"

"What does it mean?" Sheila questioned. "Who is this man, Mason, Daddy?"

"Mason is the head of the parole racket," Strang explained grimly. "And Markus being freed means that someone is going to die tonight. Someone is going to be murdered, in spite of the fact that I know it and your father knows it—in spite of any precautions either of us can take...."

A PECULIAR GLARE—THE sheen of molten steel—was glowing in Mr. Strang's eyes as he threaded his way through the tables in the café to where Resa Kent was sitting.

She smiled, and the fire abated slightly in Strang's eyes as he noticed again—it was always new to him—how beautiful and how lovely she was.

But his first words showed how truly little her smile had affected him. "You're in danger," he announced bluntly, as he spread his napkin. "Martin Quinn is dead, but the evil he engendered has found a new champion, Steve Mason. The parole racket—the horrible business of freeing desperate criminals and charging them for their freedom to prey upon society—is again in full operation."

"But why am I in danger?" Resa asked. "No one knows that I had anything to do with Martin Quinn or Johnny Lester."

"They are dead," Strang pointed out. "They are dead and you and I are alive, together. Steve Mason is no fool. He will guess what that means."

"That I am the Lady of Death—?"

"And that Strang Cummings, art dealer, is really Mr. Strang."

For a long moment, the girl looked into the man's fiery eyes. "Sometimes, Strang," she said, "I wonder if you're human—and sane."

A suspicion of a smile lurked on Strang's lips. "Sometimes I wonder that myself, Resa. Sometimes I wonder if our plans to marry are not a huge mistake. For I shall not be a very good husband to you, dear. My mind is still that of the little boy who saw a paroled convict shoot his father down in cold blood. A little boy whose mind was somehow changed by the bullet which lodged so close to his brain. You should remember too, Resa. Your father was with mine, died by the same hand."

"I know," Resa answered softly. "But it is so long ago, now. And the man who did that murder is dead—punished. He can pay no more fully than he has already done. And the system which paroled him and produced him is finished too. The bill which you wrote—the bill which will free the innocent and keep the veteran criminals in prison—is to be submitted to the legislature in a few days."

"That's true."

"Don't you think, then, that perhaps it's time to let the doctors remove that bullet, dear? As it is now, it may kill you at any moment. The operation would be a simple one— safe, beneficial. Why don't you take your chance for happiness, with me?"

"I'm afraid, Resa. Not exactly afraid, but there are so many possibilities. Perhaps my bill will not be passed. Perhaps even now Steve Mason has plans for burying it in committee. Perhaps Mr. Strang must once more carry his war to the underworld in person.

"And that bullet. What would happen to me if it were removed? Would I still have the singleness of purpose that has carried this far?"

"I know," Resa whispered. "Perhaps you are right."

"I'm not sure, yet. Do you see?" Strang queried. "This afternoon, when I went with Commissioner Barton and his daughter to visit the prison, I saw Slick Larry Markus being released—paroled. Do you know what that means?"

The girl nodded. "He's a notorious killer. It can mean only one thing. Someone is to die."

"Right," Strang agreed. "My men are working, trying to get a line on his activities. They've had no success so far. But as long as men like Markus—"

He stopped. The headwaiter, a plump little Italian named Giuliano, had approached the table. "Signor Cummings," he said, after a discreet cough, "there is a telephone call for you. Shall I have an instrument brought to this table?"

"Please," answered Strang.

One of the waiters brought the handset, plugged it in at a wall socket. Strang picked up the instrument, said: "Yes?"

"Mr. Strang, is that you?"

"Yes."

"We have a line on Markus, now. He's casing the home of Elmer Helverson, the lawyer. You know?"

"Yes, I know."

"That's all."

"That's fine. Thank you, Kendricks."

He rang off, and the telephone was taken away again. "I'm sorry, Resa dear," Strang said, "but I have to go now. Take the usual precautions."

"I'm sorry too," the girl returned. "Don't worry about me. Take care of yourself. And good luck!"

SLICK LARRY MARKUS was well pleased with himself. Twelve hours ago, at eleven o'clock in the morning, Slick Larry had been in the prison shop, running the huge press which turned out metal license plates for motorcars. Now he had a loaded gun, a thousand dollars in fives, tens, and twenties, and a ticket on an express train for Kansas City. It was a big day in Larry's life.

Also, it was something like the turning-point in his career. No more of this fifty-now-and-fifty-when-he's-dead business. Slick Larry had made the grade. He was in the big-time now. The boss had given him the gat and the ticket and the money and said: "Get Helverson—tonight." That meant that when the newspapers got through howling, Larry could come back and do some more jobs. If things went wrong, all he had to do was to keep his mouth shut and take a vacation in the big house. Not much work to do there. Plenty to eat and drink and read—they even brought in a girl occasionally!—and then when the boss had a really important job, he'd get paroled.

So Slick Larry paid off the cabbie and walked up the walk to Elmer Helverson's house. He waited in the darkness of the entranceway long enough to draw on suede gloves and pull out the .45 automatic. Then he thumbed the doorbell.

There was a short wait; then the padding of bare feet crossed uncarpeted floor. Elmer Helverson, in an old-fashioned nightshirt, inched the door open. Markus hurled his strength against it, lunged into the hallway. The hand which held the gun was as steady as a rock. It yawned straight at Helverson's little round tummy.

"What—what do you want?" the lawyer asked. He was very nearsighted, and he squinted painfully in an effort to see.

"Where do you want it?" Markus growled. "You've crossed the boss for the last time, Elmer. This is the payoff."

"But—but—!"

"Where's the door to the cellar? I don't want to smear you all over the hall. Go on—to the cellar."

"But my wife! My two little girls!"

"Upstairs?" Markus snarled.

Helverson nodded numbly. Then: "My wife's ill."

"That's tough," the killer said with a smirk. "You should have thought of that when the boss asked you for a little favor."

Helverson, his brain paralyzed with terror, stumbled into the kitchen, at the end of the hall, unlocked the door which led to the cellar stairs. He groped his way down into darkness, pawed the air until he found the light cord hanging beside the furnace. He pulled it on.

Slick Larry was halfway down the cellar steps now, gun still aiming at Helverson. Silently, he descended to the cement floor. Silently he glared at the man he was going to murder.

Helverson was the first to speak. "Don't kill me!" he begged. A note of hysteria was in his voice. "Don't kill me. I've got money. I'll give it to you."

"I've got money," answered Markus. "Take it, rat!"

Gunfire racketed like thunder in the gloomy cellar. Smoke feathered from the snout of the gun. A red period was in the middle of the lawyer's forehead. His eyes were popping, blood-rimmed. His mouth was wide-open and red. And then he began to crumple to the floor.

Markus turned on his heel, fast. Footsteps had crossed the kitchen overhead. Bare feet started coming down the worn wooden steps. And then the woman's face came into view, flushed with fever and illness and horror. She didn't look at Markus; she had eyes only for the man lying in a spreading pool of blood.

Markus didn't bother to speak to her. He just pulled the

trigger again, twice. The woman pitched forward, sprawled across the body of her husband. "Damn!" thought Slick Larry. "Two kills for the price of one. That's bad business."

He turned, started up the stairs. And that's when he learned what really bad business it was. A form was standing at the head of the stairway, illuminated by the light behind Markus.

A man in black. With black, tightly combed hair. With black eyes which glowed in the murk like live coals. Markus knew that form. It was a legend in the underworld. There was no other like it. Mr. Strang!

Markus felt cold fingers clamping around his heart and brain. He snapped the .45 automatic up, triggered it wildly. He was still trying to fire an empty weapon when the bullet ploughed into his brain....

MR. STRANG CUMMINGS lay on his hospital bed and gazed vacantly at the white ceiling. Commissioner Barton was there, and Sheila, and Resa. Strang lowered his gaze, looked at them.

"I don't want to know how you happened to be in that house, Strang," the Commissioner was saying. "But I'll admit you did a good job."

Strang realized, detachedly, that Barton was speaking to him. But something was wrong. Something was wrong with his head. He untangled his arms from the smooth white sheets, explored his skull gingerly with slim, tapering fingers. It was swathed with bandages.

"What happened?" he asked. His own voice—a husky croaking—startled him.

Resa answered him. "You were wounded, dear. A bullet in the head. Very near the old one. A great surgeon. Dr. Le

May, removed them. Both of them. And a small portion of the brain. You will be all right now. All right, do you understand. Aren't you glad?"

Strang tried to understand. The bullet! The old bullet which had made him what he was! The bewilderment must have shown in his eyes.

Sheila must have seen his puzzlement and hurt. She said: "Leave me with him, just a minute, will you?"

A surprised expression crossed Commissioner Barton's face, crossed Resa's too. The Commissioner nodded, reluctant. Resa smiled a trifle bitterly. Together, they walked out of the room, leaving Sheila beside the bed. She leaned over Strang, looked a long moment into his eyes.

"This will not change you, Strang Cummings," she said, almost savagely. "It must not change you. The fight you started must be finished."

And it seemed to the girl as she looked down at him that he was shrinking from her gaze, retreating into himself. It almost seemed as if he were afraid…!

2

WASHED UP

RESA KENT SAT very erect behind the wheel. She stole glances at the man who crouched low beside her. His coat collar was turned up, his hat pulled far down, his dull, frightened eyes flashing from side to side. Occasionally he stiffened, started, clutched at her arm as a car, halted by traffic, slowed down beside them.

The man was Strang Cummings. He was also—only a few people knew both names—Mr. Strang.

The girl thought of the bullet that had been so close to his brain, imbedded in his head—of the modern surgery and the deft assurance of the noted surgeon who had removed that bullet and a section of the brain with it. Weeks—months—and now this. A man who had created immeasurable fear in others lived now in a world of fear of his own....

Resa turned her head slightly. She had to speak to him, and to believe that the thing was only temporary. Yes, she must actually convince herself that the man who would be her husband within twenty-four hours was not a coward. She said:

"Buck up, Strang. You have Doctor Le May's promise

that time will make you completely well. Just see that nothing jars your head—now."

"I'm not thinking of my head. I am thinking of my men—to whom I no longer give orders—no longer see, though they must wait for me day and night. And then Mason—Steve Mason. Oh, Resa! I could know every move he makes. It's you, Resa, whom he will kill. He doesn't know me—has never seen me. Go away. Take a long trip for several months. By then—"

"By then," Resa interrupted, "you would have succumbed to your own morbid thoughts.

"I promised Commissioner Barton to keep you on the job. Not even a week end for our honeymoon until Senator Bixby pushes your Parole Bill through. It's big, Strang! And you are the only man who could have done it. Your bill neither takes the right of rehabilitation from the deserving nor turns loose the vicious."

"I'm washed up," Strang mumbled, slumping lower in his seat. He clutched her hand. "Our wedding, Resa—it's madness—just a duty you feel you owe me! I'm not a man any longer—I'm a muddle. It would be better if I threw myself from some cliff—let that bone fragment crash through my useless brain."

"No!" Resa gripped at his hand now, her fingers growing colder and colder. "We'll be married at once. We'll go away together."

"I can't. I can't." Strang buried his head in his hands. "That would be admitting that I'm a coward. I have to stay. I have to fight it out here with myself—if I can."

She tried to laugh—rather unsuccessfully. She said suddenly, in spite of herself:

"I wonder, Strang, if you really love me?"

He answered at once, without feeling:

"If the brain I now have and the body I now own are capable of such an emotion, I love you." Blank eyes turned toward her; dull lifeless eyes seemed to study her—so different from the fire that used to be in them. While she drove through traffic, though she did not turn her head, she knew those lackluster eyes were there. She was not greatly surprised when he spoke again. "And you don't love me, Resa. You think of the name I might make, of your position beside me. Yours must be the hands that thrust me forward—yours the mind that rules."

"Yes, yes," she agreed softly. "I want the fulfillment of my ambition. You must do that for me!" Then trying to be reassuring, she added: "You can't sneak out of it, Mr. Strang!" She pretended she did not notice that he shuddered at the name. "I should be jealous of the Commissioner's daughter, Sheila, only that I know you are not capable of human emotions." She paused. "Except one—the power to hate."

STRANG CUMMINGS SMILED. He was thinking of Sheila Barton. A sort of mystery, that girl. It was only with her that he felt no fear, no pain—that constant gnawing pain in his head.

Resa Kent spoke as if she guessed his thoughts.

"She couldn't protect you, Strang—couldn't drive you forward as I can."

"No, no!" He almost screamed the words. "I never knew fear before. I liked to face it—always. I never minded pain. I enjoyed it because of my mission—the Parole Evil.

Don't you understand now, Resa? I'm afraid I live in deadly terror."

She bit her lip. He was getting more difficult to handle. Still—he could have a brilliant future—a great hidden knowledge. She said:

"You could tell me where that ledger is. The book that you filled with names and crimes."

"You told Barton about that book, Resa?"

"I hinted about a ledger which you had and he should have. You're not well, Strang. That book—"

"That book is where I have not been able to get it—have not had the courage to get it."

"But Commissioner Barton could send men and—"

"No. I am not man enough to go myself—But someday I must go—must go myself or—or—Resa! Ambition or no ambition, you are too fine a woman for marriage with me!"

They had reached the house of Senator Bixby. Resa Kent shut off the motor, locked the ignition, and, placing the key in her bag, opened the door and stepped out onto the street. Then walking around the front of the car, she reached the window behind which Strang Cummings sat and tapped on it to attract his attention. She knew, of course, his fear of stepping out onto the sidewalk at night without first looking up and down the block.

But what was there to fear now? Nothing except in the warped imagination of Strang Cummings. Commissioner Barton said a new parole racket was forming—far more dangerous than the first because of the influence and ruthlessness of the men who headed it.

Resa Kent's hand, half raised to tap on the "silly" bulletproof glass of that window, dropped quickly. Her mouth, opened to call to Strang behind the glass, remained open. But no words came. She instinctively felt the danger. Now, as she swung, she saw it—saw it and shrieked in the night.

Five men were there. Two of them seemed to have come from the little areaway before Senator Bixby's house. The other three had come from a big car that had drawn up ahead of her machine at the curb.

Resa saw them all plainly before they fired. Fired directly at her—through her—beyond her. Bullets crashed into her body—crashed into it as Strang Cummings peered through that bullet-proof glass with dull, horror-stricken panicked eyes.

Yes, Strang Cummings, looking through that window, saw it all. He saw the men, recognized three of them. Automatically, the other faces were stamped in his memory.

His brain was dulled. Beads of perspiration broke out on his forehead. The icy, moist hand with which he sought to open that door—for he did try to open that door—shook so that the fingers could not grip the handle.

Resa Kent was not standing on the sidewalk now. Her body was lying very still on the sidewalk. Three men stood above it, looking down, aiming their guns at that broken figure. They fired a shot apiece; three bullets that jarred the body as they struck.

Three men did that. Three men whose faces Strang Cummings saw distinctly, and recognized. Now they were moving slowly toward the door of their car. Maybe they saw Strang back in the darkness. Maybe they didn't. But they did raise their guns and fire. Clear bullet-proof glass was covered with spreading white stars.

Strang Cummings did not see so clearly after that.

He did not know that one of the men stretched his hand toward the handle of that door.

He did know that the door would open and that lead would pound into his body—pound and jar into his helpless, tired body just as it had hammered into Resa Kent.

Then a siren shrieked. Light flashed from the open doorway of the Senator's house. Lead was fired and that fire returned. Feet beat hard on pavement. A motor roared and a car raced away. It was then that Strang Cummings pitched to the floor of the car and lay very still....

AFTER A WHILE, a voice said: "Mr. Strang! Yes, by thunder, Mr. Strang, Commissioner! And he has fainted—fainted like a woman!"

Then another voice, which Strang recognized as that of Commissioner Barton: "Not Mr. Strang, Senator. We would have found Mr. Strang leaning against the car, blood-spattered and bullet-ridden, but surrounded by dead men on the sidewalk. The man lying there is Strang Cummings, art collector. You were right, Senator. My dream of turning a terror loose in the underworld, is over. He's washed up."

And finally, with a bitterness which Commissioner James Barton had not felt in years: "Yes, he's washed up—and to hell with him!"

3

AFTER THE MURDER

THE COMMISSIONER OF Police paced his living room, took his cigar from his mouth and pointing it straight at Senator Bixby, said:

"Six weeks since they buried the woman who was to be his wife. Three weeks since I looked him straight in the eyes and called him a coward. You didn't know him very well in those other days. His name struck terror to criminals, big or small. He hated them then—golly, how he hated them! And—" A frown and a pause. "Yes, he made me Commissioner of Police."

"Yes." Senator Bixby took off his glasses, twirled them on the thick black ribbon. "But we might as well face the thing now, Barton. I tell you we've got to have him put some place—sent some place."

"No!" Barton barked. "Not until we get that book. Don't you realize what that book means? He used many men. They died for him. Men who were doomed to die through disease; men who had no claim other than a few short years—even months—of life. And those men faced death recklessly, eagerly for him; faced it with the hope of meeting it. For they had Mr. Strang's promise that if they died by violence in his service, their wives, children, mothers—

any loved ones—would live free from poverty, would be taken care of by Mr. Strang. Mr. Strang," he repeated the words, a deep sarcasm in his voice and then, "But it is his book we must have, Senator. That ledger that holds so much information—the names and the misdeeds of the criminals which Strang collected over the years. The thing's an obsession with him. He's got the book where he's afraid to go and get it—and damn it, it almost seems he's more afraid not to go!"

The Senator coughed, nodded his head toward the girl who had entered the room.

"Well—?" Barton reddened slightly, turned and took both his daughter's hands. His smile was a twisted grimace. He said, "I hope, Sheila, you were your father's daughter tonight. A cop's daughter. This Strang Cummings is at ease only with you. Did—did you get him to tell you where the book was?" And, when the girl did not speak, "There was no other purpose in your seeing him!"

"From your point of view, no." The girl looked steadily at her father. "But I have no interest in the book. I am interested only in the man himself—the first Mr. Strang, whom I knew as much about as you did. I kept every newspaper clipping, every little detail pertaining to his work. The invaluable information, the limitless help he gave you! Why, the debt you owe him—that society owes him—can never be repaid!"

"Of course, my dear, of course." Commissioner Barton was coughing uncomfortably. "I am not ungrateful. But today—this is not the Mr. Strang. The man in that hallway is a coward. He—"

"That is not true," Sheila objected quickly. "Mr. Strang

is a sick man. Mentally sick." She went on before Barton
could interrupt: "You know it's the truth, Father. You are
the Commissioner of Police of a great city. You see crime
sweeping the city, rising to engulf you and the Department
and the people themselves. You are angry that Mr. Strang
is no longer able to help you. You miss him. You want
him. You need him. Well, you've got to stand alone. Strang
Cummings—Mr. Strang—is going away. He is going to a
little place upstate."

The girl's face brightened as she went on.

"It is on a high cliff; great rocks and rotted trees and
jutting branches lead straight down to the water below.
He's going to fight it out there—most of the time alone.
If he needs me, I will go and help him. Mr. Strang will be
leaving tonight. Will I bring him in now?"

SHE SWUNG, OPENED the door to the hall, said, "Mr.
Strang, please. Father and the Senator wish to bid you
goodby and wish you luck."

And the man who had been called Mr. Strang came
from that hall. His lips were blue and rough where his
teeth had bitten into them. His eyes were shifty, covering
the room in quick, furtive looks. His body was bent and
his hands rubbed together. His lips twisted when he spoke
the thought that haunted him:

"I didn't understand what the men were doing there—
not until after they—shot. I had no gun, understand. I felt
sort of sick and—and—"

Sheila Barton stepped forward, took his hand as she
looked defiantly at the hard, stern, unsympathetic faces of
her father and Senator Bixby. Then she said:

"You have nothing to explain, Mr. Strang. Nothing to

apologize for. Your courage and daring have been demonstrated too many times. It is simply that you are not well now. We all understand that."

Strang Cummings straightened, looked at the girl as she gripped his hand. Barton scowled, felt the touch of Senator Bixby's hand on his arm, smiled, said:

"We all get down at times, Strang. Country air the like will build you up. Now those men you saw—the men who killed Resa Kent. You called out their names when we took you from the car. Remember? Eddie Owen and Gunner Keen, Steve Mason's trigger men." And seeing the fear creeping into Strang Cummings' eyes again, he said: "Come, come, Cummings!" Barton could not bring himself to use the name "Strang" now. "Hell man! We need your testimony—at least a signed statement." Barton suddenly jerked a folded legal paper from his pocket. "Just sign and we'll let you know when we need you."

And when the cringing man drew back, he roared: "Good night, man! You wouldn't let them kill the woman who was going to be your wife and get away with it. When you have only to open your mouth to condemn them both?" Barton pushed his face close to Strang. "Come on—simply a signed paper and we'll make the arrest. It's all written here."

"No, no, no!" Strang Cummings looked at the girl. "They'll kill me and—"

Sheila Barton thrust herself between Strang and her father, turned and faced Strang, forced him erect.

"Tell them you're going away to think; that Mr. Strang never had to sign papers—that you'll make a decision later. Tell them that you're going away to forget."

And swinging suddenly around and pushing her father back across the room, she whispered hoarsely to him, "Do you want to kill him! Do you want him to drop dead here in the living room? Leave him alone! He's going away to find what he lost—what is missing in his head. Then he'll talk; then he'll tell. It would be murder to ask him now. Father, remember what he did—what he meant to you—to me—to our home."

Barton growled: "He only served himself by serving me." But Barton didn't move from the corner of the room when the girl returned to Strang Cummings, took his arm, spoke softly to him.

Barton's teeth came down on his lips too, but for a different reason. His hands clenched. Mr. Strang, eh? Mr. Strang Cummings! If he had him for ten minutes—even five—beneath that light in the basement below Headquarters, he'd have everything out of him.

Then he shook his head. He knew that he could very easily prevent Sheila from taking the cringing Strang from the house. He wouldn't admit it even to himself, but he wanted it that way. No, he knew he could never sweat or beat anything out of Strang Cummings. That broken man had meant something to him. Barton was incapable of doing anything to injure Strang Cummings—anything except talk. But he hated a coward, and anger made him see red.

The girl took Mr. Strang's arm, led him to the door. He said:

"Goodby for a while, Barton. Good-by, Senator. I must catch the ten-ten train." And after a dry tongue wet still dryer lips, "I'm going away to—to forget."

4

OF THE NIGHT

COMMISSIONER BARTON STRETCHED out a hand and took Senator Bixby by the shoulder. "Wait—don't leave yet!" He hesitated, smacked his lips, then directly faced the Senator. "What are you going to do about Strang's bill? They are still turning men out of prison by the hundreds—vicious, desperate criminals. Yes, I know the prisons are crowded beyond the danger point, that men must be released to make room for others. But they are not turning out the right ones. By thunder, Bixby, the system is more evil than ever!"

"More evil?" Bixby's eyes widened. "Good grief, Barton, the Parole Board can hardly be more careful! For the longer term prisoners, there is the deportment sheet of the Warden. It is taken directly from the reports of the guards, I know, but who else can supply it? Then a reputable citizen or firm must offer them employment. The thing's becoming an obsession with you, Barton—much like it was with Mr. Strang. Surely you wouldn't have all criminals imprisoned for life. Your job, Barton, is here in the city—even if you don't see it that way. Crime prevention. If you wouldn't fill our jails, we wouldn't have the problem of turning the wrong men loose."

"Crime prevention, of course!" Barton spoke irritably. "But the greatest prevention is quick and certain and lasting punishment. It's said that Steve Mason can spring any man he chooses in less than two years—even lifers. We've hardly got them safely convicted when they're back again!" He went on:

"Take Eddie Owen and Gunner Keen. Both paroled—both marked as killers by Strang—when he was really Mr. Strang. Couldn't you have used your influence to keep them in? They made good—from Mason's viewpoint—when they came out they killed Resa Kent."

Bixby's shoulders moved. "Strang said they did. Then he said they didn't. Switched his story. I wonder if it was fear of death which made him withdraw that statement—or if, in his distorted, fear-crazed mind, he thought they were the men—believed they were the men?"

Barton clutched at his head. "I don't know. I don't know!"

"We'll straighten things up without this changeable Mr. Strang. I've done my part about parole. I lent every bit of influence I have with the Governor to back Kirkman Billings—philanthropist, humanitarian, worth millions—as chairman of the Parole Board. No one could criticize him."

"I could," rasped Barton, "—and do—and have to his face."

"Surely not his honesty, nor his motives. You were for him, you know. He's set men free, of course, but certainly you can't suspect him of anything—except a great heart and a dull head. A dull head—"

The Senator paused. "I don't mind telling you, Barton, that I looked up a great many of the criminals he turned loose. They got jobs, they made good on them. The books of the company show that."

"Yes, I know." Barton scowled. "Strangely enough, a great many of these men knew or worked for—or were associated with Steve Mason."

"But you have nothing definite against Mason. I know him well. He makes money running night clubs. Not a laudable profession perhaps—yet hardly criminal."

"Senator Bixby," Barton said very slowly and seriously, "there is hardly a big criminal the police do not know. I am positive that Steve Mason is the most dangerous man in the city today—yes, in the whole state."

Barton spread his hands far apart. "I rose quickly to be Commissioner of Police. It wasn't politics. Politics couldn't even stop me. My daughter, Sheila, was right. Mr. Strang, the broken man you saw here tonight, gave me—yes, forced me into the position I now hold."

"Silly, that!" Senator Bixby switched his cane to his left arm as he put his right about the Commissioner's shoulders. "You're just what you always said you were—an honest cop. But you must also be diplomatic. Don't ride rough-shod over men who have studied politics all their lives. Don't try to reform a city over night. Let down the ropes a bit; give yourself a breathing spell. Drive crime off the streets, drive it from the public view. No criminal, no gambler, none of the slot machines and similar rackets wish to operate in the open if they can operate in private, undisturbed. Then, when things are right—when the time comes, and your knowledge has become evidence—strike! Take a politician's advice. Play ball with the politicians and they will play ball with you."

"Do you mean play ball with crime—criminals?"

"No, no, of course not! But don't run blindly into things. Don't crack down on people like Kirkman Billings—especially to the Press. Sit tight for a while. I'll build you up with Billings."

COMMISSIONER BARTON HAD turned from the open door when he swung back, pounded his right fist down on his left hand. "I don't have to be built up by anyone! I'll stand or fall on my own two feet—now." He was thinking of Mr. Strang when he added that now.

"All right. All right. But having powerful friends never hurt anyone. Good-night."

Senator Bixby nodded, consulted his watch and walked hurriedly down the steps. When he reached the sidewalk he turned right and crossing Center Street at a rapid pace, swung down the block and was almost running when he entered a drugstore.

He darted into a telephone booth. He got his party, spoke very quickly:

"The man once known as Mr. Strang," he reported, "is leaving on the 10:10 for upstate. That gives you time. Yes, I think you should attend to him yourself. Of course, he's useless, but what he leaves behind isn't. Whatever is in the ledger can't concern me personally or he wouldn't have trusted me, but it might concern you or one of the boys." And after a bit, "I'd like to know you were on the train yourself."

There was an interval of silence while Senator Bixby listened, and when he did speak, his voice was surprised, shocked:

"No harm to the man! I won't tolerate that. Of course, if

he won't talk alive, he can't talk dead. And if he doesn't talk, he won't ever tell where the cursed ledger is. You can't miss him. Watches all the time—furtive side glances. Light gray hat, black overcoat, tan shoes. A woman may or may not go to the train with him. That's fine. Be aboard the train first. It will stop at East Junction. That's right, Stephen. I'll leave everything to you."

And just before he hung up, "Be careful, Stephen. A severe blow on the left side of his head might kill him—might show that he died from natural causes. I don't know where he's going or when he'll return—if ever."

Senator Charles Philip Bixby hung up the receiver, pulled his hat down over his forehead and turning up the collar of his coat, passed out of the store and into the night. Odd business, he thought as he jerked down his collar and straightened his hat. Imagine his sneaking through the city like a criminal! He laughed at that thought, but it was not nice-sounding. He called the whole thing politics. And there was money in politics. Money that for a long time had been going to someone else.

Senator Bixby had a warm feeling in his heart toward both Barton and Strang Cummings. They had really showed him just how the whole thing could be done. And they had shown him just what a big man Mason was. But he in turn had shown Mason what a really big man looked like.

Yes, Senator Bixby was pretty proud of himself. Of course, he got around a bit, knew the right people, had accepted a favor here and there. But, in a few short months, to head the greatest organization in the underworld, if not a feat to be actually proud of, was certainly a remarkable accomplishment. Nothing wrong in it, understand? Simply politics. Wrong people got out on parole anyway. He lent his services at a price to see that the "right people" got out!

It was very safe, and very profitable!

5

A SINGLE SCREAM

SHEILA BARTON, AT Strang Cummings' request, drove him to the dark side street. She gripped both his hands as he climbed from the car, looked toward the dimly lit tunnel that led below the high office building to the railroad station itself.

"Strang," she said. "Mr. Strang! The world needs a man like you. You've got to look at the sea and the stars and fight it out alone."

"Sheila! Sheila!" His voice was husky; fearful. "I can't— can't go up there alone."

"You must," she replied. "You have just one person who believes in you. I am that person. You need only one other to believe in you—that is yourself. You must go!"

Strang Cummings looked up and down the street, ahead over the low buildings to the brilliant lights of the Bus Terminal two blocks away. Then he looked straight at the girl.

"There will be shadows there at night—and Eddie Owen and Gunner Keen. Yes, I saw them, Sheila. I was afraid and I lied to your father about that. I won't be able to forget."

"Then don't forget," she told him. "Perhaps that is not the way. You have plenty of time to catch the 10:10—

almost forty minutes. Get something to eat. Let me see you start and I'll leave." She gripped his hand.

Strang Cummings turned and looked at the long black hole of the tunnel with the single spaced over-head lights. Although the night was pleasant, he shivered visibly. He looked once at the girl, then turned quickly and started into the tunnel. He had hardly entered when he stopped. A full minute he hesitated. Then fear struck him. He felt that death lurked beyond the darkness. He always felt that way when he went any place. But this time he was right. Death was already hurrying across the city to the station— to the gate marked 10:10, and the train beyond that gate.

He stepped forward with determination—and stopped dead. Moving figures along that wall—both walls! Figures that made no sound on the stone walk. It was his head, of course. But he'd go on. Must go on. If he faltered tonight, the thing would beat him, would— And he suddenly turned and ran back toward the sidewalk, out onto it, onto the street. There was a figure there now. No shadow, but a real figure, for he heard the tread of feet; feet that suddenly stopped and made no sound upon the sidewalk.

Strang Cummings had difficulty in not running madly across the street—down the block. Then he looked and saw the figure, the blue of the uniform, the gold of the buttons, the steady uncompromising look in the officer's eye. Strang Cummings ran across the street, down it. Once he turned his head, but the uniformed figure still stood there.

Strang Cummings stared straight ahead. Right before him were the lights; the lights of the Bus Terminal. And he knew the truth then, as his legs gathered speed rather than lessened. The police officer, no doubt, thought that he was running to catch the upstate bus.

And the police officer was right....

IT WAS EARLY fall and if the weather had been brisk and sharp back in the city, it was cold and a biting wind swept the shore. Strang Cummings looked from his small, well-built cabin out to the heaving ocean beyond the great rocky cliff. It always seemed bleak to him even when the sun shone brightly.

Bleak too was his mind and his body—yes, and even his soul. He had not walked to the edge of the cliff to look down at the pounding surf on the rocks so far below. The temptation was too strong; far too strong for his meager will power. There was a way to end all the bleakness—to forget. He frowned. To forget what Sheila Barton had said to remember....

Two days before he had sent her a letter telling her to come. He knew to the minute when she would arrive. He was not sure when he wrote the letter if she would meet him or—or find him down there below the cliff. And somehow, he thought it was best that she should find him there.

Alone in the wilderness and he had no gun. Not that he forgot to bring one. There were plenty in his apartment. Guns that had burnt hot in his hands and had taken the lives of those not fit to live. But now! Guns—the very sound of guns—drove him nearly mad.

Half way between his cabin and the cliff he sat down upon a mound of earth. He leaned against the peculiar short growth of a tree which had long since died. Yet it was firm and hard and seemingly had life—much like the short, dead thick branches that grew from the side of the cliff itself.

From his pocket he drew a letter and read it again. Then he replaced it in the envelope. He wanted to be sure the directions for getting that ledger were clear. After reading it, Sheila could give her father the exact location. She'd find the letter, all right—find it there not far from the edge of the cliff under the stone. He had written her about that stone and the message awaiting her there.

It was all clear. The other letter which would tell her the truth was safe in his bedroom. He consulted his watch, backed slowly from the edge of the cliff a good hundred yards. There were a few hours yet—a good three hours anyway before the driver would reach the clearing over the rutted narrow road from the station.

For long hours he sat without moving. His thoughts were of Sheila. He looked toward the cliff—the sea beyond—and he knew the truth. He wouldn't do it; couldn't do it—yet. Sheila had believed in him. He'd talk to her again—once again.

Thoughts, thoughts, thoughts!

He looked up, jumped to his feet as two men climbed from a big, dirt-covered car and walked straight toward him. Sheila was not with them. There was no one else in the car, and the car had come from the opposite direction.

Strang backed away—toward his cabin. They came nearer. Strang swung to the right and walked toward the cliff, his feet quickening with their running feet. One of the men called out, shoved a hand beneath his armpit and Strang saw the gun!

It was not a rifle, such as a native might carry. It was a

heavy, black, snub-nosed automatic. And Strang knew that
what he had feared had actually happened. The past, that
he had tried so hard to forget, had caught up with him. He
heard the armed man shout his name, saw the gun rise,
even saw the tiny yellow-blue flash which turned into a
puff of smoke in the sunlight. Then he heard the roar and
was running madly toward the cliff.

They didn't gain on him. They didn't have to. They sepa-
rated, one running left, the other right. Strang laughed.
They thought that he would have to turn when he reached
the edge of that cliff, but he didn't. He didn't have to. The
excuse he had wanted had come. He was not taking his
own life now—he was saving the lives of others. For if he
were caught here, killed here by these men, the letter in
his pocket would fall into the hands of Steve Mason. Yes,
they were Steve's men—and they would kill him, of course.

What of the letter if he ran straight off that cliff, fell
crushed to the rocks below? They wouldn't try to climb
down. They couldn't at that point. His body would be found
later—when Sheila discovered him gone. The letter in his
pocket, the information where the ledger was, the book of
names that would open things wide in the underworld—
and in politics!

Strang Cummings was only fifteen feet from the edge
of that cliff when he knew fear again. Certain death was
ahead. Maybe life was behind if he offered the men information about that book. Perhaps Sheila was right and it
was only a sickness—a mental sickness that would pass
with time. But he didn't fool himself. He was a coward. He
was yellow. A few minutes ago he had planned his death.

Now he was unable to run wildly out, fling his body far into space, as he had planned.

No, he'd live. He'd— And Strang Cummings knew another truth, as he dug his feet into the ground, slid toward the end of the cliff, felt the dirt and rock give. It was too late to change his mind!

Just a single shrill scream, and he was over the edge, disappearing into space…!

THE TWO MEN far behind ceased their advance upon the cliff and came together. The taller of the men shrugged his shoulders.

"That's that, Owen," he said. "We laid lead in his girl friend and chased him right into hell. Now what did Steve go to the trouble to have Ike trace him from the bus and then send up us here?"

Gunner Keen said sarcastically:

"That lad was at one time the terrible Mr. Strang. He's got a book or some dope or something. The boss wanted to pull it out of him."

"It wouldn't have taken much persuasion to get all a yellow rat like that had. Funny. He rubs himself out."

"Maybe not funny to Steve," said Gunner Keen. "I can't just see him laughing. He wanted him alive."

Owen moved his shoulders, said: "A few months ago you could have raised fifty grand along the Avenue for Mr. Strang's death. Now what?"

"Let's have a look at the body."

"What for?" Owen looked up and down the cliff, along the far distant road that stretched beside the bottom of it. "Just to see if it floats?"

"Listen, fat-head," Gunner Keen pounded a finger

against Owen's chest, "Steve will want to know that we saw the body."

"Okay." Owen stepped forward indifferently and started toward the cliff. "We seen him go, we seen the rocks, and we seen the ocean all before. He's deader than hell and—" Owen stepped, gripped his companion by the arm, pointed far down to his right in the opposite direction from which they had arrived.

A car was making its way slowly along the shore, heading toward the steep climb to the top of the cliff, then the winding, twisting, rutted road to the cabin. One figure, two figures, or five figures—? It was impossible to tell at that distance, and in the glare of the sun, how many occupants were in that car.

"Come on!" Owen pulled Keen far back, crouched slightly. "It's ten to one they didn't see us. Let's beat it along. Hell! Here's a guy does a high jump for us and we open ourselves up to being accused of throwing him to his death."

The two men ran back toward their car, their speed increasing as they neared it. It took Owen less than a minute to swing that car, back it off onto the hard rock soil and shoot back the way in which they had come. "If they see anything," he said, "it'll be just dust."

If they had waited a few minutes longer or perhaps not raised so much dust as they sped away, they might have seen that the old touring car that bounced up the road behind them was occupied by a single figure. And that figure was a girl.

Sheila Barton stepped out of that car and walked straight toward the cabin. It was very silent, just the distant beat of the surf upon the rocks—a roar that she had grown accustomed to on the drive from the station, and now it seemed to accentuate the silence rather than lessen it.

Sheila was almost running when she reached the cabin, pushed at the door without first knocking. She was running, too, when she came out. Then she stood still, looked toward the cliff, the white caps on the water, then walked slowly forward. She was right. It was sickness— just sickness. A sickness that she could not cure, that only Strang might have cured—and he had failed.

She moved faster now toward the cliff overhanging the sea. She hurried on, running, faltering, stumbling slightly. It was not like her to act that way. She was always so calm, so sure of herself, so able to meet any situation. But now—she actually was unsteady as she ran and pictured the height of that cliff, the jutting rocks, the great stones with the waves beating on them below.

He would be dead, of course—even before the water came, got him, sucked him in, tossed him back and forth across the rocks. There was no use to look. It would be too hard to look. She could drive back to the nearest town and get a man—many men.

Then she came to the rock, close to the edge of the cliff. She could have stepped a few feet further and looked over. But she didn't, couldn't then. She was relieved at the sight of the rock. The letter he had written her about—something very important in that. She had thought about the book. Now—it might—it—

And it wasn't there! Nothing was there. She felt in the softness of blacksoil beneath the heavy stone. He hadn't put the letter there. Why? She came to her feet, looked out over the ocean. Perhaps—perhaps he had not "done it" yet.

Sheila braced herself, stepped to the edge of the cliff and looked over. Nothing but rock and water beneath. Nothing but the beating waves. Could they have so soon carried him out to sea? But not that treacherous coast. It caught its victims, pounded them ruthlessly, but always gave them back to the land from which they came.

If she knelt down, held tightly to the jutting roots she might see better, might— And she saw him; saw him plainly. Her mouth opened to scream, but no scream came. Then she fell to her knees and buried her head in her hands....

6

THE RUB-OUT

THE GARAGE WAS dirty, ill kept and damp, yet the heavy doors could slide quickly and quietly back. The freshly painted, expensive car stood just inside those doors. Joe Parelo leaned against the hood and spoke to the man who came out of the cubbyhole of a small dimly lit office.

He said:

"The paint job looks good. It would never be recognized as a stolen car." He poked a finger against the manager's chest. "It's a rub-out tonight—Kirkman Billings, head of the Parole Board. Then Steve Mason's own man will head that Parole Board."

The manager picked his teeth with his grimy nails, said:

"Here comes the boys now. Expert gunmen both of them. Mason sure springs the right lads for the right jobs."

Two men entered that garage from the rear. Their faces were cruel—but white; the deadly white of the prison pallor. Parelo said to the first of the two as he opened the rear door of the car:

"Ever seen them things before, Fink?" And when the man leaned in and lifted out a Thompson machinegun. "Well, you know the racket. I'll drive," and to the other man, "There's the mate to that Tommy for you, Dill. Okay, climb in."

Fink climbed into the rear without a word. Dill paused on the step, his hand on the door as Joe raced the motor. He finally said:

"It ain't the job that bothers me, Joe. It's the smell afterwards. This Kirkman Billings is a big name—friend of the Governor."

Joe shrugged his shoulders. "No man's too big to take a load of lead. Anyway, this is the job you were sprung to do. You were told that when you were pulled out of stir. If it wasn't for Mason, you'd be rotting in there for life. Here's your chance to pay him off—after that you'll make money. You're alibied. Mason has the city in his pocket now. Let's get going!"

Joe shifted silent gears. The big garage doors swung open. The car glided into the shadows of the street. The men in that car were silent for a long time. Then Dill in the back let down the window.

"Hell," he said. "Mason or you, Joe, must have planned this ride to the second. It don't look like we'll have to drive around no blocks to kill time. Let's see—this Billings comes down his steps and walks straight down the block toward us—nothing fancy about him—one of the people, eh?" He chuckled, and suddenly, "There he is now—coming straight toward us! Hell, not that slow, Joe!" He raised his machine gun, watched his friend's gun lift too. "About fifteen miles an hour should do the trick. We'll put a hundred slugs in him—me and Fink. Eh, Fink?"

Fink nodded, crouched low. The deadly noses of two

guns were almost, but not quite in line with the open window. Fink said:

"We'll give it to him coming and going—about fifty feet ahead, on a direct line—then fifty feet behind. It's an open and—"

Both guns jarred up as they neared the little man who walked so erect, his brief case beneath his arm, his steps as nimble as a man half his age.

And the blast came. But not from the guns in that murder car, Two men had stepped from a doorway and running into the street directly in the path of the slowly moving car had suddenly and without warning opened fire.

Dill cursed, switched his Tommy-gun, hesitated for the fraction of a second. It was the appearance of those two men that got him. One was almost staggering on his feet, had difficulty in keeping his balance—yet, his hands were all right, his fingers too, for heavy forty-five caliber revolvers were belching lead from both those hands.

Dill closed his finger tightly on his machine-gun, felt the sudden jar in his own body as the man in the street dropped under his accurate rain of lead. He saw the other man, too, as he turned his gun, saw plainly the sunken cheeks, the almost hidden eyes far back in his head; saw him twist and turn, then bounce into the air as Joe swung the car and struck him.

Maybe he was dead before Joe swung that car—maybe he wasn't. Dill didn't know. He only knew that there was a terrific pain in his head—blood running down his face.

The car swerved, jarred, leaped forward and went dashing down the street. But there was another jar; a jar that sent Dill to the floor; to the floor with a body on top of him—a dead body—the dead body of Fink.

Very slowly, almost indifferently Dill twisted from under that body. Then, just as slowly, he laid his head on that dead shoulder. Dill was very tired—and a dead man didn't care how he laid.

7

GREASING THE WHEELS

STEVE MASON WAS a big man with broad shoulders. He was in his early thirties and had come a long way in the racket. As a younger man he moved fast, shot faster and blasted his way up with gun-fire during the later days of prohibition. After that, he became more cautious. His name was known now; he didn't have to use a gun so much.

Steve was one of the few big racketeers who didn't believe in luck and didn't toss his money away on gambling tables. He found it wiser to give it away to some coming politician who had to grease the wheels on his way up. Steven Mason believed in using plenty of grease.

Now, as he sat behind his desk back of the Black Knight Club, he looked up at his closest associate and perhaps crudest killer of all his men. He said to Rudolph Weber:

"Send in the Senator. Give him a big blow, lots of respect—and set some lads who look important at the choice table outside—close to the girl show. I'll want someone to throw out of the best seats for him. He laps up that hooey."

Steve Mason's broad, thick lips parted and his shoulders bent forward. Fish-like, filmy eyes opened wider in what was meant for a hearty welcome, as hearty as Mason could make it.

"Sit down, Senator, sit down!" He beamed the words, pulled out a great leather chair, shoved it beneath the Senator, opened a box of expensive cigars. His smile broadened, but he withheld a wisecrack when the Senator, unable to shake off earlier habits, gathered up three or four cigars.

"Well," he said. "What's in that keen brain of yours, Senator?"

The Senator puffed up his cheeks, moved his glasses. Steve Mason flopped into the seat behind his desk.

"Politics," said the Senator with pompous dignity, "is a great burden upon the man who wishes to serve the public. To serve the public honestly, one high in the archives of the state must at times resort to little tricks of the political arena rather than be a victim of those tricks."

Steve Mason nodded and looked Senator Bixby straight in the eyes for the next five minutes, yet he did not hear a word. Then he picked up the finishing sentences. The Senator was saying:

"This Mr. Strang, and Commissioner Barton, first showed me how easily one might take advantage of the Board of Pardons and Parole. And I met you, Stephen, and we decided on a little partnership."

This was Steve's cue to bang his hand upon the desk.

"Partners!" He laughed aloud. "You showed me a boss that was a boss." And tapping the ends of his fingers together, "There's this Marty Henderson—he's a good boy. I'm set on getting him out. The Board meets Thursday."

The Senator shook his head.

"We must not," he said pompously, "kill the goose that

lays the golden egg. Henderson's past is simply scandalous. I won't say he hasn't reformed, but Billings' secretary, Jackson, is rather botching things now—a thorough man."

"Henderson's past doesn't count," Steve Mason snapped. "He's set for a spring all along the line. The guards will give him a fine record. The Warden or his deputy can't be reached, but we won't bother there. Mortimer Jackson, Mr. Billings' secretary, will look Henderson up and be surprised at his clean record—and the unfortunate association with bad company that got him into his little murder jolt."

"But I thought you were going to see that Jackson would leave town for a better job?"

Steve Mason was thoroughly familiar with the Senator's pretended, childlike belief that he never knew of a man being killed.

"Jackson will get a better job," Mason said. "He'll stay with Billings, but he'll work for me. That's settled."

The Senator coughed. "Entirely settled?" There was more than a simple question in his voice.

Mason frowned. When it came to pretence concerning money, the Senator had none of it.

Mason watched the Senator for a long moment. Then he came slowly to his feet and leaned across that desk.

"If you want to beat around City Hall when we talk, go ahead. But I'm going to give it to you straight from the shoulder. It was all right for a time slipping you a few grand here and there—and the parole racket was easy money with you handling Billings, head of the Parole Board. But that's out now. You and I are through with that. We've got something big—a chance for us—for you to control this entire state. Millions where we had thousands before. Power, Senator—power for you!"

He watched the Senator's lips close and open with a silent smack. He watched the greed in the man's eyes, on his whole face. Mason spoke now very slowly and clearly— making each word count:

"First you're going to head the Parole Board. Do you know what that means? Not the small scale business we do now, when each man gives us a percentage of his earnings after release. It means that each man—that is each man worthy of our attention—pays ten percent of his earnings before he ever goes to jail. A sort of an insurance. It will not be hard to collect. The underworld is used to paying for protection and here is the best they can get. The assurance that when they go to prison—they won't have to stay. And it doesn't mean simply gunmen and swindlers and high-class confidence men. It means the big boys with big rackets—the politicians and even brokers and bankers and lawyers and men with secrets—secrets that that will be yours.

"Other men have controlled entire states. Other men have made laws that suited them and disregarded those that didn't. You're the logical man for it, Senator. You're the only man fitted for the job. Senator Bixby, you're to be the next Governor of this state!"

SENATOR CHARLES PHILIP Bixby toyed with his glasses, jerked down his vest. He had had such thoughts—had them still—but they were a fleeting something that he only grabbed at, but didn't expect to catch. Now—Mason— He coughed once or twice, said:

"Really, Stephen—really! You flatter me. Maybe I do not have the brain and wit of a Lincoln or the—"

"We won't need speeches," Mason snapped in. "We'll need action."

"I see." The Senator cleared his throat. "First I head the Parole Board—you told me that before. If it wasn't for Billings—Billings being so strong and healthy and apt to live for so many years—I could have gotten that appointment."

Steve Mason grinned. "Billings' health is not as good as you believe. He won't live very long." Mason took out his watch and looked at it. "A month—a week—perhaps only a few minutes—just a few minutes longer."

"What—what do you mean?" The Senator didn't mean to speak those words. Oh, he wanted the answer to the question, but he wanted it without asking the question.

"I mean—" Mason paused, lifted the ringing phone, said gruffly: "All right—talk."

The voice on the other end of the wire evidently did talk. Twice Mason opened his mouth to speak, but changed his mind. His eyes grew narrower; his skin tightened over his forehead. He finally said into the mouthpiece:

"Both Fink and Dill dead, eh? No, no—wait." He sat looking toward the ceiling for a full minute, then he said into the mouthpiece, "No—we can't afford to have those bodies of paroled men found yet. You've got to bury them deep or take them out beyond the three-mile limit and sink them."

Steve Mason dropped the phone back. He didn't inquire if Joe was wounded or not; he didn't congratulate him on being alive. He wasn't interested in that. He said either to the Senator, to the wall, or to himself:

"Two of Mr. Strang's men—two men who not only didn't care if they died, but seemed to want to die." And suddenly to the Senator, "Senator! Mr. Strang is behind this—Mr. Strang still controls these men."

"Ridiculous!" The Senator shook his head. "Mr. Strang went away for his health. What have you heard about that?"

"Nothing—nothing." Mason got up and paced the room. "They turn up every place. There seems no end to them. Shoot one to death and another takes his place. Shoot him and—"

"You're afraid of these men?"

"Fear and common sense are two different things. The thing's unnatural, uncanny—unbelievable. There was Dutch Fritz—a careful man—never a fool with a gun. And a man walks up to him—right smack on the Avenue in board daylight. He puts a gun against Fritz's stomach, laughs, and they both died there on the street. A dozen people heard that laugh."

Senator Bixby shook his head.

"They're paid to die," he surmised solemnly. "But you don't have to worry, Stephen. They have been acting without their leader, I imagine—acting in hope of seeing him again." Another cough behind his hand and the Senator continued. "I was hoping to hear something about—er— Mr. Strang's health and—"

The phone again.

Steven Mason grabbed it up. A minute later he put it down.

"It's Strang." Even Mason, who prided himself on not showing emotion, made no attempt to conceal that emotion now. "He's dead—deader than hell at the bottom of a cliff." And laying both his hands on the Senator's shoulders, "I don't mind telling you he bothered me. Now—the last obstacle that stood between you and the governorship of this state has been removed. From tonight on, it's you and me—and power."

Power! A girl, too, thought of the same word—thought of it as she stared down with dilated pupils at the body of a man—an unconscious man who hung so perilously on dead branches less than twenty-five feet beneath her. Power. It was in every muscle of Sheila Barton's body; in her mind: in her steady feet that swung over that cliff. Mr. Strang was not dead—was not going to die. Or if he did die, she too would die, with him.

Power. That was what she thought. That was what she saw. For now as she gazed fearfully down, Mr. Strang's eyes opened. Days, weeks—months flashed back. She was looking into malignant, blazing globes of hatred. Fires so long dead were burning again. It was not Strang Cummings she saw now. It was the man of vengeance. The fearless man who hunted and killed in the night. She hesitated. Was this what she wanted? Had she the right to turn this killer of men loose in the city again? Her lips set grimly. She hesitated no longer. Only one question now. Could she reach him in time?

Mr. Strang was alive; alive in born body and soul. The black soul of death....

8

MR. STRANG'S BOOK

SENATOR CHARLES PHILIP Bixby sat back in his chair, his thumbs rested in the armholes of his vest. He regarded Steve Mason with a kindly, fatherly air. So he was to be Governor of the State, eh? Mason would put him there, but Mason wouldn't be his boss. No one would rule him. No one would tell him—once he was in.

"So you like the idea, eh?" Steve Mason patted the Senator on the back. "And you won't forget the boys that put you there—won't forget your old friend, Steve Mason?" Mason's laugh grated, his blue eyes narrowed. "No, you won't forget Steve Mason." And after a full minute, "About this Marty Henderson being released by the Parole Board—you'll see Billings. We need Henderson out, Senator. And there's thirty grand right smack on the line for his release." He raised his hand as the Senator's eyes sparkled. "Nothing in it for you, Senator. The organization needs that money too badly. It's sort of your campaign fund. You see, Mr. Strang's men have been gumming up most of our plans; plans that meant money. Now that Mr. Strang is dead why—"

"Yes, yes—" Senator Bixby pulled at his black ribbon. "Marty Henderson, eh? Someone must want him out pretty badly—that's a lot of money."

"That's right." Steve nodded, grinned broadly. "An old uncle—very rich." And with an emphasis that Senator Bixby did not understand at the time, "An uncle who is a judge."

"Commissioner Barton won't like it, Stephen. He'll make trouble. He never expects to see Henderson on the streets again—alive."

"And he won't." There was a sudden downward thrust of Mason's head. "Marty Henderson is going home to die with his uncle." And when the Senator opened his mouth in surprise, "Want to know the details?"

"No, no—!" Senator Bixby said quickly. "I know anything you manage will be quite honorable, Stephen. But what of this bad report on Henderson—from Billings' secretary?"

"I'll attend to that report." Mason shrugged his shoulders. "Mere detail. And Billings will be for anything that Barton is against."

The Senator leaned far forward, his yellow-gloved hands clasped about the head of his cane. "This book of Mr. Strang's. Now that he is dead—did you get it—? There are names in that book—facts, too, I understand. Nothing about me, of course, for Mr. Strang trusted me. But there are names that might embarrass you—or your friends."

"No." Mason hesitated. "I haven't got it yet. But I think I know where it is—at least where we might get a line on it. Interested?"

The Senator was interested. Although his name was not in that book, he knew that the lowest criminal—even one who did not know where his original orders came from, might involve a criminal a little higher, who to save himself might involve another—and so on up the line to "Stephen" himself. Yes, he knew the story of a chain and its weakest link. And the chain of crime with its links of death—so strong, so well welded together—could fall to pieces if one man wanted to live badly enough to turn on another. It was Stephen Mason who held together this vicious chain of crime, and the Senator liked to look on himself as the man who held the key that could lock that chain leaving himself outside. He had been very careful—very careful indeed.

The Senator said "Tell me about the line you have on this book."

"I've been going back into Mr. Strang's past even if I never saw him. There was a fence who worked for Strang—Simon Becker. He was killed, but a brother came on from Philly, took over his establishment. That book will be worth millions to the guy who knows how to use it. I couldn't come straight out and ask this Aaron Becker about it—only hint around. Simon Becker's old shop would be the natural place for Strang to have kept this book hidden.

"Now—I have thrown Aaron Becker a lot of business, tossed him some nice stuff. Wanted him to make money and move downtown. He did. After he left, I was with the boys when they tore the old place apart. The book was not there."

"Yes?" The Senator was disappointed.

Steve Mason went on. "I have a feeling Mr. Aaron Becker located this book before he moved. He's smart—too damned smart. A guy called Lorey shook down Rudolph Weber for a single grand. Lorey is a hop-head, been hanging around Aaron Becker's shop. The information Lorey had on Rudolph he saw Becker copy out of a book."

"And Rudolph paid the money? You permitted that?"

"Sure. I encouraged it. Even put up the dough. We trailed Lorey to Aaron's shop." Steve shook his head when the Senator voiced an opinion about the shop. "No, it's not a pawnshop. Aaron is wise—very wise. He sells vases, rugs, antiques of all kinds. Yep, that junk he has in his store pays his rent and shows up well on his income tax return. He's one receiver of stolen goods who doesn't pay out good money to the cops. He doesn't have to. Yep, we permitted that, even slipped Lorey—that's this hop-head—a couple of grand."

"That's not your way, Stephen!" There was half reproach, half unbelief in Senator Bixby's voice. "Very commendable to the unfortunate drug addict, but hardly your way."

"What the hell!" Steve Mason started and stopped. He had forgotten for the moment how he had to handle the Senator; talk around things, never directly at them. In the racket, Steve liked to be all business. He was not interested in the Senator's pretended virtues.

He said: "Lorey did see a book. We don't know that it's Strang's book, of course. But Lorey is hanging around that shop, doing odd jobs there. If he spots that book, even discovers it's in the shop—then we'll crash down."

"Couldn't you put pressure to bear on—this Aaron? Your influence—your persuasive power over men?"

STEVE MASON'S EYES narrowed. Torture, eh? Of course that was what the Senator meant. But he never expressed his suggestions in clear concise words. In a way, Steve had to admire the man. He could talk one way and mean another, yet drive home his meaning with a meat axe.

"I don't know for sure he's got the book," Steve explained. "Aaron's a good man. Why antagonize him if I'm wrong? I can use a man like that plenty. That book is worth a million to us—to any guy. If it pops up in wrong hands, if Barton got it, it would make him the strongest Commissioner the city ever had. I want to see a lad now." And as he pressed the bell, "You will want to be seeing the girl show. It's safe for you to come here. It's the most popular and highest class place in town. Men like you coming here make the club big—important."

Senator Bixby straightened. He wanted to know more about Strang, but he wanted Steve Mason to tell him. Now, he looked at Rudolph there in the doorway, heard Steve say:

"The best table for the Senator. Rudolph. No, not just a front one—the very best, in the center, close to the girls."

"I'm sorry." Rudolph's voice was apologetic. "Very prominent people occupy that table tonight."

"Nonsense!" Steve Mason came to his feet, placed an arm around Senator Bixby's shoulders as he walked toward the door. "Senator Charles Philip Bixby honors us tonight, Rudolph. No one is more important. Be nice to the people, but they must go, under the circumstances."

"Now, Stephen, now, Stephen!" The Senator's smile was very broad. The club was a popular one. He was a popular man. Someday—well— Once again he thought of his earlier ambitions to be Governor of the State. But he paused at the door, waited until Rudolph slipped into the hall beyond, then turned to Steve Mason.

"I was wondering about this Mr. Strang."

"So was I. You never told me actually who he was in real life—though you know."

"I don't mean that. I don't mean that," the Senator said

irritably. Even the feared Steve Mason bowed before him, recognized his power, his brains. And it all came out of the Senator at once, "My soul, man! What became of Strang? What happened? You're sure he's dead?"

"Sure." Mason moved his shoulders indifferently. "And you don't have to sit up tonight and wrestle with that great heart, that magnificent conscience of yours. I sent two boys up to talk with him." And with a sneer, "The ex-Mr. Strang was no good—a yellow rat. He did the Dutch act, jumped to his death. Crashed down on the rocks below."

Senator Bixby shook his head; his bulging eyes rolled.

"It's too bad—really too bad! He might have had fine things in him if he had overcome his criminal—his vicious criminal tendencies. I really liked him, Stephen. Liked him a lot. You say he jumped over a cliff?"

"That's right, Senator—and there is no cause to worry. Two men saw him do it. Gunner Keen and Eddie Owen. They came back to the city by plane and went right to a job I put them on, watching for that hop-head Lorey's signal that he has located Aaron Becker's hiding place for that book. They both carry heavy guns and will—"

The Senator cut in: "I'm not interested in that—not interested at all. So Strang committed suicide? Dreadful, dreadful!" Senator Bixby wanted to know enough, but not too much. He felt that he controlled a great organization, but was not a part of it—would not be a part of it if anything went wrong. He had protected himself well. He had even invited Barton to join him at the Black Knight Club that very evening.

"I'll see you later at the table," he told Mason. "I've

invited Barton over. We've become quite good friends—almost allies, you know."

"As long as you're allies, that's fine. I'll drop in and see him. And, Senator—"Mason coughed, winked and twisted his lips—"that little girl—the third on the right. She was speaking about you. Wanted to meet you. Her name's Vera."

The Senator wrinkled his forehead, played with the ribbon on his glasses. He pretended to forget that he had spoken about her to Mason.

"Vera—dark? Oh, yes, yes—a nice little girl. So she wants to meet me, eh? We must take an interest in youth, Stephen. They need the encouragement and it keeps us young. I might take her out some night." He eyed Mason shrewdly. "Just a quiet little supper up at my apartment. She'll like that of course?"

"She's hoping for it." Mason ignored the question in the Senator's voice. He poked the Senator in the ribs, said to himself, "If she don't, I'll knock all her teeth down her throat." Though he didn't like it, Mason couldn't do anything about that. When it came to women, the Senator was stubborn—no one changed his mind. And the dark-haired Vera was not easy to handle. When Steve first spoke to her, she had made remarks about the Senator that both amused and annoyed Steve. Annoyed him, yes, for Senator Bixby was a real politician with a front that had fooled the Avenue for years—still did for that matter.

Why some of the big boys hadn't grabbed him up before, Steve could only guess at. And his guess was that the Senator's front had even succeeded in fooling those same big boys.

There wasn't a person who even suspected the criminal

association of Steve Mason and Senator Charles Philip Bixby. Mason frowned slightly. At that, the Senator wasn't so dumb. He could drop from under any minute and leave Mason holding the bag. Could now—but later?

9

PAROLED TO KILL

THE SENATOR GONE, Steve Mason returned to his desk, lifted the phone and said: "Good evening, Alice. Get me the Trafalgar Hotel. Ask for Mr. George Stamp."

After he had gotten his number and been connected with the room he said: "Benny Ries there, George? Okay, put him on."

He hummed for a few minutes, and then: "Hello, Benny? This is Steve. Sure, Steve Mason. I've been thinking it over. It'll come high as 'dusting offs' go, but it's a natural. Fifty grand." He stuck twenty thousand dollars extra into his own pocket without even a thought of the price he had told Senator Bixby.

Steve Mason made a face and held his hand clapped over the receiver for nearly a minute, then he said:

"Judge still bothering you, eh? Going to make it hot for you? Oh, that hot? No, Benny, I can't cut it a penny. But I can make it so you'll never be suspected. Damn it, man! Will you listen? I tell you it's a natural. Yeah, a lad coming out on parole. A lad who once threatened to kill the Judge the very day he was released. Of course, they've forgotten that now, but they'll remember it after the killing. You can't possibly be suspected. You never even met this gun.

Sure—I'll have to have the cash now. Just send someone on with it."

There was some talk back and forth after that—"my word," and "your word." Steven finally said: "If it's a bust, you get back the jack. But it won't be a bust. It's best that you don't even know his name. Just be around places— when we make the date. Everything will be handled from this end—except the money. Sure, he's an experienced man." A low laugh. "Don't try and run my business for me, Benny. Of course I expect he'll be shot to death. If you own half the cops in district—as the Judge is going to prove publicly that you do—my man should be shot to death in a courageous, but futile attempt by the police to save the Judge's life." And just before he hung up the receiver, "Cripes, Benny, he never even heard your name. You'll come out of it as white as Mary's lamb."

Steve Mason hung up the phone, started toward the door, turned back and picked up the other phone that was ringing.

"Oh, hello, Gunner!" he said. "What's the story?" And after a bit, "You got the signal from Lorey? This Aaron Becker has a room under the summer house in back, eh? Sure, I'll—" He paused, looked at his watch. "I can't be there, Gunner. I can't. Commissioner James Barton will be here. Don't dust off Aaron unless he gets really mussy. I like his work. I wish I could be with you. I know—I know you will."

Steve Mason listened to some more talk from Gunner Keen about someone who had been digging around in Simon Becker's old quarters further uptown. No, he didn't think it was a cop. Yes, it might have been Barton—or it might have been a lad from the Meyers mob.

"Either way you look at it, it's bad," Steve told him. "Someone else has the same idea. The book would cost us plenty if the Meyers mob got it—plenty money. And cost us plenty in health if Barton got it. You got to get the book tonight. You got to, Keen. Aaron's death or not—horrible or not— If the book's there, I want it."

Keen finished speaking and Mason laid down the phone.

Keen and Owen were great boys for a knock-over. Boys who were satisfied with their jobs—with the handsome hand-outs. Never squawked for more money, just went out and did their trick. But why should they squawk? He'd be handing them twenty grand to split if they got the book tonight.

They were killers who never failed. No, he wouldn't take a hundred grand for the two of them. Take tonight, for instance. Here they were back in the city only a few hours after chasing the "feared" Mr. Strang clean over a cliff— and right back on the job they had left for the Strang kill.

Steve Mason smacked his lips, picked up a cigarette and smoked for a minute in silence. Maybe a minute and half—certainly not more. He didn't have time—hardly time to sleep. No, a lad had to push himself in this racket. Power—that was it. That was what he wanted—and that was what he'd get! Yes, he'd control the entire underworld; the upperworld too, if Senator Bixby became Governor. If the Senator became Governor? He stamped his cigarette viciously out in the tray on the desk. *When* the Senator became Governor.

He pushed the button on his desk, said to Rudolph

when he opened the door: "Bring that shrimp secretary of Billings' in. He's cooled his heels long enough. It's better when they wait to see me, Will he need it rough?"

Rudolph Weber grinned—at least his lips parted and white showed—but his eyes remained mean; cruel. He said: "Nothing rougher than a dash of lavender. He's a pushover; lives only for his two daughters."

STEVE MASON LOOKED across his desk at the trembling bent little man before him. He said simply: "There isn't any use to whimper about it, Jackson. You got a receipted bill for your wife's operation, plenty of money with which you sent her and the two girls south. And an eleven-hundred-dollar car to run them out in the country when they came back. I'd have made it a high-priced boat, but that might create talk. You're a modest man who wouldn't like that."

The little man shook, said: "I didn't know what the money was for. I thought it just came from some good—"

"A good fairy, eh?" Steve Mason tilted back his chair. "Imagine that at your age, believing in fairies! You never mentioned getting the money. Yes, I know the suggestion that you shouldn't was in the letter with the cash. We won't argue. How long have you worked for Kirkman Billings?"

The little man looked at the ceiling, finally said: "Seventeen years. Six as confidential secretary since he has given up active business. He trusts me in everything, Mr.— Mr.—" When Mason just stared at him Jackson stumbled on. "He takes my word—the report I give him on the men he's interested in having paroled."

"Of course he does." Steve Mason opened a drawer, pulled out a thick wad of bills. "There's a thousand for you

now. The name of the guy to be paroled is Marty Henderson, the finest boy you'd ever want to see." And shoving
a tightly folded sheet of paper across the desk, "That's
your report to Mr. Billings on Marty Henderson. It may
overlook a few facts, but mainly they're near enough. You
simply have met and talked with his mother—a grand
lady—poor but proud. Don't be too enthusiastic, understand? Just a little surprised that such a fine boy wasn't
paroled before."

"But Mr. Billings' trust in me, sir." Mortimer Jackson
began to tremble visibly. "I can't break this trust—"

"You won't have any trust to break," Mason told him,
"if you don't take that jack and make that report when he
asks about Henderson. You'd have hard work explaining
to Kirkman Billings why you took my money."

"I'd tell him the truth, sir. Yes, I'll tell him the truth."

Steve Mason got up slowly from the desk, walked
around it, looked at the crouching, gray-haired man. He
spoke through tight lips:

"Jackson, there is one thousand dollars for you. You've
worked for Billings for seventeen years and get sixty-five
dollars a week. You've got a wife and two nice girls."

"No, no. I'd see them starve first!"

"Hell!" Steve Mason stifled a yawn "What do you take
me for? The old-time villain that puts the starving family
out in the cold. I'm your friend. I'm taking orders from a
guy who sent you that money." He paused a long time. "He
said to tell you to take that dough, make that report—or
go home the next night and find those girls of yours filled
with lead. You—"

The man was on his feet, staggering, clutching one of Mason's arms, begging, his voice breaking.

Steve Mason pulled the man erect, pressed the bell on the desk. "Cut it!" he said sharply. "Do you want to break my heart?" And to Rudolph Weber who opened the door, "This is Mr. Jackson, Rudolph. Doing a little stuff for us. Put him down for a drawing account of a hundred— hell, make it two hundred a week. He's a valuable man. There, there, Jackson. Don't thank me. You're forgetting the money and the paper." And as he led the man toward a little rear door, "You're the kind of a father who wants to make a place for his girls—good college education, meet the right people, marry the right boys." And with a laugh as he patted Jackson on the back, "Now—I ask you, honestly. Who'd want to marry a girl who had been filled with lead?"

Mason shoved the little man out the door, looked at the clock, sighed. No big executive ever worked harder. He was on the job twenty-four hours of the day and night. But it was going to be worth it. He wanted power—not rest. The rest would come later. Now—just the little book, the death of Billings—and things would be rolling straight toward the Governor's mansion.

Steve Mason stuck a cigarette into his mouth and half sat, half leaned against the desk. A guy had to have a few puffs—and then the big room below—Senator Bixby and Commissioner of Police Barton. But he was ready for the job—anxious for it. Things were too close to success now to slow down. No more slick, clever work. That had been going on for years. It ended tonight with the death of Mr. Strang. From now on, death to those who stood in his way.

Yes, he'd blast himself right to the top of the pile—and what a top—and what a pile!

For a moment he paused before a mirror, straightened his tie, picked at the end of his handkerchief in his breast pocket. He let his face slip easily into a smile—yes, slip in as if his features entered a groove; a groove that was rather hard and cold—and cruel when one looked very closely at it. Then he left the room.

10

DEATH UNDER GROUND

AARON BECKER WAS a tall gaunt man whose sharp eyes, which were too closely set on either side of his nose, gave him the appearance of being cross-eyed. But he was not cross-eyed. His eyes were very direct and straight.

The book that he had found had made those eyes widen to bulging proportions. It read like a *Who's Who in Murder*—with particular stress upon parole violators, dates of their release, jobs they did, and in many instances, dates of their death with the simple letters, *"Mr. S."* after many of them.

He weighed every possibility of the use of that book to the best financial end. He was not familiar enough with the city to handle each case personally, nor of a trusting enough nature to organize his own little group of black-mailers, killers and extortionists. He liked to work for others. It took him exactly ten days to decide that the man to handle things for him was Steve Mason. Mason's name was not in that book. Aaron believed that twice as much is gotten out of a man who works for greed as one who works through fear. No man would ever kill an active and lucrative account, but men killed through fear.

Now Aaron was a shrewd man. He knew that this book

was being looked for in the underworld. So he pretended to take Lorey, the cringing snow-bird, Lorey into his confidence. The one grand extorted from Rudolph Weber, the man closest to the great Steve Mason, was nothing—nothing but a cryptic message to Mason that Aaron had that book, or knew where it could be obtained. He would much rather have Mason come to him and make the proposition than to go to Mason himself.

As for Mason having him killed.... The thing was ridiculous while Mason even suspected that Aaron knew of such a book. Yes, he'd make Mason come to him and so have the upper hand. The book was worth a fortune.

But Mason did not come and Aaron was annoyed. He had that book well hidden. He had planned that hiding-place when he made his move from his brother's place to the little Italian home downtown with the pretty little summer house in the back; the summer house which proved after careful examination to have a large vault-like room below it. That that vault had been used to make and store wine which was sold at a low price around the neighborhood during prohibition, had nothing to do with Aaron.

He'd give Steve Mason another chance. Yes, he'd tear a leaf from the book itself, put it into Lorey's hands and send him to Mason to see what he'd pay for it. Damn it, Mason would be a fool if he didn't strangle out of Lorey the information as to where he got it.

Now Lorey was out in the shop in front and Aaron was down in his damp cement vault below the summer house. He had removed the stone block from the wall, even had his cement mixed to put the book back in its place again.

The book was small, though the word Ledger was written upon it. And just below the stamped word Ledger was a name—some writing below it. It was faded but he made it out clearly.

Mr. Strang's Ledger. Don't Open It. Don't Use It.

Aaron Becker grinned. No threat, no word of danger, not even a warning—perhaps just a request. He shivered slightly. A request more fearful, more dangerous, more deadly in its meaning than if the words read: Death lies within.

But Mr. Strang was through, washed up—dead or something. No one seemed to bother about him anymore—least of all to fear him. No man fears the dead.

But there was other business. The business of taking a page from that book to send to Mason. There were many names, some known to Aaron, but most of them not. It would be foolish to pick the best of them with their crimes listed, the double-cross they had pulled on friends. There were a few that made Aaron whistle softly—shootings and stabbings and brutal torture murders he had read about in the papers. One murder in particular that even made his eyes narrow and seem to press closer against his hooked nose. Johnny Weber, the fast coming Johnny Weber, the man who had threatened to turn Steve Mason out of his power.

Aaron still could hardly believe his eyes at the name of Johnny Weber's murderer. The man who had leaned over from behind the back of his chain and slit his throat. But the name was there—the name of the man who was closest to Mason now. And that man's name was Rudolph Weber, Johnny Weber's brother.

Horror—well, it wasn't exactly horror that Aaron Becker felt. It was something else he couldn't explain, nothing moral, of course; nothing that effected that keen brain of his. Rather it caught him in the stomach. His brain knew that anything was possible at a price. He wondered what Mason had paid for that kill, and he wondered what it would cost to have a man like Rudolph kill his own mother. Aaron didn't doubt it could be done, but surely it would cost plenty. Greed knew no relationship—except money.

He stopped thinking, jerked up his head, stood crouched there on the cold hard floor listening, the book upon his knees; his ears strained to catch the sound again. His eyes on the wall that dripped dampness; his back to the stone steps that he had come down.

Aaron Becker let the book slowly to the floor with his left hand, covered it with his knee. He'd give Lorey, drugged or not drugged, a lesson in spying on him this time. His right hand went beneath his left armpit. Spying, eh? And his mouth opened and his yellow teeth showed. Why not? He had encouraged that spying so that Lorey would report it to Mason. But then he hadn't expected Lorey to leave the shop. Maybe if Lorey reported where the book was, Mason might not make a deal at all; not the kind of deal Aaron expected anyway, but a deal between a live racketeer and a dead fence.

Aaron Becker grinned. There were many other loose blocks in that wall and he was quite adept in sealing up those blocks again. The bit of dirt, a slight rub, the appearance of age between the concrete blocks. Yes, he could bury a body there. And he could get a body—now.

His hands jerked out; his body half swung and a voice said "Don't do it, Aaron. That's right. Drop the rod."

Aaron Becker was no expert with firearms—that is, when it came to a quick draw. The voice was not the voice of the twitching hop-head, Lorey. It was a strange voice— yet not entirely a strange voice. He had heard that voice once before in the street, close to his shop, speaking to Lorey. But he held his gun for a second as he turned his head.

He saw the gun before he saw the man's legs. It was not an ordinary gun. Gunner Keen was not in the habit of carrying ordinary guns. It was a Thompson sub-machine gun, and its black nose with the great circular drum of steel was directly on Aaron's middle. Aaron's mouth fell open. He recognized the face above that gun now; the face of the other man who stood beside the machine gunner. They were both grinning broadly; both suspected in the killing of Resa Kent; both known as high-paid gun-artists employed by Steve Mason.

Aaron Becker didn't grin any more. His gun fell to the floor with a single crack, but his teeth chattered audibly. Even as he felt death very close, he tried to push the book toward the darker corner of the room. Yes, he was frightened, horribly frightened. The gun was still directed at his middle as Gunner Keen spoke.

"Get on your feet and don't try hiding that book. Hell, man, stop throwing dice with them teeth of yours. I'm a nervous man."

Owen said: "He sounds like the car we used tonight."

He picked up the book, flipped the pages, whistled, said, "This is it all right! Jordan killed the cop just like you said. The cop had a sick wife, two kids, and—Hell, this lad Mr. Strang went in for detail." It was peculiar how everyone spoke of him as Mr. Strang, even in the underworld. But the *Mr.* was not a title of respect, but more as if it were the man's first name—used in awe a few months before; used simply as habit now.

"You're okay," Keen said to the shaking Becker as he looked up at the huge supporting beams of the wide room. "Your little stunt to attract Steve's attention with the one grand shakedown of Rudolph didn't fool him any. He just played dumb like he didn't understand, but he may make use of you—the book being his, not yours."

"Listen to this." Owen's eyes bulged. "It's your name, Gunner—and I never thought you done that job. Must have hated Old Man Stern to cut the—"

"Give me that book!" The Gunner crossed the room, tucked his machine gun under his arm. "We'll tear that page out and—" He grabbed the book in his right hand, gripped the page with his left when a voice spoke on the stairs behind him.

"It would be a crime, gentlemen, to destroy that book. It is a very rare volume—the only one like it in America— not another single copy." And though his words seemed humorous as single words—as single sentences—there was nothing of humor in the speaker's voice.

Owen said: "It's—" and jerked up his gun.

There was a single shot, but it was not from Owen's gun. Keen stared wide-eyed at Eddie Owen, who faced him. His pal, his partner, his buddy in every worth-while killing in the last three years. There didn't seem much wrong with him then, when he dropped his gun. There didn't seem much wrong with him as he twisted slowly and sank to the floor. It wasn't until Keen saw the small round hole straight in the center of Owen's forehead that he realized Owen was dead.

The man on the stairs spoke again.

"Your friend, Owen, is rather impetuous, Mr. Keen— or should I, say 'was'? But it really didn't matter. He had to die, as you have to die." And with a viciousness that stopped Keen in his sudden whirl, his dropping of the book and his tossing up of the nose of the tommy gun. "My intention was to put heavy lead piecemeal into your rotten body. That's right. I was sent by a dead man—a Mr. Strang Cummings. Ah, that is better."

Aaron Becker pitched himself forward on his face as the machine gun spouted lead; spouted lead harmlessly against the hard walls, even the high ceiling—thumping into the great beams.

Aaron knew that those bullets did not endanger the man upon the stairs. They might have, for the gun was spitting lead as it swung with the turning body of Gunner Keen. But the man on the stairs fired once. Gunner Keen still held the machine gun straight out before him, but no shots came from it now. Keen was dead then, Aaron thought. Dead on his feet.

But he wasn't dead. His fingers closed again; the staccato notes of the machine gun jeered horribly. His body turned toward the man on the stairs, was almost facing that man with the deadly weapon crashing like bolts of thunder in that underground vault.

The man wasn't on the stairs anymore. He was coming down them. The blackness of his body; his two guns now firing orange-blue flame from two hands; the white blotch below the black felt hat must have been a face.

Aaron's ear drums seemed shattered, his nostrils raw and his throat burnt by the thickness of the powder. He was crying too; his eyes were wet, but he was crying out his fear, begging for his life as he backed to a large barrel, forced himself between it and the wall.

The room was a dull haze of smoke, yet Aaron saw things plainly. Keen wasn't firing any more. Keen was dead—dead from any one of the many bullets that had pounded into his body.

Keen hit the wall before he took the final dose. But it didn't hurt him any—couldn't hurt him any. There was no more lead needed then. The wall couldn't hold him erect. His knees gave; he knelt a moment on the hard cold floor, then flopping sideways lay there—a huddled, bullet-ridden, distorted bundle.

The man with the guns still held in each hand turned and peered for a full minute straight at Aaron. He must have seen him through that haze, for Aaron Becker saw him. He saw the legs spread far apart, the guns—black, ominously outlined against the white of the man's hands, and the white of his face, the black holes; burning holes that must have been his eyes.

Aaron Becker screamed out in terror; dilated eyes nearly popped from their sockets as he tried to force his body back into the cement of the wall. The figure with the two guns was walking toward him.

"It seemed a bit brutal, that second killing, eh?" the man

asked. Then he shook his head. "It was nothing really—nothing to the way I had pictured it myself. Do you know why?"

"They killed the girl—Resa Kent! That was why?"

The man laughed. A chill ran up and down Aaron's back. Gun powder was in his throat—yet this man in the center of that terrible haze breathed easily, seemed to gulp great mouthfuls of the foul air as if it were refreshing.

"Perhaps," said the man, and now words choked in his throat. "But they killed also the best friend I ever had—the only claim I had to life. They drove him in shrieking terror over a cliff. They never gave him a chance to fight for his lost courage; his right perhaps to live a normal life."

"Who was that?" Aaron coughed. He did not want to speak, but he had to. Those eyes; those terrible eyes!

"Who was that?" The man spoke slowly. "That man who dashed over the edge of that high cliff was Strang Cummings." And as if he thought aloud, "He must have died rather horribly. I mean with his thoughts—the thoughts of a coward—plunging into space. With Strang Cummings went my only claim to life, the only thing that made me—made—"

The white hand with the gun still in it came up and ran across a white forehead. And then "You have rope—long, thick, strong rope—somewhere among those barrels?"

Aaron Becker found the rope and Aaron Becker tried to help. The bodies were so-limp that the arms and legs moved as if they were trying grotesquely to walk by themselves. And as he helped the man who had brought death so suddenly and so violently, he saw that the ledger had gone from the floor.

Aaron remembered little of those terrible minutes. The man didn't seem so large and strong, but he handled those bodies as if they were children. It was over then, and Aaron Becker collapsed upon the floor. For the first time in his life, he fainted, passed out cold without a violent hand being laid upon him. But he had already seen the thick white cards with the bold words printed on them.

What he read on those two cards seemed without meaning—yet it struck a paralyzing fear into him. The words were

THE LEGION OF THE LIVING DEAD WALKS
AGAIN TONIGHT!

Those fearful words, and then Aaron Becker remembered no more....

11

THE BOYS WHO TOOK THE DOSE

STEVE MASON WALKED across the brilliant dance floor
with an easy air, a walk that turned into a swagger when he
saw the Commissioner of Police, James Barton, turn from
Senator Bixby and look directly at him. Steve Mason had
come up a hard road. He could act like a man long used to
meeting the best people as if they had been his associates
all his life. But when Barton looked at him, things were
different. Steve Mason swaggered then. He was a man
who had done pretty well for himself and wanted Barton
to know it.

He stopped at one table to pat a noted sportsman on
the back, at another to call familiarly to a famous comic
of radio and screen; he moved to a banker who sat rather
stiffly erect with his wife and daughter, said:

"I'm having Rudolph bring you over a couple of bottles
of champagne—Paul Roget." Steve whispered the date, let
a hand rest lightly on the banker's shoulder.

The banker nodded stiffly but did not speak and Steve
went his way toward Barton's table grinning. If the truth
were known, Steve would have given fifty grand—yes,
right smack on the line—if that banker had ever called him
"Steve" and asked him to sit down and chat for a moment.

Commissioner James Barton was biting his cigar and saying:

"He's dead, Senator. There's not a bit of doubt it was suicide. I got a wire from the Chief of Police. Identification by letters in his pocket, a card and—"

"Anything about—any letter giving information concerning that book?"

"No, no. Hell, I've been on the phone for the last hour, have men on the way up there. I wired the Chief to say nothing if he found a letter."

"Sheila will take it hard. Didn't she rather like him?" The Senator coughed when he mentioned Barton's studious daughter.

The Commissioner laughed. "Not Sheila! She's not the type for it. I don't mean she isn't true and loyal and a fine girl. But since she was a child she liked to meet and study odd people. College put her bugs on it. Why, there are times when I'm stewing around and she pops right out with the very thing on my mind!"

Senator Bixby smiled. "Just as I might now. You're thinking more of Strang Cummings' death than you are of that book."

"Not me!" The Commissioner jerked down his vest which was riding up on him. "I'm all for police work and—" Suddenly bringing his hand down on the table, he exclaimed: "Senator, you're right! I thought a lot of that boy. It floored me when he went to pieces that way. He was a different man—mentally sick. If I hadn't have been so set on that damn book, he'd be alive yet. He just needed time. Who's that?"

"Eh? What?" The Senator turned from Barton, looked

*"Drop the phone, Commissioner!"
a harsh voice called. "I sent
you that telegram myself."*

at Steve Mason a few tables away from them. "It's Mason. Be courteous to him. Barton. He's coming along in the city—politics and all that. Oh, I know your views—hard, iron-handed law. But there's got to be some handshaking and back-slapping. Politicians, for all your thoughts of them, are really diplomats. They keep the wheels oiled; the wheels of a great city."

"You're seeing a lot of Mason. Senator, and—" Barton stopped. His eyes brightened, he lifted the cigar from his mouth. "Good Harry, Senator, I had always put your visits here down to—well, just to be seen. But Mason is head of this new parole racket, and you're trying to be clever, play the detective, catch a word here and there?"

SENATOR CHARLES PHILIP Bixby's laugh was loud and hearty. "It's good food, fine wine, youth and gaiety, and people who know people who know voters. No, I don't think Mason heads any parole racket—any racket except for his own protection, that is. He makes money on these supper clubs. His ambition now is social—yes, social! I think he'd give me the run of this place if I'd introduce him at my club. And I would too, Barton, except that he wouldn't get in." He leaned forward. "Stephen Mason talks to me freely at times. I think you're dead wrong about him. He can't control me and certainly not Kirkman Billings, and surely not the Governor, and I doubt— Ah, Stephen!"

The Senator shook Mason's hand, said: "You know the Commissioner, of course."

"Of course, of course!" Mason waved in a friendly fashion. "I'd offer you the courtesies of the Club, Commissioner, only I know you'd refuse. I admire you for that."

"I'm afraid," Barton growled bluntly—for at heart he was still an honest, straight-talking sergeant—"that I don't admire you."

Mason shook his head, laughed pleasantly. "You let a fellow know where he stands, all right, Commissioner. I'm glad I run a high-class place. But I want to ask a favor of the Senator, and as long as you're here—well, maybe you'll put a bug in his ear. It's about parole."

Barton stiffened, said: "About parole, eh? Maybe I *will* put a bug in his ear."

"Good!" Mason nodded and spoke rapidly. "It's mercy more than just simply justice. Senator. More an appeal to your heart than your head or the law. The boy wasn't bad, just got mixed up in things. I know a man who's been putting up for his family while he's been away, is willing to put up for him when he gets out. I'm talking about Tommy Flint. You see, he changed his mind about that robbery, and dropped out before it was committed. The judge sentenced him anyway."

"Tommy Flint?" Barton took a new interest. "That's funny!"

"Funny!" Mason bristled. "It's a damn shame!"

Barton said: "You're right. I know all about that boy. I was saying only the other day that if Billings has to let men out, why not—"

"There!" Mason cut in. "The Commissioner's for it. Just a word to Billings and— I know it will have to come straight from the Governor, but you and Mr. Billings, Senator— and with Commissioner Barton in favor of it." And turning to Barton, "You will back it, of course? Just your name to Billings, Commissioner?"

"My name would not help that boy." With an effort, for Barton was an honest man, he continued, "That boy never should have been tried, let alone convicted. If the jails must be emptied, why are the laws fixed so that only the most vicious come out?"

"I'll do everything I can, Mason. Everything." Senator Bixby opened his eyes wide as he looked at Barton. "If the Commissioner thinks— But there, who has been taking care of his mother?"

"Oh, he doesn't even know the people, just heard about the case, spoke to me and—"

"But his name!" insisted the Senator. "Come, come, Mason. It lends an air of respectability and has influence when—" And suddenly, "By thunder, Stephen, you're as red as a beet! You've been doing this yourself."

"Oh hell," said Steve Mason making little lines in the white cloth with a long finger. "That won't lend him any air of respectability. Besides, I don't go in for those things. Don't know how I did this time. Just leave me out of it."

"But Stephen, why not let—?"

"Mason is right," Barton said sharply. "I know these people. The mother came to see me. Take the responsibility or the credit yourself, Senator. The boy deserves freedom."

"He does?" The Senator's eyes widened. "You knew— and what did you do?"

"I told Billings that the law was wrong, the judge a dunce, and—well, then I told Billings other things. About men he turned out. It was the last talk Billings and I had. After that—"

"After that?" It was the Senator who spoke.

"After that—I guess I just neglected it."

"Of course you didn't!" Mason's voice was low and soft; his right hand started for the Commissioner's shoulder, but he never let it reach there. "It's not your job to get people out of jail, Commissioner. You're too busy putting them in!"

"It's my business to protect the citizens." Barton's voice was low too, but it was hard and grim. "I neglected that boy. There is no excuse."

A WAITER TAPPED the Commissioner on the shoulder. Inspector Gilligan was calling on the telephone.

Commissioner Barton came to his feet, said quickly to the Senator: "This will be the upstate police chief's message. I'll be back for a minute, even if I have to fly up there tonight."

As the Commissioner disappeared, the Senator raised his eyes and looked straight at Steve Mason.

Mason nodded, ignored the question in the Senator's eyes and said: "I knew that crack about the Flint kid would get under his skin. Every word of it was true. I've given that damned woman twenty-five dollars a week, and told her to see Barton." He fired a cigarette. "So they're shipping the body back to New York, eh? Well, at last I'll get a look at the great Mr. Strang—at the morgue where he belongs!"

Steve was almost ready to leave the table when Commissioner Barton returned. The lights had dimmed on the dance floor. The Senator had straightened his tie, turned his chair slightly, and was cleaning his glasses to ogle the little black-haired, slim-figured beauty, Vera, third from the end.

Bixby was annoyed and he showed it, but his annoyance disappeared when Barton called to Mason. He read the tenseness in Barton's face, the sudden outward thrust of his chin. Things were going to happen or had happened. The Senator gulped slightly. He thought that he knew the truth. Mason had lied to him and Strang Cummings had been murdered—shot through the neck.

But Barton said to Mason: "You know Gunner Keen and Eddie Owen."

Though there was no question in Barton's voice, Steve Mason seemed to think there was. "Keen—Owen? Yes, sure, the big fellow and the little fellow who go around together. George Keen, did you say?"

"I said Gunner Keen. You ought to know them. You or your lawyer have stood behind them enough."

"Have we? Oh, I won't deny it, Commissioner. Mine is a big and a complicated business. If you say it's so, it's so. Sure, I remember now. You were in here the other day—hinting that I knew something about that girl who was killed; hinting that I sent Keen and Owen to do it."

"Well," said Barton grimly. "I won't ever hint about your

using them to kill anyone again. Both of them were killed tonight. I don't know exactly how, but I understand it was a nasty job. Goodnight, Senator. Goodnight, Mason—unless you want to come along."

"Me? I guess not, Commissioner. I'm not strong for—" And suddenly, "But if it's for official identification, I'll go of course. But there, Commissioner, I warn you. I haven't got a strong stomach. I'll get my hat and coat—not a second."

Steve Mason glanced at the Senator, hurried down the hall. He was glad the Senator had understood his gesture, was holding the Commissioner's attention. He was even moving toward the cloak-room with Barton and was quite evidently going to join them on their visit to the dead.

Steve Mason moved quickly. He had Rudolph at his elbow the moment he slipped into his private room. He was talking, walking to the side door as he put on his hat and coat.

"No questions, Rudolph. Take a couple of boys and go out and get Lorey—the dope. You've got to find him and bring him here. He'll hide out in some joint to get hopped to the ears." And as he reached the door, "No, I don't know he isn't dead already, but I know if he isn't he'll talk. It's Gunner Keen and Eddie Owen. They've both been given the dose."

His words to Rudolph Weber were just twisted syllables through the side of his mouth. But Rudolph heard.

Mason said, the moment he caught up with the Senator and Barton:

"Ah, the Senator is coming along! This your car, Commissioner? But of course it is. In a way I feel sorry for both those boys—just unfortunate kids, victims of environment."

"Well, their environment is changed now," growled Barton. "I understand it was a brutal affair."

Steve Mason was not sure, but he thought that there was a certain grim note of satisfaction in the Commissioner's voice.

12

CHAMBER OF HORRORS

SENATOR BIXBY STOOD far back by the foot of the stairs. A policeman, recognizing him, asked him if he wouldn't like to get some air. Steve Mason regarded the bodies, shaking his head and twisting his face at the whimpering Aaron Becker. Becker, though not bound nor gagged, still crouched against the wall close to the blue-coated leg of a uniformed man. The policeman gazed vaguely around the small room; eyes avoiding the swinging bodies. Steve Mason did not speak; his lips were set very tightly; his face was white. He stared now at his two dead friends.

They were not a pretty sight. Hanging head downward from the ceiling, they were suspended by a rope attached to their legs which ran across a thick, wooden support. That rope had been carefully adjusted so that Keen's feet were higher than Owen's—so their faces were close together, dead eyes staring at other dead eyes. Lieutenant Dawson touched Keen, the taller of the dead men.

"It was no accident we found them," he told Barton. "A lad telephoned in for us to look under the summer house here. That simpering guy there—" he jerked a contemptuous thumb at Aaron Becker—"couldn't 'a' done it. He was tied up in a ball when we came in. Everything else was left as you see it."

"Yeah—" The Commissioner ran a hand across his mouth. "Shot to death, then hung head-down from the ceiling. I guess the killer wanted others to know they died hard."

"He wanted *them* to know it anyway—the way their faces are almost touching. But here's the trick." He took a dead arm, moved the body of Keen, set the other body of Owen swinging.

Steve Mason's breath whistled in his throat. He leaned forward read the clearing printed words on the white cardboard; read them aloud in puzzled bewilderment.

The Legion of the Living Dead Walks Again Tonight!

"What the hell does that mean?" he asked Barton.

Barton turned, noticed the two reporters. He glared at the man from the *Transcript*, but he knew he couldn't glare down Halerhan of the *Record*. So he made his voice soft:

"These men are paroled convicts. The taller one, Gunner Keen; the shorter one, Eddie Owen. I want you to keep what information I'm giving you now in confidence— especially about those two cards. It might—"

Halerhan of the *Record*, long, thin with a crooked twist to his mouth leaned forward: "That won't wash, Barton," he said quickly. "We had a peek at those cards before you came—sort of crawled under and looked the boys straight in the face. And as for knowing them—hell, we've taken more cracks at them for murder, chanced more libel suits than you cops ever did. As for the Gunner, you cops did everything but carry the machine-gun for him and—"

"You mean to say you're going to print what's on that card? We've been friends, Halerhan. If you—"

"Cut it, Commissioner." Halerhan said. "You can't give me anything in confidence about those cards. Why, it's the best story in years! Who are the Legion of the Living Dead? Why do they walk again? Bluff?" He laughed hoarsely. "Anyone who looked at those two birds wouldn't think so. Look at Steve Mason. Look at the sick puss on him! He doesn't think it's bluff."

And when the Commissioner would have cut in, "No use of telling me it's for the good of the citizens. I already rang up my editor. Yeah—that's right. I used the phone in the shop in front. It's burning the wires now. England, Germany, Japan. Hell, that story will be carried into the savage villages of Africa. What a spread! *The Legion of the Living Dead Walks Again!*" He glanced at the bodies, "And how!"

Barton shrugged his shoulders. This was no story to try to kill. He said: "If you wanted to make a guess, Halerhan, what would you say it meant?"

"The sign?" Halerhan raised his eyebrows, spoke with some disgust: "Even the editor wouldn't make a guess at that. But if you want me to guess who did it, shot those birds to death and make one damn good killing of it—well, six mouth ago I'd have said it was Mr. Strang."

"Mr. Strang is dead," Barton said.

Halerhan let his hands drop. "Then he didn't do it. Besides, his stuff wasn't quite so—well, 'vicious,' perhaps, is not the word. Say 'artistic.'"

Barton cleared them all out of the room, even the cops before he spoke to the trembling Aaron Becker. "Well," he said. "Let's have the story—all of it!"

Becker said: "I wanted some rope I kept out here and came out. Then these two men came down and attacked me—wanted money."

"Don't shake like that. They can't do you much harm now. What then?"

"*He* came down the stairs after them. Don't ask me who *he* was. I didn't see his face—just his blazing guns, the dead man on the floor, the other dead on his feet, staggering—erect—pounded dead against the wall. After that, he tied me up like this."

"Anything else?"

"He was laughing," whispered Becker.

BARTON LOOKED AT the bodies, thought of the many times he had tried to get those men for particularly brutal slayings—of Resa Kent, dead on the sidewalk, and Keen and Owen above her firing into her body. He said, and his face was hard: "Maybe it isn't such a bad joke if you look at it that way. Did he say anything to you?"

"Yes, he talked some. The place was chocked with smoke. I could hardly breathe. He spoke without difficulty. He said these men had killed his last link—with life, I think."

"He did?" Barton's thoughts ran riot in his head. If he had not seen Strang broken, if he had not seen that telegram telling of Strang's death, he would have believed the impossible. He spoke quickly, thickly, though the last of the gun powder had gone from the room. "Did he say it was a woman? Did he say—?"

Aaron cut in, his voice high-pitched. "He said—the

man they had killed—his last link with life was named Cummings. Yes—yes—!" He tried to think. "He said they had killed Strang Cummings."

Barton nodded. If Strang Cummings were dead, naturally Mr. Strang could not be alive. So it was murder upstate, after all! Maybe one of men that Strang Cummings had befriended as Mr. Strang had struck back; struck back hard and sure—just as Mr. Strang might have struck.

At that moment the medical examiner, Doctor Farrington, came down the steps. He was humming softly, stopped as he looked at the two bodies, said: "Nothing new under the sun, eh, Commissioner? The lad that got off that crack didn't see much of the night. Well, you don't expect me to climb up on that beam to pronounce them dead? Come, come—send down a couple of men. Don't forget I was your best friend when you were a sergeant."

The Commissioner shoved Aaron Becker ahead of him up the steps as two uniformed men came down, followed by fingerprint experts and a couple of camera men.

Aaron was glad to get into the open air. He said to Barton, despite the presence of several men including Senator Bixby and Steve Mason: "I don't see him here. Commissioner. The man I left in charge of the shop, I mean. A little drug addict—Lorey." Aaron stopped. He saw Mason staring at him, saw Mason's eyes grow icy cold. But he didn't care then. Lorey must have come from Rudolph Weber or Steve Mason. Lorey had let Gunner Keen and Eddie Owen in to trap him—maybe kill him. If Lorey talked—well, the harm it would do Aaron Becker would be far overshadowed by the harm it would do Mason.

Barton gave quick sharp orders. "Sergeant," he said to

a heavy-set officer. "Buzz Headquarters for me. Have an alarm broadcast for Lorey—what the hell is his full name?"

"Why," nodded the sergeant. "Everyone knows that little snifter. He won't be hard to find. We'll send it out as wanted for murder. The dump that hears the news will chuck him out on the street."

A few minutes later the medical examiner appeared. His mood was jocular as he patted Barton's back.

"Not very difficult to find the cause of death, Commissioner," he said. "You can remove the bodies at your convenience." And as he started toward the street, "I'll tell you just how dead they are tomorrow." And then he was gone, black bag swinging merrily at his side.

"The old ghoul," Barton mumbled beneath his breath. "There are times when I think he kills them himself just for the pleasure of kidding me about it. Come on, Senator. Mason can walk back. I want to have a talk with you."

The Senator turned toward Mason, started to speak, then didn't. Mason was whispering swiftly to him: "Come down to my place later. We'll have to get Lorey. Don't forget!"

The Senator said under his breath: "Yes, yes!" And in a louder voice. "I daresay you can get back, Stephen. Barton and I wish to have a talk. I'm as interested as he is."

"Of course you are." Barton threw an arm about the trembling Senator's shoulders as he pushed him into the car. "Not as used to it maybe—but after all, they were two of the state's babies—both paroled men."

"But—they're dead," the Senator choked.

"I'm not denying that." Barton nodded. "And I'm not

complaining about it either. It's the manner of their deaths that bothers me."

"Gangland," said the Senator. "Only common gangsters would make things so gruesome."

"Gruesome!" said Barton. "You're right, of course, Senator, but I hadn't noticed that."

HALF AN HOUR later the Senator sat opposite Commissioner Barton in the library of the Barton home. Just a few minutes before, Sheila had put those penetrating eyes upon him and left him mentally confused, but emotionally stirred.

The black-eyed girl, Vera, whom the Senator had seen at the Black Knight lost some of her appeal when he thought of Sheila. Then he looked at Barton. At that hard stern face; honest face. Yet, the Senator knew that within a very short time he would have to use every bit of influence he commanded—yes, and that Steve Mason commanded—to keep Barton as commissioner. Barton did things in such a rough offensive way.

The Senator looked dreamily toward the ceiling as he thought of what a girl of Sheila's type might do to keep her father in that high office. To be sure, she crossed and she defied her father, but she loved him greatly; admired his rough almost indifferent honesty. Yes, if the Senator didn't actually have a wife traveling in Europe he might—just possibly might marry Sheila.

The Senator's pleasant thoughts were turned to more disturbing ones as Barton spoke: "By thunder!" he said suddenly, looking straight at the curtains to the dining room. "If it weren't that I know he's dead, I'd be willing to swear that Mr. Strang—the former Mr. Strang—walked the city streets again tonight."

"You know he's dead," the Senator snapped irritably. "You have the telegram from that Chief of Police."

"But I haven't got the answer to my telegram. You know, Senator, that Mr. Strang had friends. Many of them had only months to live—other perhaps a few years. Most of them not strong in a physical sense, but a man needs only to press a finger lightly upon the trigger of a gun to cause the destruction of life— And these men—"

"Yes, yes, I know! He paid them—supported their relatives if they died by violence serving him. It must have cost him something."

"He had," explained Barton, "become a very wealthy man."

"But look what that man—was it Aaron Becker?—said. This brutal killer spoke of those horribly murdered men as the killer of his best friend, Strang Cummings."

"Keen and Owen," Barton mused. "They certainly killed Resa Kent, whom Strang was to marry. Say, I wonder if they went up there and tossed his body over that cliff?" He looked at the phone on the table. "There's no use calling my office again. But I would like to hear from the Police Chief upstate. Oh, I'll call again."

Barton reached for the phone—and his hand froze to the receiver. He didn't turn at first. He couldn't. The voice that spoke from behind him; from between the curtains that led to the dining room was so ominous, so foreboding of evil, so hard, so cruel—and yet so familiar! A voice that he used to hear—used to—The voice said:

"Drop the phone, Commissioner. Your telegram was

never received by Police Chief Sheridan. There is no such police chief. I sent you that telegram myself."

Barton saw the Senator's popping eyes, the quivering hands, the fingers of which bit into the arms of the chair. He saw, too, the dead whiteness of the Senator's face—not a sheet-like whiteness, for there were large yellow spots in it. The Senator was breathing very hard through a mouth that hung open.

Then Barton turned to face the man who had entered the room. His gaze ran from the black trousers to the black coat with the peculiar clerical collar. All resemblance to the clergy ended there when Barton's gaze reached the man's face.

Barton was conscious only of the flaming eyes—piercing eyes the color of molten steel—or steel just before it cools.

Barton stared. He was a man without fear, and perhaps he did not feel it now—for himself. But his voice was choked when he spoke:

"Strang—!" he said. "Mr. Strang-back from the dead!"

The Senator said like a man in a horrible nightmare: "But you—you went away to forget!"

Mr. Strang let his head sink slowly onto his chest.

"That's right," he said. "I went away to forget. But I've come back to remember."

13

MR. STRANG RETURNS

FOR LONG MINUTES Senator Charles Philip Bixby and Commissioner James Barton looked at the cruel, hard face and burning eyes of Mr. Strang. They looked down at his hands too—hands that were empty. Then they looked at each other. Barton thought: If Mr. Strang was half mad before he pushed Barton up to be Commissioner, he was entirely mad now. Thin eyebrows never moved; thick lashes never closed over restless eyes. It seemed as if Mr. Strang were capable only of a direct stare.

Barton finally spoke: "Those dead men tonight—you killed them?"

Mr. Strang smiled, but he did not speak. Then Barton's own right hand slipped down on his right leg. He was an old-fashioned cop; his gun was in his hip pocket. He said, as his hand crawled slowly up his leg: "You put those signs upon the dead men. The signs that read: *The Legion of the Living Dead Walks Again Tonight?*"

"So you didn't guess what it meant?" Mr. Strang asked. "My dear Commissioner, it means your future—perhaps the future of the entire city. It means that you, Barton, will decide if, in one great stroke, the entire crime ring that encircles the city is broken. It means— Barton, if you move that hand another inch I'll shoot you to death!" Barton's eyes widened and both hands popped to his knees. "Let me repeat to you the story you know so well. Some three or four years ago I came to you with a proposition. I would tell you where wanted men could be found—where men who broke their parole could be picked up, exactly what evidence you could use to convict murderers and when the occasion warranted I—"

"You shot them to death—for me?"

"I shot them to death for a purpose—a mission—to rid the state of the Parole Evil. Then came the operation that removed the bullet from my skull and the forcing out of the bone that pressed against my brain. After that I was a new man. A broken, fearful man. You called that man a coward and you called him yellow. He had been your friend. Yet you did not try to help him and make him whole and normal again. Those men you saw dead tonight killed Strang Cummings, but brought Mr. Strang to life."

Strang laughed and the Senator came part way to his feet. But Mr. Strang went on talking: "Yes, they chased me, a frightened coward, over that hundred-foot cliff, but not to the rocks below. Dead branches, buried for perhaps centuries, blocked my fall. They broke beneath the weight of my body, but one held. Held me there alive; unconscious from a single blow on the head. And where, gentlemen, do you think that blow was? It was on the very spot where Doctor Le May, the great and eminent surgeon, had pushed out that bone. Did it pierce my brain and kill me? It did not. It pierced my brain, perhaps, but it killed only Strang Cummings, the man who crept about with fear and watched Resa Kent, the girl he was going to marry, shot to death. Shot to death by the same two gunmen, remember, who drove him over the cliff. So, Strang Cummings, the noted connoisseur of art, died—and, Mr. Strang was reborn. The selfsame Mr. Strang who made you commissioner. The Mr. Strang who can keep you there—and who alone can keep you there—if you trust him again."

"You are—" gagged Barton—"going to kill more men?"

"I am," answered Strang. "Perhaps many men. Certainly those men who killed Resa Kent including the man or men who directed and instigated that killing. Only two died tonight. Five participated actively in the murder."

"You know them then?" Barton was sparring for time. The first Mr. Strang had been dangerous enough, but this man—

"I know another of them," Mr. Strang said. "I recognized him running from the scene of the murder. From him I will get the names of the others."

Barton's smile was not quite real. "You don't expect for one minute that he would talk—to you?"

"He will be eager to talk. He will fall on his knees and beg to talk." Mr. Strang spoke very slowly now. "Commissioner Barton," he said. "I am the same Mr. Strang you knew—with one vital difference. I am out of control."

"You mean to say you are going to kill wantonly?"

"I am going to kill those men."

"Without giving them a chance?"

"Without giving them a chance."

"Man!" the Commissioner choked, "that would be murder!"

"The word 'murder,'" said Mr. Strang, "applies only to humans—not mad dogs. I intend to kill mad dogs."

"But that is not law and order!"

"We must separate the words." Mr. Strang shot his head forward. "Tonight I was the law. Two murderers are dead. They— What was that?"

PLAINLY THERE WAS tapping on the front door—on the rear door, too.

"That," explained Barton very slowly, "is the police. I have been surprised before. There is an electric button beneath my chair. I am not quite as stupid as the day you found me a sergeant. Give me your gun, Strang, and they will not bother you. They will never know your true identity." Barton paused a long moment, and then, "You were never beyond the power of reasoning. I do not believe you are now." Barton leaned forward, looking into those blazing eyes. Then he exclaimed: "By Thunder, Strang—you are mad!"

Strang laughed. "Mad enough to kill twice tonight— mad enough to kill again. You wouldn't care for me when I needed care—now, you have what you wanted. A man of iron, you said. A man who would frame a bill—even back that bill—so that murderers turned loose by the state would no longer prey upon the honest citizen. And now you would have me put away."

The Commissioner spoke very low as he imagined a doctor might talk. "Just for a little while. There will be no story in the newspapers—not even a disclosure who you are to the men outside. Just a couple of policemen will go with us. Later, when you are yourself again, I—" There was a crash of glass. "Don't let them find you threatening me like this!"

Mr. Strang said very slowly: "You are bringing men to

their deaths. You are causing your own death. Call to them that there was a mistake."

Barton never took his gaze off those flaming eyes.

"I have saved no money to retire on, but I have plenty of insurance money for my daughter, Sheila. You are not fit nor safe to be free. You have come here with your hands stained with blood, perhaps quite justified, but one-man law is never justified. I will not turn a madman loose in the city. I have my duty. They're coming. Drop that gun—or shoot. There are many of them."

They were pounding at the door now—at least the front door.

Senator Bixby spoke for the first time as he came to his feet and staggered toward the door which led to the hall and so to the front door and escape. His legs were shaking; his extended hand trembling violently. He was saying over and over: "Strang! Not me—not me!"

Mr. Strang said: "Not you. Barton's life will be sufficient protection for me. Go open the door. That's right." And as the Senator staggered out into the hall, "You may be of some use to the citizens without me—but Barton will be none."

Mr. Strang stepped to that door, closed it quickly after the Senator, turned the key in the lock and returned to his position before the heavy curtains of the dining room.

He heard the front door open and close and he knew that the Senator was gone, but that many others had entered the house. They were pounding on the door to that room now.

Then—steps behind Mr. Strang, quiet, furtive steps that were crossing the dining room behind him, nearing that curtain before which he stood. Mr. Strang listened. One man—one man only. Mr. Strang turned; his gun swung from Barton toward the curtain.

The curtains moved as Mr. Strang pressed himself hard against their heavy folds. Then they parted in the center and a head came through. A head and a hand and a gun. Maybe Mr. Strang smiled grimly as he realized that the uniformed policeman had removed his hat in the house of the Commissioner, but he didn't know, of course, that that same bald-headed policeman had entered the house before on false alarms, crossed wires or electrical defects.

The cop saw the Commissioner sitting straight in the chair. He smiled, turned his head slightly and half raised his gun. Mr. Strang struck once; steel cracked against bone. The police officer made an odd face—and started toward the floor.

Mr. Strang cursed softly as he cleared the dining room, dashed through the butler's pantry to the kitchen. Then the little hall and the back door which led to the street—and to his right the rear stairs that went above.

Something struck against that back door. Strang sprang quickly across the semi-darkness of the kitchen, for a tiny light burned close to the rear door. He thought that he saw a face at the window by the foot of those stairs, but he wasn't sure. Then he was, for there was a light, a flash pressed against the glass, a pencil of light was creeping into the kitchen, wandering about it.

And Mr. Strang did it. He jabbed his gun into its shoulder holster, grabbed up a kitchen chair and hurled it toward that window. Shattering glass—splintering wood. The light and the face disappeared.

Mr. Strang jerked open the door to the stairs, pulled it to behind him and bounded up the steps. Trapped? Of course he was trapped! He could hear the servants moving above—two floors above.

The police were coming from below. Strang thought it was the beginning of the end....

14

MURDER PLAYS NO FAVORITES

SENATOR CHARLES PHILIP Bixby very nearly knocked down a policeman as he threw open the front door and tried to crowd his way out of Barton's home. That is, he nearly knocked down a policeman on the first rush; on the second rush, a policeman succeeded in spreading him all over the hall. Only the approach of a sergeant who recognized him saved the Senator from a nasty crack over the head.

His hurried explanation that there was a maniac with the Commissioner cleared a way for him. Senator Bixby was not a man to be stopped by the police.

He signaled a taxi, drove straight to Steve Mason's club. The information that Mr. Strang was alive could not be told over a phone. It should be told straight to Steve Mason—

The Senator opened his mouth. Should he tell Mason? Would he have to tell him? Maybe later. Certainly not tonight. Perhaps Mr. Strang was already being taken away by the police; take some place where he would be kept a raving maniac.

That would be it! That would be the thing. Barton would surely tell the Senator if there was a chance of Mr. Strang's getting well and reappearing. Then, perhaps Mr. Strang would meet with an accident.

Even to himself Senator Bixby did not admit that he was a criminal.

But the Senator had to be careful about Steve Mason. Of course, Mason could never tie him up in anything. He had been very shrewd about that—and Mason had been stupid. Mason could never tie him up with his criminal activities.

The car drew up to the curb and Senator Bixby had made a few quick decisions. He would have a few drinks to straighten him up, call up Barton to see how things came out—and not see Mason tonight.

Senator Bixby stepped from the taxi and walked directly into Steve Mason. "My dear Stephen!" he started and stopped. He was surprised to find himself back in the taxi—to hear Steve directing the driver to go to the Black Knight Club.

Steve Mason was explaining. "Didn't want to waste time. I know you always come to this club when you expect me to call you. But I came directly here instead. I've got a surprise for you." He clapped the Senator on the back.

"A surprise?" the Senator gasped. "But my dear Stephen, I was going to bed—just dropping into the club to see if you called."

"What about the little dark-eyed girl, Vera? Maybe she's crying her eyes out for you now."

"Really?" The Senator was not interested now. It was not because of his interest in Sheila; it was entirely because of his interest in himself. He wanted to know what had happened at Barton's house. If Mr. Strang was a prisoner or shot dead—and if the book was found. But he said:

"That was very thoughtful of you, Stephen. I always have an interest in youth. But tonight—with your—those two dead men. They might have been quite innocent of any evil."

"They were guilty as hell, Senator. They killed Resa Kent, and they killed Mr. Strang. I'm ashamed to think they're from the same street that I came from—sorry that I ever helped them."

Steve Mason seemed in a particularly pleasant mood.

Senator Bixby did not seem to notice it. "After all, they were your friends. To belittle the dead is—"

"Dead friends are no friends. And it isn't bad policy to run them down. I'll make a statement about them in the morning to the papers if my name is dragged in."

"But if the Commissioner knew that I returned to your place tonight—to fun and frivolity after such a tragedy—It would be unforgivable."

"Oh, tell Barton it was your interest in Vera. Tell him you pretend an interest in women to get information from them—maybe about me. Barton's set on riding me." And after a pause and through tightly set lips, "I'm set that he won't."

"Good grief!" the Senator blurted. "You're not thinking of killing Barton!"

STEVE MASON LAUGHED. "Not me. He's the best Commissioner of Police the city ever had—at least from my point of view and from every regular guy's point of view. Give him a few more months and he'll have walked all over the pet corns of every big-shot politician or every meddling millionaire like Kirkman Billings. Then he'll be lucky if he gets his old beat back across the bridge in Prospect Park. He rides rough-shod over everything—everybody."

"He's honest." The Senator contended. "Absolutely honest."

"That's right—and that's his trouble. He's so honest he bends backwards. A good politician leans a little forward for the right guy and makes good. An honest man may keep himself erect and hold his job through respect for that honesty. But a lad who bends backwards—can't even stretch a point for a friend, flouts his honesty by making it tougher for a friend than an enemy—is out before he starts."

"He's the Commissioner of Police," Bixby reminded.

Mason laughed. "He was dead on his feet—a sergeant who'd never have moved another step forward if it hadn't been for Mr. Strang. Now Strang's dead—and Barton's ready for the toboggan. Kill him? I'll bend every effort to keep him in office. But when he starts down the slide, it'll be one fast ride!"

"Oh, I don't know." The Senator was willing to drop that sort of talk. "This girl now. Can't I meet her some other time?" They were climbing from the cab now.

The doorman of the Black Knight said: "The visitor has arrived, sir. Mr. Rudolph Weber said to mention it."

Mason nodded, said to the Senator: "You're not going to keep your appointment with the doll. Your interest today lies in crime and crime prevention—and the stricter enforcement of the parole laws. There isn't any girl tonight. We've got a different visitor. A hop-head called—Lorey."

"A hop-head called Lorey! The one the police want?" And as Mason shoved him down that long dark side hall where the hum of the music just reached them, "Really, Stephen, you exceed yourself tonight—and I don't particularly like it!"

Mason cursed, said:

"It's my duty to you, Senator. You take me into your full confidence and I wish to take you into mine. If this Lorey talks—you see the danger? He knows something about Rudolph Weber."

"That," said the Senator, "would be Rudolph's problem—not yours and I must say hardly mine."

"Wrong." Mason gripped the Senator's arm, held him steady as his thick fingers clutched a doorknob in the heavy dimness. "It's that chain—the crime chain we were talking about. Lorey shook down Rudolph from the pages of a book. A certain book we still want. If Lorey talks, he can involve Rudolph. If Rudolph talks, he can involve me, and if I talk—well, I *could* involve you. I think you are entitled to the assurance that you won't be involved, Senator. You'll sleep better for it. I always do."

"Yes, of course, but—!"

The Senator stepped back, gasped as he was pushed into a room and the door was closed behind him. It was a small room, no windows, no other door but the one they entered. That door was heavy and evidently padded for silence. But what bothered the Senator was Lorey—Lorey the drug addict. He had seen the man only once before, but he recognized him now. Eyes with pupils enlarged, quivering lips, fingers that ran under his nose as he made queer animal-like noises.

Rudolph said: "A piece of luck, Steve, though I'd found

Lorey sooner or later. But he came around to the side door. No one saw him come in."

"Not a soul?" Steve Mason was thoughtful.

"Not a soul. Steve." And with a smile and smirk Rudolph added, "So we're sure Lorey's safe."

"That's fine." Mason hardly started speaking before the Senator puffed out his shirt, adjusted his glasses and said in his most senatorial manner: "It was nice of you to show me about the place, Stephen. The little odd hidden places made useless by repeal, but I must get on. I must—" And in a hoarse whisper, "You fool! This man must not see me here."

"Nonsense." Mason raised his voice. "Lorey's a fine boy. You needn't be a bit afraid, Lorey. I like your work. I'm going to take you over—stand behind you, Lorey."

"You will—you will, Mr. Mason?" Lorey leaned far over a table, his hands trembled, his fingers twitched. "But what if they get me, put me over the jumps, take away my stuff and—?"

"You wouldn't talk anyway, Lorey. You'd die first, wouldn't you—for Steve Mason?"

"I want my stuff. You gotta see that I get my stuff." Lorey's fearful attitude had taken on a slightly pleading, slightly threatening tone. He looked at each of the three men, dug a hand in his pocket, turned his body, bent low. It was a full minute before he came up again. His breathing was louder, then regular. He stood very straight, spoke almost sharply:

"You got me right, Steve. You take care of me and I'll take care of you—and you." He looked at Rudolph, then turned little malignant eyes on the Senator, "—and you too, big boy—Senator Charles Philip Bixby."

"That's the boy, Lorey! We just wanted your word—to know you were right." Mason was grinning from ear to ear. Rudolph, too, was smiling. The Senator was perplexed, angry—afraid. He said: "But you can't take this man's word like that, Stephen. He knows nothing detrimental to me, of course, but he'll—"

"Soon find out." Lorey ran a finger under his nose. "Damn soon, big boy—and I'll be seeing you. Okay, Mason—you got sense. I'll need—need a couple of centuries just to keep in shape."

"Maybe a grand or two?" Rudolph Weber suggested with an ambiguous smile.

"Three grand," said Mason. "It'll never be said that Steve Mason didn't take care of his friends. Especially Lorey. I've watched you, Lorey. You're going to be big—damned big someday."

LOREY SWAGGERED AROUND the table. His face took on color; his chin shot forward. He said melodramatically: "I'll play ball, Steve—them that knows Lorey knows that. But five grand is what I get now or I—well, you can just deal me out and take your chance."

"Five grand?" Mason frowned. "But I guess you're right, Lorey. You could make it tough. You might even go over and head the Meyers mob." Then he set his teeth. "Make it four, Lorey. Rudolph and me and the Senator might dig up another grand tomorrow, eh, Senator?"

"Me, *me?*" The Senator, who was amazed at the whole proceedings, was startled now.

"You see how it is, Lorey." Mason shook his head very

sadly. "We can only raise four and you won't take it. You want five. Tough, very tough. But take this anyway. It'll be as good to us as if we'd given you the five grand."

And then Lorey knew the ghastly joke these men had been playing on him. He screamed in terror, started to drop to his knees as he saw the black object suddenly jump from beneath Steve Mason's left armpit. The Senator cried out too, but it was just a whistling noise to his throat.

Lorey never reached his knees; never reached them alive. Steve Mason's finger closed and the gun exploded so close to Lorey's head that it knocked him over backward. Rudolph stepped sideways to avoid the body. He grinned his appreciation, but there was something behind that grin, a look of doubt.

"Did you see that, Rudolph? He never even got to his knees—just bent them. Yes, only bent them and he was dead! I haven't lost any speed."

"No, you haven't lost any speed," said Rudolph. "No speed at all. You're still the fastest drawing man in the racket, Steve—high or low, professional killers or just plain 'guns.' There's none can tie you."

"Remember that, Rudolph." And as Rudolph's face grew white and his chin came forward, Mason changed the meaning of his words; changed them deliberately. "I mean, of course, remember to tell the boys about my speed. I can't tell when I might want to use it—or when they might least like to see it. What the hell, Senator?"

The Senator was bubbling words. His glasses had dropped from his nose, his gold-headed cane had fallen to the hard stone floor—one yellow glove beside it. But he got his words out just the same:

"Good grief, Steve! Why did you do that? Why did you kill him?"

Steve Mason looked up. "I kind of thought you didn't like taking his word, Senator." He smiled very pleasantly. "I wanted to assure you that you need feel no more danger from that chain. The weakest link is gone. There, there, Senator—no thanks. Both Rudolph and I are glad— damned glad to oblige you."

The Senator wanted to speak, but he couldn't. Oblige him? What did they mean? But his lips were too dry to ask. He knew that he and Steve Mason left that room, that Mason said something about Rudolph arranging for "finding the body." He knew too that Mason handed his gun to Rudolph, said:

"The ballistic experts at Headquarters can tell if a bullet *isn't* fired from a certain gun."

The Senator heard a voice speak, realized it was his own. The words were: "But can't they tell from which gun the bullet is fired?"

"No," said Mason as they went down the narrow hall. "They can't, Senator, when they can't find the gun. My motto is one shot to a gun. Expensive, I admit, but then it costs quite a bit more to fry a man up in the electric chair."

The Senator had walked more than a block from the Black Knight Club when the surprising and—yes, terrifying thought struck him. He had been present at a murder—a brutal and horrible murder. Yet, Senator or no Senator; important personage or no important personage, his tongue was sealed as tight as any racketeer's, any gangster's—any common hood's who slunk through the night.

He had suddenly discovered with a shock that crime and murder play no favorites.

But after that first terrifying shock was over, he discovered something else—and even though the fear still remained, it was pushed far back into his brain. Murder! There was no crime worse than that. He was in it up to his neck now. It gave him a sort of abandon—a freedom that he hadn't felt before. Nothing would stand in his way now. The lust of greed and the obsession for power gripped him more than it ever had before. Steve Mason was right. Senator Charles Philip Bixby would be the next Governor of the State....

15

FEET ACROSS THE FLOOR

COMMISSIONER BARTON EXAMINED his ruined windows and broken doors as the servants huddled on the stairs to the third floor. He looked too at the dazed police officer, O'Brien, whom Mr. Strang had struck on the head. He finally said to Sergeant Parslow:

"You searched every spot, eh? Of course you did. He got through you then—out the pantry window—after he threw the chair. Then over the fence to the next alley?"

"Well," Sergeant Parslow twisted his face grimly, "O'Brien was by that window and said he didn't. But O'Brien crashed back hard against the fence, has a bump on his head as big as a goose egg. It's possible that he was knocked sillier than usual." The Sergeant glared at the blank face of Officer O'Brien.

O'Brien said "I heard the crash and I seen the chair and I felt the glass, but there wasn't no man unless he leapt clean over me and the fence together." And straightening rather stiffly, "I could have shot him dead too, Sergeant, but it was your orders that there was to be no firing."

The Sergeant snapped: "Then he did jump out the window! Otherwise, how could you have shot him?"

"I could'a' fired point-blank right through the window opening and—"

"Enough!" Sergeant Parslow turned to the Commissioner. "There's been a couple of false alarms you know, sir, and I didn't want things unduly disturbed. Senator Bixby sort of disrupted things in the hall. You've always said not to shoot. Did you know him?"

The Commissioner hesitated a long moment, finally decided to keep the name of Mr. Strang to himself for a bit at least. He said: "He was just the usual type of fanatic—an idea that a relative was being persecuted by the police."

The Sergeant snapped out his book, stuck a pencil to his tongue.

"Did you get a good description of him, sir? We'll have a general alarm sent out and—"

"No, no—" The Commissioner seemed very thoughtful. "I know who he is, Sergeant. Yet I can't remember. I've seen his face someplace. You've had the same thing happen to you, of course?"

He waited so long that the Sergeant had to nod. "So we'll do nothing—then quietly pick him up when I remember. Did you look in my daughter's room—here?" He walked toward the door. It opened suddenly. Sheila Barton looked out.

"He did, indeed, Dad," she said. "That is, I opened the door and talked with Sergeant Parslow. My door was locked so he could not have escaped through here. I heard the noise and your talk. Is there danger, Sergeant?"

"No, Miss." The Sergeant was very polite. One white bare shoulder showed above Sheila's negligee. "I'm sorry I made such a disturbance. But when I found the door locked, I thought maybe he had run upstairs and hidden in a vacant room. Did I scare you much?"

"Such words to a Commissioner's daughter!" Sheila had a lovely smile, the Sergeant thought. "I wouldn't admit it if I were frightened—any more than Father would. Don't bother me, Dad. Get your sleep." The head disappeared, the door shut and a key turned in the lock.

Sheila Barton stood for a moment by the door after she removed the key from the lock. She heard the servants ordered to their rooms, heard the Sergeant assure her father that they had already covered the house from cellar to attic. Then she went to the window and looked through the glass. Nothing but a blank wall. She lifted the window and looked out. A policeman stood in the alley below; his bright buttons showed plainly. She smiled as she went to her bed and lay down. The police protection was good—at least for the Commissioner of Police it was extremely good.

For a long time, Sheila Barton looked at the closed closet door—the closed door that she had left open. Then she reached up and turned off the small bed lamp, plunging the room into blackness. She lay in bed for a long time listening. The clock struck one. Then hours seemed to pass—ages even—and the clock struck two. It was on the second strike that she heard the closet door open.

The girl listened for some time after that. She thought, too, of that other day along the top of the cliff; thought of looking down and seeing the body there—the body of Strang Cummings, hanging so perilously on those cracking branches....

She didn't know, then, and she didn't know, now, how she had climbed down that steep cliff to reach Strang

Cummings—the man she had sent away. She remembered, though, that she did climb down and that she dragged the body back.

Maybe it was the dead body of Strang Cummings that she had held there close against that cliff—but it wasn't a dead man. Closed eyes had opened. Not the dull listless eyes of Strang Cummings, but the burning ones of Mr. Strang!

HE HAD KNOWN her, of course, for in these two person-alities the one remembered well the deeds of the other. Nothing unnatural or mystic or Jekyll-and-Hyde about this man. Just a case for medical attention—and a surgeon who could relieve the dread pressure against the brain. She knew, then, as she looked at him, that he was Mr. Strang—the man she had seen through tightly drawn curtains at her father's house a year or more ago. Not the Strang Cummings who had found such a child-like comfort in her presence. Not the man who lived in a world of fear. This was the man who lived in a world of courage, dominated, perhaps, by a world of hate.

Mr. Strang had looked into her eyes, come erect despite her restraining hand, then swept her up under his arm and climbed quickly and surely straight to the top of that cliff. He had left her there by the cabin and taken her hired car into town....

Sheila stopped thinking, stiffened in the deep black-ness. Feet were crossing the room. Feet she would not have heard if she had not been expecting them. She strained every faculty to hear that doorknob turn, to hear the slight pressure upon the door, even the smothered curse far back in the man's throat when the door did not open. She heard him groping for the key as she pushed that key deeper beneath the pillow. Then she did two things at once: She turned on the lights and she spoke:

"The key is not there, Mr. Strang."

The man whirled. There was a gun in his hand, hatred in his eyes—nothing soft and kindly for the girl who had done so much for him during his illness.

"Don't move—don't cry out—and give me that key!"

"The key is hidden." The girl sat up in bed, pulling the covers close about her throat. "I have no intention of screaming. I got up and locked the door as soon as you were safely in the closet."

"You heard me come in then? Guessed who it was? You knew I was there when the police were at the door? You were afraid to tell them; afraid of me? Afraid of the Frankenstein monster that you created?"

The girl looked straight into those burning eyes, blazing, hateful balls of fire. She said: "I was not afraid to tell them. I was not afraid of you then. I am not afraid of you now. I suppose you came to apologize for leaving me there on the cliff after I saved your life—for I did save it, you know."

Mr. Strang stared at her a long time. He had the feeling, as the Senator had it, that she looked back behind his eyes—inside of his mind.

"Yes," he said. "You *did* save my life. And you are not afraid of me—I am quite sure of that."

"Why did you come here tonight?" Sheila demanded.

"I came to offer your father a proposition. I came to renew our former alliance. I would offer certain criminals—many parole violators—to the law. In return, I wanted to be let alone by the police. I wanted the right to kill."

"To kill or to murder?"

"It was all the same," Strang said.

"Did you murder those men tonight?"

"No." Strang shrugged his shoulders. "It was only their quickness with guns that made it a killing."

The girl smiled. "I think," she said, "you were much easier to handle as Strang Cummings, the frightened child, than you will be as Mr. Strang. But Mr. Strang you can do much good." She leaned over and reached for the phone beside her bed.

Mr. Strang raised his gun, then dropped it into his pocket, moved quickly and clutched her wrist.

"I've changed, Sheila," he said, almost desperately. "You don't understand; can't understand. I have things to do. Things that *must* be done! I could—I would never let you lift that phone and call for help."

"If I wanted help, I could have obtained it long ago—less than a minute after you entered my room."

"Don't you understand what it meant when your father refused my aid?" He still held her wrist, leaned very close to her, his breath warm against her face. "I am going it alone, Sheila. I am going to destroy this rising criminal organization that grows in power every day. I will destroy Steve Mason, who controls it."

"Yes," Sheila agreed very seriously. "I think you will destroy it. But are you sure Mason heads it?"

"What do you mean?" Mr. Strang demanded, and when she did not answer, "Do you believe, as your father does, that I am mad? I—" But he did not go on. He would not tell Sheila the truth—that he was never saner in his life— never more in control of himself and those who served him.

Those who feared him now might fear him more if they thought him mad. He was waiting for Sheila's answer, wondering if he could fool her. But she did not answer him then.

16

THE LAW OF DEATH

SHEILA LOOKED AT Strang, and her eyes did not waver. Finally she raised her other hand and jerking out the light climbed from the bed.

"Come to the window." She pulled at the silken cord and the drapes parted. She leaned out, whispered, "There is one man there below—there—his brass buttons shine. He is watching for a man to attempt entrance—but he can also see if a man *leaves* this house."

Mr. Strang drew a gun from beneath his armpit with his free hand, held it close to the window.

"I could shoot him from here," he said solemnly.

"That is true," said the girl. "Take your hand from my wrist. I will go and open the door and listen when you shoot."

Mr. Strang hesitated; his breath sucked in. Was this a trick of the girl's? Yet she seemed so much in earnest. He said "But my shot would be heard—"

"No one would know where it came from, and certainly not suspect the house of the Commissioner. You could escape even by the front door in the excitement that would follow the shooting of the policeman and—"

"But the man might tell. He might see the flash of the gun. I would have to kill him!"

"Yes, I suppose you would."

"Sheila!" The man turned and dropping her wrist gripped her by both shoulders. "You talk as if you wished me to kill him!"

"I?" she exclaimed. "But isn't that the purpose of Mr. Strang's return to life? He blocks your escape from this house, blocks the death you plan just as much as I did. Yet you threatened me."

"But *you* stood in my way. *He* represents the law. I cannot kill him, for I am the law also—the very law he represents. You—!"

"I was planning a way for you to leave here safely. If I did not wish you to go safely, I would not have let you stay here in the first place. I am going to telephone Doctor Edgar Robinson. I promised to look up some things for him and give him an opinion. I intended to give him that opinion tomorrow, but I will call him now."

"And he will not think it strange—this time of night?"

"No." She shook her head. "He will simply think that I am in the mood to discuss it—or rather simply to enlighten him. You are fortunate that my hours are so irregular, and my life moved by impulses rather than the clock."

He held her hand again when she reached for the phone. "And a medical doctor will come to you for advice, ask your aid, come from his bed this time in the morning? How can you help him?"

"Because," she said, "to him the human body is made up simply of material things. He is a very clever man—if the disease—is there he will see it. But I can see what is not there—not visible. I have a library and laboratory down-stairs."

"But you never told me this, Sheila!"

"It would hardly have interested the Strang Cummings I tried to help."

"And this doctor is to examine me?" There was a queer sound in Strang's throat that might have been a laugh. When Strang looked at her now—her hair down, her face white—she seemed older; much older.

"No," the girl said. "You know that I have rooms down-stairs, and a private entrance on the side street. Doctor Robinson will come by that entrance. A few minutes later, you will leave as Doctor Robinson. The police will hardly question me or my visitors."

Without another word she lifted the phone. Two minutes later she turned and faced Mr. Strang.

"I wish," she said very calmly, "a price for the service I am doing you now—to say nothing of saving your life there on the cliff. I want your word that you will not kill except in self-defense until you see me again."

"My word!" He gripped her hand; she held it a full minute.

It was exactly twenty-five minutes to four when, now fully dressed, she opened the little side door for him. The Doctor was in the library. He was pouring over some closely typewritten sheets of paper. He heard nor saw nothing.

Strang was surprised when she followed him across the sidewalk, gave a cheery greeting to the policeman who sauntered up, then stood with his back against the iron fence along the house.

Sheila Barton leaned in the window and watched Mr.

Strang feel around uncertainly as he put the key in the ignition lock.

"Don't worry about the doctor," she said. "Just leave the car around the corner. And, Strang, you are not even fooling yourself this time."

"What do you mean?" He raised his voice slightly as the motor started.

"The gun—the policeman—my suggestion that you shoot. No, you may succeed in creating the illusion of your madness in others, but you can never create that illusion in me. Don't forget your promise. Goodnight."

The car shot from the curb. Mr. Strang's lips parted, but his eyes remained hard, steady. So Sheila knew.

He needed sleep too—plenty of rest. For the Legion of the Living Dead would walk again. Many criminals would die.

His eyes brightened, burned to glowing flames.

Sheila who could look into the eyes of men and see behind those eyes. He laughed a little shrilly. If what she said was true, she would see behind Mr. Strang's eyes the countless eyes of many dead.

Strang was to be the *law*—The only law the underworld understood. The Law of Death.

17

AT THE BIG HOUSE

STEVE MASON DROVE his car to the great door of the State Prison. Steve thought he visited the prison for the purpose of cheering up a former associate. But actually his trips were caused by an overwhelming desire to stand before those huge gates, pass inside and walk out again. It was odd the way Steve felt about that. It was nice to feel that no prison door had ever or would ever close on him but for a few hours. Yes, he was drawn to those gates sometimes like a bit of steel to a magnet.

Today he was visiting on real business. He had to see Marty Henderson—poor Henderson, a nervous, sensitive sort of man to be shut up behind those grim walls. He wondered how the poor lad stood it. Henderson, the best man for a bit of killing—real out-and-out killing that had to be done quickly—than any other man Steve Mason knew—and Steve's knowledge of killers was large.

The guard who took him to the visiting room, with its high sheets of double netted wire, whistled softly when he heard the names of the men Steve Mason was to see.

"Henderson and Fiester—and young Flint too?" he breathed. "I didn't know you knew Henderson, Mr. Mason."

"No, no!" Mason winked at the guard—there was no

pretence about Mason. "I understand he hasn't many friends and I like to visit the unfortunate."

The guard nodded, said: "About Fiester. I understand he's up for a parole too."

Steve Mason turned on the guard sharply, said: "He isn't in your section."

The guard paled. He had spoken out of turn and it could do him a lot of harm. "Sorry, Mr. Mason!" he murmured apologetically.

Mason nodded briskly and they went on.

Marty Henderson was a thin, nervous little man whose eyes blinked continuously and whose fingers laced and interlaced as he talked.

"Sure. I know you, Mr. Mason Never worked up your alley—never got the chance. You notice me kind of late to do you any good."

"Only dead men are no good to me. Mason leaned as close as he could to the iron mesh. "You're up for parole, Henderson—right?"

"Right." Henderson grinned rather sickly. "Some guy wrote me a letter I should have a try at it. Even sent up a mouthpiece to talk to me. But it's no wash. They're laughing their heads off all over the prison. The mouthpiece ain't showed up again since we first talked."

"Tough, boy!" Mason lowered his head and his voice, but he didn't mention that the letter and the mouthpiece were both sent by him. "Haven't you been behaving all right?"

"They wouldn't let me out anyway—under any circumstances." And when Mason's gaze held his "Oh, I've raised hell a bit. I get nervous."

"Huh!" Mason spoke slowly and distinctly and though

his lips moved the words were more formed than spoken. Yet, Henderson caught every one of them. "You're to be sprung. Things are fixed all down the line—right to Billings himself. Know Billings?"

"I know of him. Head of the Parole Board—one tough baby." And suddenly, his eyes blazing, his face reddening to a vivid brightness against the prison pallor. "What's the racket? I ain't got no dough."

"That's right." Mason nodded. "It'll cost just fifty grand for your out. I can get the fifty back in one payment. After that—I pay you to work for me. I want you to do a killing—a tough killing, a—"

Henderson laughed, choked it off as a guard looked toward him, whispered hoarsely:

"Get me out of here and I'll walk into the White House in Washington with a machine gun and—"

Mason grinned. "It ain't that hard, but it's a judge—a guarded judge—and he's got to be knocked over right on the bench. It's got to be sensational. We've planned for an in and out for you. But there's a possible chance if you're not clever that there will be no out. It's Judge Freedman K. Rawley."

"Him!" Henderson cursed. "He give me my ride and I swore I'd—"

"Yeah, I know. I'm not setting up fifty grand for your pleasure. Will you do the job as told?"

"It's done," Henderson said thickly. "I'll pop him over when the court room is packed if you want. Hell—" He clutched at the bars, "what's a chance at death—to this? Look—I give you my word. You must know my word's good?"

"Sure, sure," Mason said easily as he looked toward the top of the wire mesh. "Your word's good with me, Henderson, but if you don't make good, we'll bust your parole or lay a row of bullets in your back. I was just wondering if you were the type to—" And as a guard started toward them, Steve Mason leaned forward and spoke rapidly, giving Henderson directions as to who would meet him when he came out.

"All right." Steve got up from the hard bench as the guard drew near. "You'll be sprung. Goodby, boy." And to the guard, "Glad I talked to that lad. He don't belong in here."

The guard smiled pleasantly. "He don't belong in here no more than you do, Mr. Mason." And it was hard to take offense at the soft voice and the apparent easy pleasantry of the guard's words.

Steve Mason looked at the guard a long time and wasn't sure. It wasn't like this guard to crack wise. Should he get him fired? But Steve shook his head. He had made it a rule not to let little things bother him—and where he might get this gray-haired old veteran thrown out of his job, it would put nothing in Steve Mason's pockets. Just a favor he'd have to return some day. No, it was small-time stuff like that which put the skids under the big-time names quicker than anything else.

Mason's talk with Fiester was pleasant and easy. He had known Fiester for some time—the best box man in the country. He could open a safe blindfolded and not leave a scratch on its highly polished surface. Of course, the big burglar-proof ones—well, that was different. Fiester was noisy, but he split the box clean and with only one blast.

Fiester was sure of his spring. It was just advice Mason had to give him. He said:

"You and me have been close, Fiester—too close. Your orders won't come directly from me. My good friend Senator Bixby is giving you the out—through Billings of course. You'll be watched. Oh, I don't mean followed, but how you work. Billings has gotten you a job with the American-Canadian Cash Register Company. I'm clean out of it, except to suggest where you might sell your products. Listen."

Steve Mason didn't have much interest in seeing the Flint boy. That was just part of his racket. He'd let the world know who gave Flint his second chance, who spoke to Barton about him, who gave his mother money and who got him a real honest job when he came out.

No, he had no use for the Flint boy. He was dumber than hell. Tommy Flint was simply to be a walking sandwich man advertising Steve Mason's big heart. "Steve Mason's boy who made good—went honest." And Flint would go honest too, or Steve Mason would lay a hunk of lead in the back of his head.

He didn't let young Flint miss any of his generosity. He told him his mother had received good care and that he had personally seen the Commissioner of Police about him, talked with Senator Bixby—and that he would be free. He was a little annoyed when the fool kid promised to keep secret all that Mason had done for him. He didn't think they came as dumb as that. Of course, the boy was honest—he was too dumb to be crooked.

Mason swung back as he walked away. All this work and nothing out of it. He was too good a business man to take all this trouble and get nothing in return. He said to the boy:

"After all—tell people if you want to, Tommy. I know now I'm not going to be ashamed of you. So tell the world. I'm proud you're making good."

Steve liked the pleased look in the boy's eyes—almost tears of gratitude that he was to be permitted to tell others the name of his benefactor. Yes, young Flint was crying as Steve Mason went whistling out the prison gates and climbed into his classy car....

18

POWER

STEVE MASON FELT pretty good as he drove back to town. He was the biggest man in the rackets today. Maybe the Meyers mob made more money at the moment, but he'd soon drive them out of the picture. Steve Mason had vision. He looked toward the future.

Mason always thought of the Meyers boys as a mob. Steve Mason's was an organization and a big one; a big one that needed more money and of a necessity must enter new fields to get that money. With Senator Bixby governor, Steve Mason would sit back and grease the wheels—plenty of wheels, but also plenty of grease. Bixby would just wear the title of Governor. Steve Mason would have—no, he would *be* power!

The Billings bump looked good—almost ripe. Even the attempt on Billings' life had not been recognized as such. The police, the papers put it down to rival "mobsters" meeting and shooting it out down the street from Billings' house. And maybe it did look like that. Joe and his two punks did make a mess of things. But at least they had left Billings open for the kill.

Senator Bixby! Mason took a grin. The Senator would no longer be hard to handle. He had sat in on a killing. "The vicious, brutal murder of a helpless drug addict," the papers would call it if they ever found out how it did happen. Still the Senator never made a peep. Steve Mason might have the pleasure of shoving his huge hand into the Senator's "mush" yet. From now on, he and the Senator would call a killing a killing and not an "unfortunate accident."

He had already taken care of the Fiester angle. The Senator had approved that parole and had made Billings see it his way. Yes, and just as Billings did in many other instances, he had obtained a job for Fiester. Cash registers. Not a bad job at that. Most of the taverns uptown needed new cash registers anyway—and if they thought they didn't, Mason's boys had gone out and changed their minds.

Mason had to have Fiester show a good sales record. Show the Parole Board that no mistake had been made in letting Fiester out. But all that had already been attended to—or at least Mason had given orders that it should be attended to, which amounted to the same thing. Mason had not gotten Fiester out to sell cash registers. He had more important things for him to do—a big job—a damn big job.

Of course, Mason could have bought those cash registers himself and distributed them around. And he would too, if it was simply a single man out on parole. Billings had dough—plenty of it, and dough had pull. Billings was a stockholder in many companies. And Billings got some of the paroled boys the damnest jobs. Steve laughed. It was only a week or two ago that he had had a downtown hotel to outfit with some pretty classy bedroom furniture for a paroled gunner whom Billings had made a furniture salesman.

Steve chuckled. Maybe he was lucky after all. Suppose Billings shoved a paroled mug into selling dredges or even locomotives. He guessed he'd have trouble clamping down on one of the big railroads. And Steve didn't chuckle any longer as he drove to the Black Knight Club. That sounded like a dream, eh? Well, with Bixby as governor it might become a nightmare. Oh, not a nightmare for Mason, but a nightmare for the railroad company. There would be no limit to the power and experience a man in his business might obtain. And Steve Mason was an experienced man.

As for the Meyers mob. There was a truce with them at present. A truce so detrimental to the interests of Steve Mason that even the swaggering Meyers might have guessed at the purpose of it. But he didn't guess it. Meyers believed that Steve gave so he, Meyers, would not take. And Steve Mason was doing everything he could to cement a deeper "friendship" between his organization and the Meyers mob. Meyers' boys would be that much more surprised when Mason pulled his massacre.

As soon as Mason reached his office he sent for Rudolph Weber. He said abruptly when Rudolph entered the room: "Fiester will be sprung next week. Give me a list of places that were glad to buy the cash registers and those, if any, who wouldn't buy."

RUDOLPH HANDED OVER a few typewritten sheets of paper, explained as he leaned over Mason's shoulder.

"The guys in blue made no squawk. Those in black took a little arguing—" When Mason looked up from the seven names in red, Rudolph said, "That's right, Boss. Those seven refused flat."

Steve Mason ran a tongue beneath his upper lip.

"Can't have that." He shook his head. "Poor business—" He hesitated a moment and then, "Get an outside mob to go up and wreck those seven places tonight. It should be a cheap job, Rudolph—just walking in and breaking things up. Then we'll see how they feel about buying."

"Okay, Boss." Rudolph Weber waited, watched Steve Mason examining the large, hand-printed name on the bottom of the last sheet.

At length Mason spoke.

"Tony Ricarro. When did he buy a place uptown? How did the boys happen to run in on him? Hell, he'll connect me up with the racket."

"That's right." Rudolph nodded. "He always hated you, Steve. You drove him down the ladder from the owner of a big mid-town restaurant to this little dump he now has. He told Fats he'd go straight to the D.A. in the morning. And Tony ain't one to bluff. Remember in that investigation when he damn near sent you—well, you remember."

"Yes, I remember." Steve Mason took a pencil from his pocket, very carefully drew a line through the name Tony Ricarro. "He's got a nerve going into business under his own name after taking a crack at me. Well, he won't go to the D.A. in the morning. It's your personal job, Rudolph, to see that he doesn't. Remember, he was always fast with a knife."

"I'll burn him down." Rudolph nodded and started toward the door.

Steve clutched his arm. "For once you're right, but not

with a gun, Rudolph. You used to do a bit of arson against the fire insurance companies before you came over with me. Can you do a sure and quick job now?"

"Sure, sure!" Rudolph looked inquiringly at Steve Mason. "Tony's got a wife and two kids sleeping upstairs. They'll be sure to roast if it's a quick job."

"Well?" Steve Mason just looked at him.

"Okay. Any special reason?"

"Must there be a reason?" And when Rudolph only smiled and shook his head, "Hell, I don't like him or any of his family. Be back here at twelve o'clock."

Steve Mason was not afraid that Tony would have police protection. He knew better than that; knew that men were very wise not to testify before the Grand Jury in racket inquiries. They were well protected while their testimony was necessary, but after that? Steve's hands spread far apart.

He sat back as Rudolph passed out of his sound-proof room, along the sound-proof hall with its heavy doors and so quietly through the side door to the alley. Mason could plainly see his own guard who sat there with a heavy caliber revolver held across his knees. No, Mason had nothing to fear.

He came to his feet, crossed to the door and called to the man in the chair; a giant of a man—Tiny Manning:

"I'll see no one until Rudolph comes back." And when the man simply nodded, "Remember, no one," and with a laugh, "except over your dead body."

"No one," Tiny Manning repeated the words, "except over my dead body."

Steve Mason hesitated, then closing the door he shut himself up in his room. He wanted to think. He had a two-hundred-grand job for Herman Fiester. It was a box job and needed both clean and fast work. Noise didn't matter if it was a fast job.

19

THE FACE IN THE LIGHT

RUDOLPH WEBER NEVER regretted killing his own brother and so pushing himself up to be Mason's right-hand man. He liked working for Mason—there was so little worry attached to it. So little loss of sleep. It wasn't Rudolph's conscience that bothered him. It was lying awake nights wondering if someone who could make the big squawk might do it before morning. With Mason there was no morning. He struck quickly. Few men would dare to talk about Steve Mason. Those who dared didn't live long enough to talk.

And Rudolph was proud of his work; he was an efficient killer. Gun or knife made little difference; he used both with equal proficiency. As for arson—well, that was his original line. It wasn't that the insurance companies got so tough, but that his big chance came with Mason; came when Mason put the finger on him, and Rudolph saved his own life by arranging to trap and murder his own brother. Since then, things had gone big for Rudolph.

It was shortly before eleven o'clock when Rudolph reached Tony's home well out on the edge of the city—the three-story wooden structure with the little restaurant on the ground floor. He had all the information necessary.

Tony was in the habit of closing up the restaurant after the dinner crowd had gone. Except on Saturday nights, when he took the wife and kids to a movie, he smoked his pipe, read his paper and went to bed a little after nine. Tony served a five o'clock breakfast. Not to many people, perhaps, but since it was on his own time, he made money on the deal.

Still Rudolph was a cautious man. A fleeting figure met him, gave him the information that Tony had retired at five minutes past nine, and being a man who saved his money had turned out all lights.

"I've eaten there quite a bit, Mister." The shifty-eyed man tried to peer at Rudolph's face, but saw nothing above the scarf and nothing but distant eyes beneath the hat. Then he asked, "What do you aim to do? Tony ain't a bad guy. There's a cellar window with a break in the glass by the lock. You just got to reach in your hand. I done a swell job, Mister. The guy what you sent to have me fix things said you'd pay me handsome."

Rudolph raised his left hand slowly and gripped the thin man's wrist, then opening the hand he shoved a roll of bills into it.

"Blood money," he said in a hoarse disguised voice. "From Meyers. Don't spend too much of it tonight, but get yourself off to some place you know—will be seen." And as the man would have jerked from his grip, not liking the coldness of that voice, "And remember, what ever happens here tonight you are just as guilty under the law as if you planned and executed the whole thing. Get going."

The thin man went. He knew something terrible was going to happen to Tony—maybe not his best friend, but

Tony in whose place he had often, as he said, eaten—but he didn't say how often he had eaten free.

Rudolph examined the little stone yard, found the window, pushed through his hand and snapped back the lock. For a long time he remained in the shadows listening. Then he went back to the car and brought his kerosene and bundle of newspapers. His last trip from the car was a very careful one. He carried a long box which he placed beside the window. In that box was his whole bag of tricks; the explosive that would toss burning oil right through the ceiling. It would take only a minute, a few more at the most if he needed time to get away from that first single terrible blast that would drop the entire building into an inferno.

Rudolph grinned to himself when he climbed in that window and shot his small flash about the floor. It was nice—easy to do a job like this. No careful workmanship was needed to fool the insurance men. No one would care what they thought, except, perhaps, some distant relative of Tony's. As for Tony and his wife and his kids, they'd tumble at the first blast right into the raging, leaping flames.

Rudolph had no kick coming. He had brought the proper equipment for a real fire. Tony had supplied the old wooden structure to make the fire a complete success. Mason wanted this job done right. It was personal ambition as well as business with him. Rudolph was sure of an extra grand or two bonus.

There were many places to hide in that little cellar, many papers and boxes of both cardboard and wood. But Rudolph had no intention of hiding. He just looked the place over, running his light in and out of dark corners. He was a careful man. The only place he did not look in was the coal bin. He just glanced at the door, saw that a padlock held it closed and went to work.

The papers Rudolph saturated with kerosene and put them about the cellar. He didn't merely toss them about. He placed them in strategic positions. He knew how to build a fire that would do its damage before the firemen arrived, would be a roaring furnace in seconds.

Yes, Rudolph was a fast worker. It was all easy and familiar work to him.

Familiar, but dangerous when he was ready for that oblong box. His flash flickered about the cellar again, fell upon a chair. Rudolph crossed to it, tried his weight upon it, didn't like the way it swayed, found another, and at length picked one whose only fault was a bad leg. Very painstakingly, he tied this leg up with thick clothesline which he lifted from behind some old iron. Then he stood on the chair, tested it, bending his knees up and down. Rudolph was satisfied.

He moved the chair to the window, stepped up on the seat, leaned out the window and lifted in his long box.

RUDOLPH HELD THAT oblong box in his arms as gently as any young mother ever held a new-born babe. His foot slid carefully from the seat of the chair when he stepped down. His movements across the cellar, directed by the flashlight that he had placed on the stairs to the floor above, were slow and deliberate and he kept directly in that light. His sigh was audible when he finally placed the box upon the fourth step, and with great effort lifted the five-gallon glass jar of kerosene and placed it upon the box with the utmost caution.

After that Rudolph worked quickly. There was the fuse, the necessity of soaking it with oil, carefully lifting a tiny circle of wood in the box and inserting the end of that long fuse.

He didn't raise his head when he had finished that job. Rather, he lowered it as he directed his light upon the floor and strung the fuse slowly out before him.

He had almost reached the window when he raised his head, gasped slightly, then shot up the flash in his hand. A man was sitting in the chair he had left beneath the window. Weber's flash shone squarely on the man's face.

Rudolph Weber, who had killed his brother without the least fear, felt the blood drain from his face, heard the wind whistle in his throat and felt it choke him.

It was not a pleasant face. It was hard, as if it had been molded in wax. Nothing seemed to move about it; nothing seemed to be alive about it. The straight black hair down over its forehead like a bang—yet it wasn't a bang. It was deadly, sinister, straight black hair, more as if it were part of the forehead itself—as if it were painted upon that forehead and not combed that way. But all this Rudolph saw only for the fraction of a second. After that, the eyes of the man in the chair held him.

Burning, deep, cruel eyes—and yes, Rudolph felt that they would be the same in the dark, that the light was not needed. The eyes were alive; too alive with hate to be just glass stuck in a white wax face that was put there to frighten him. But despite the brightness of his flashlight, those eyes did not blink nor did a lash flutter.

How could this man see him if the light was directly upon his eyes? But Rudolph could see the man; could draw a gun and kill him. Perhaps if Rudolph had such thoughts they might have been correct. But Rudolph had no such thoughts; no thought of any kind, except a fear that was growing to a deadly terror.

Like a living dead man—that was what he was. And the living dead man spoke.

"Surprised, Mr. Weber? But then the lock on the coal bin was not snapped. The name is Strang," he said slowly. "Mr. Strang." And Mr. Strang raised his right hand slowly; a heavy revolver was gripped in it. The revolver wavered slightly, then Mr. Strang's elbow settled on his knee, the nose of his revolver settled directly on that light.

"You are—you must be!" Rudolph's voice was raising to a squeak; an almost hysterical squeak. "But you can't— you—you are dead!"

The wax-like face moved, seemed to twist at the mouth. The words that came were very low, yet very terrifying to Rudolph Weber: "I am the head of the Legion of the Living Dead," Mr. Strang said slowly.

"It was you then—you who murdered Gunner Keen and Eddie Owen, and left their bodies hanging from that ceiling?"

"Yes, I killed them, Rudolph. I put the signs there. They murdered Resa Kent. There were three other men who took part in that murder. I want to know the names of two of them."

"Two of them!" Rudolph gasped. "Only two of them?"

"That's all," said Mr. Strang. "Only two of them. I know the name of the third. Don't lie—not about murder when you are so close to death. I saw you plainly that night."

"I should have killed you then—could have—"

"No, you couldn't have, Rudolph. You were afraid that night, afraid just as I was afraid then. I was a coward because I could not help myself; you were a coward because others were coming—and because you have always been a coward and will die a coward."

"You are going to—to kill me now?" Rudolph breathed the words. It was the first time he thought of the light—directly on the man's face, and his left hand that had only to cross from beneath his right armpit to shoot Mr. Strang between those burning eyes.

That was it. That was what he should have done. Why the man was mad—was always half mad and now—now! Rudolph tried to keep from laughing, it was so simple, so easy. Yet he didn't keep from laughing and his laugh held a hysterical note as the left hand which started across the chest trembled; trembled but reached his shoulder holster just the same.

What was wrong with him? He never had had any trouble in getting his gun before. Why he could draw and shoot in less than— And he had the gun, had his cold wet fingers upon the butt, was tightening those fingers for a grip; a firm grip that icy fingers refused at first to take, and then—

20

A THREE-EDGED KNIFE

LIGHT BLAZED IN Rudolph Weber's eyes. His own torch was torn from his fingers and something rapped sharply against the hand that held the gun. He closed his eyes as he felt the gun slipping from his fingers, held himself tense. It wouldn't take much if that gun went off and the bullet went in the wrong direction—no, not much to send them both—with Tony and his family, to a living hell.

His gun never hit the floor—at least Rudolph didn't hear it strike. He surmised that Mr. Strang had caught it, but he didn't know. Now he faced the light and Mr. Strang was invisible behind that deadly glare.

Mr. Strang was saying easily: "No, Rudolph, I am not going to kill you if you answer these few questions. One—is Kirkman Billings absolutely on the level?"

"Hardly. Of course not. I'm sure of that," Rudolph said almost eagerly. It was good to get Mr. Strang's attention elsewhere.

But Mr. Strang did not seem excited, he only said: "Steve Mason was behind the killing of Resa Kent. I am almost sure of that. But was he at the killing?"

"No, no—he knew nothing about it."

"The important question—and be sure you do not lie this time—who were the other two men besides yourself?"

"I can't. I can't tell you that," Rudolph cried out. "I wouldn't live a—"

"I am sure," said Mr. Strang, "that you will at least live longer by answering now than you will by not answering—"

"I'm to be free—I'm to leave here free if I tell? I can't believe that after the way Keen and Owen died. You don't know—don't know how Steve Mason would kill me—the method he'd use if I talked."

"But you don't know, Rudolph, the method I would use if you didn't talk. And you can't get away from me."

"I couldn't get away from Steve—no matter where I went. I—"

Strang said: "My method would be to tie you on this chair, place you and the chair directly over the long box which you so carefully handled, set the fuse from the window and—"

"You wouldn't do that—not you, Mr. Strang!" As Mr. Strang moved the flash so that it shone upon his own face, he whispered hoarsely: "No, no, you can't! Tony—his wife—his kids."

Mr. Strang moved the light again so that the flash showed his shrugging shoulders, his twisted lips, his narrowing eyes of fire. "I am hardly acquainted with Tony and do not know his charming family at all." His words were a sneer.

"But you came here to save them!" Rudolph's voice was quivering now.

"You flatter me, my dear Rudolph. I came here to kill you or listen to you. The method of your death you supplied yourself. I saw you above Resa Kent's body that night. Tonight I followed you here."

Mr. Strang let the light from the flash fall upon the floor and Rudolph acted. Not any sudden great courage that was hidden in the man, but the fierce fear of the terrorized rat. It was Rudolph's right hand this time that shot to his left armpit; shot there and stayed there. He didn't know that Mr. Strang's right hand went up and down; he only knew that the light was in his face again—after that, something crashed on his head and he knew nothing.

Rudolph opened his eyes with a dull sort of consciousness that something unpleasant had happened or was about to happen. But whatever it was Steve Mason would fix that—would— And Rudolph could not move his legs nor his arms.

He jerked his body quickly, felt a hand grip his shoulder, and a voice say:

"Steady, Rudolph. You could have died then, your mangled body would had decorated Tony's house. Be still, very still. You don't know the trouble I had in getting you and the chair on the cellar steps, your back against the wall, your face looking at the kitchen door above; the door that you will never use, because the box—the box that you handled so daintily is directly below your chair and—"

Mr. Strang clapped a hand tightly over Rudolph's mouth before the scream came. It was some time before he released that hand, and while he waited he talked.

"You helped kill Resa. Perhaps your bullet actually killed her. You—yes, it is in my book that you stretched an arm about your brother's neck and cut his throat. I am afraid I may risk my own life tonight until I see you— What was that?"

Rudolph muttered as great beads of perspiration ran down his forehead: "Tiny Manning was the other man."

Mr. Strang's eyes widened. He felt that was the truth. But he said:

"You mean the big fellow—Mason's personal bodyguard? The man who—"

"Who sits behind the alley entrance to Steve's room at the Black Knight, with a gun in each hand. Just him—the other lad was—was—I can't think of his name."

"It was Mason."

And Rudolph suddenly grew hard. "I don't believe you'll do it. You can't do it. Go on, blow everything to hell. I'm going to holler my head off and—"

THE SCREAM WAS low, gurgled as Mr. Strang shoved the handkerchief into Rudolph's mouth and bound it there with a length of the heavy clothesline.

"All right, Rudolph," he said and his voice sounded pleasant for the first time. "You gave me one name. After all, I'd rather kill you and learn the other for myself, for I feel sure it's Mason anyway."

Mr. Strang talked as he placed Rudolph's flashlight on the steps so that it shone back upon Rudolph's face, sprinkled down his right side which was nearest Strang and the window. Mr. Strang was very careful about adjusting that light. Then he lifted Rudolph's right hand so that the wrist held it straight up in the air. He tied his neck tightly to the back of that chair after turning his head so it would face the window.

"We are set now, Rudolph," he said as he looked at him. "I am going to leave, go to the window, pull the fuse through, just as you would have done. Keep your right hand high. If you wish to talk, drop it down and I'll know."

Frantic eyes looked at Mr. Strang; the handkerchief moved, cheeks bulged as if the man would talk. But Strang looked at his right hand. It remained up. He said:

"You should know better than I how long it will take the fire to reach this box. But after the fuse starts burning I can make a very good guess at it. If it seems to me that your hand remains erect too long for my safety, why I'll be leaving you. But it's for you to decide."

Mr. Strang bent quickly and snapped the fuse off close to that long box. Of course, he never intended to blow Tony and his whole family to death.

Now—he cursed softly. The thing would have to work or it would get back to Mason and the others that Mr. Strang bluffed, threatened a death that he did not give. Yes, Strang would have liked to drag Rudolph to the center of the floor and put a bullet in his head; even through the back of his head.

He didn't know if he could actually kill the man in cold blood like that. Murder him there in Tony's cellar. But that he would have liked to remained the truth—even if he had given a promise to Sheila Barton, the Commissioner's daughter, that he would not—well, "murder" was the word, until he had seen her again.

Mr. Strang didn't believe Rudolph would be able to take it; watch the sputtering fire cross the room toward him; the sputtering fire creep toward the box of death. Strang would make the thing real enough—and if he didn't, what? If he didn't—

Mr. Strang climbed upon the chair, was even noisy as

he lifted the window that swung down from the top, then turned once to look at Rudolph.

Rudolph's eyes were on him. Rudolph's hand was still raised. The light shone directly along his right side, from below the hand up over the right side of his face and head. His nose was just about the dividing point between light and darkness—just the edge of it remained in the circle of light; the other half of his body disappeared slowly into darkness.

Mr. Strang pushed up the window, raised his knee and there was a dull thump. He lowered the window silently and turned his head. Rudolph was very still, but his hand was down. That was the thump then. He was ready to talk.

Mr. Strang sighed with relief as he crossed the room. He'd tell Rudolph the truth. That his freedom was for twenty-four hours only. In those twenty-four hours he could do as he pleased. After that—well, Rudolph was a man of the world and didn't have to be told the facts of life—or perhaps the facts of death.

Rudolph's eyes were still open; there was still fear in them, but no pleading. A misty sort of glassy fear probably from the light that hit directly on his right eye.

Mr. Strang stumbled over a step, steadied himself against Rudolph and the chair, expected momentarily an explosion from that box. None came. He leaned over and started to look into Rudolph's eyes. But his attention was distracted to something else; something that struck his arm as he bent forward; something that must protrude from the other side of the chair or—

And something did protrude. It protruded straight from Rudolph's body; from his heart. Red was surrounding that something; gathering about it, leaving it in little rivulets and flowing down Rudolph's chest. Yes, Strang saw the thing plainly. The hilt of a knife. A three-edged dagger was driven deeply into Rudolph's body.

Mr. Strang stared into Rudolph's eyes though he didn't need to. Before he recognized that glassiness of death, he knew the truth. He knew that Rudolph Weber was dead. The knife had been driven or thrown with great force, evidently when Mr. Strang had had his back to those stairs.

He knew what the thump had been. It was not the falling of that hand as he had thought. It was the plunge of a knife; a knife hard into Rudolph's chest.

Mr. Strang looked up those steps, climbed them and tried the door above. It was locked. It would not be hard to force. But he shook his head as he returned, passed the dead Rudolph and went toward the window. He could not wait much longer; he had much to do that night. Then he paused, walked back to the stairs and looked up at the locked door, put his flash upon it; put it finally upon Rudolph Weber.

He shrugged his shoulders, shook his head. After all, Tony Ricarro and his wife would have no use for that corpse. It wouldn't do for it to be found there by the police or one of his waiters or cooks—or even a guest, for Tony's was not a high-class place and the washroom was in the cellar.

No, Tony didn't want that corpse—and certainly Strang didn't. He hesitated, then lifted the chair carefully from the box, carried it to the center of the cellar floor and started rapidly to untie that dead body.

He had suddenly decided that he wanted Rudolph—the dead body of Rudolph—very much indeed.

21

OVER A DEAD BODY!

STEVE MASON HAD plenty to do. He was figuring out a speech he would make, a short pep-talk that would be memorized by Rudolph and several other of his best—not big—leaders. Steve Mason allowed no single man to get too big. Ambition followed too quickly then and Steve knew that ambition was too often meant the murder of the head man, in this case, Steve's own murder.

At the same time, Mason examined a list of figures—figures that represented his entire fortune. He scratched his head and compared those figures with the list of men he controlled.

Wrinkles crowded his forehead as he thought of the words he would say: "Boys, our organization is closing down for a bit—that is, the parole end of it. I want you to cut your expenses, too, until I get other things rolling. Then parole again, but this time, the biggest racket the country ever knew!"

Steve Mason had come to a decision. He was going to have Billings killed, was going to get Senator Bixby in as head of the Parole Board, then push him right smack into the Governor's chair. Why, he'd make parole a more deadly and better paying racket than it had ever been!

The only hitch was that, during the first six months Bixby headed the Parole Board, things would have to be slowed down. The papers would feature the Senator up as the toughest man who ever kept a criminal behind bars.

But when things opened up again. Steve Mason would run the city, run the whole state! Men wouldn't be paroled in hundreds—they'd be paroled in very small lots. But each parole would put one hundred thousand dollars in Steve Mason's pockets. Some of it would have to go to the Senator, of course. That was only common sense. But the Senator had witnessed a murder and from now on Mason would give the orders and the Senator would obey them, willy-nilly.

The thing was so big that Mason sat back and stared at the ceiling. He wouldn't even think too much about it now. He'd see Senator Bixby first, get that straightened out. Then the simple matter of eliminating Kirkman Billings, millionaire, philanthropist, great humanitarian—and the city's biggest dim-wit!

Big! Steve's eyes brightened. He felt very proud of himself. He could think of a dozen men—two dozen, perhaps fifty—right at this moment who would pay one hundred grand to see certain men free. It was a great racket—the world's greatest racket—and Steve would own it!

He went back to his figuring how to keep his organization satisfied while things went slowly. Let's see. Something like this:

"Boys, Steve Mason has always played square with you. Now he wants you to play along with him. For a time there will be no money." Steve bit his lip, changed it. "For a time

These were Mr. Strang's men—a motley army, the Legion of the Living Dead!

there will be little money." Then he changed that too. "For a time there will not be so much money."

Hell! His hand came down on the desk. It would be cheaper to knock over the small fry. They were the ones who talked most, who'd spread it around that things weren't going so well for Steve. They'd try to go over to Meyers and—but Meyers would be dead by then.

Steve looked up suddenly to see his door opening. He yelled:

"I told you not to bother me, Tiny!" He blinked then at the partly open door, said: "Rudolph, eh? Hell, come in, boy!"

The door opened and a man came in. He left the door wide behind him, walked slowly toward the desk behind which Steve Mason was seated. There was something very familiar about the man's face—even in the shadows. Steve's eyes darted to the hands by the man's sides—two white hands that were empty—and then his gaze went to the heavy black snub-nosed automatic upon his desk.

He smiled through his teeth, said: "No visitors tonight. I don't see strangers without appointment. And if I did, they'd wish I hadn't—afterwards."

"But I—" said the man very slowly, as steady bright coals of fire stared at Steve Mason, "—I was invited to see you."

"Invited?" Steve's eyebrows raised. "That's a lie to begin with. I told Tiny Manning that no one was to come in except over his dead body."

"Exactly. That's what I mean. I took the invitation literally and came in."

"You mean—?" Mason's hand rested on the desk, but did not move at once toward the gun.

"I mean that I came as requested—over the dead body of Tiny Manning—who helped murder Resa Kent."

"OH!" STEVE MASON did not shake with fear. He sized up the situation quickly, saw that it was five minutes of twelve. Rudolph was due back at twelve o'clock at the latest. And he guessed the man's identity. He said:

"You're the man who left the signs on Gunner Keen and Eddie Owen. 'The living dead walking again' or something like that?"

"I," announced the man, his gaunt face showing hollows; his eyes a blaze as if oil were thrown on a dying fire and sent the flames up again— "I *am* the living dead—the leader of the living dead. I brought you a present, Mason."

And suddenly, as Mason's hand moved along the desk, closer to his gun, the man rasped: "By lifting that gun and trying to use it you would confer on me a great favor."

"Yeah?" Steve Mason was disconcerted. He had never had an invitation of that kind presented to him before. Finally he managed to say:

"Just how would that confer a favor on you?"

"Because," said the man, "you are the man I most desire to shoot to death. Understand?"

"Sure, sure!" Steve Mason wondered if the man was mad. And what the hell was this story of the living dead anyway? "Of course!"

Steve Mason was sorely tempted to reach for that gun. "You are a former associate of this Mr. Strang," he hazarded. And leaning forward, "You believe that in dying by violence, by my hand, that you will be rewarded? Is that it?"

Mason waited for the answer, waited for that single short word of affirmation. Then he would grab the gun and shoot.

"No," answered the man. "My reward will come in killing you, not in dying myself. The gun is very close, Steve, but you're pretty yellow when the time comes to die."

Steve Mason tried a laugh, abandoned that attempt at once. It did not ring true, even to his ears. He wondered, also, why he didn't jerk up that gun and fire. Certainly, no man could beat him to a shot under such circumstances.

But he didn't move his hand nearer the gun. He watched those deep eyes, knew the man thought, at least, that he could beat Mason to the draw. Then suddenly, Steve felt better. If the man intended to kill him, he could have done so the moment he entered the room. Time—that was all Steve needed. Time enough to discover what sort of man he was dealing with.

Mason tried to make his voice easy:

"I don't understand exactly how you got in. Tiny Manning downstairs—the bolted, barred door to the alley.

Manning had a chance to look through the slot and spot a stranger."

"He looked through the slot, but he didn't see a stranger," replied the man with the burning eyes. "He saw Rudolph Weber and opened up. Joked about entering over his dead body—"

Steve Mason's eyes glanced toward the gun again. "And Tiny Manning—you didn't actually—?"

The stranger leaned forward. There was death in every word he spoke:

"He wanted to use his gun, Steve Mason. But I shot him directly through the head. I hope you won't try to use a gun—at least, not right now."

Mason straightened slightly in his chair, asked: "You have not come here to kill me, then?" There was a new ring of confidence in his voice.

The man answered very slowly: "I have never lied to a man about to die. Yes, I have come here to kill you."

"Murder—murder me?"

"Execute you, Mason, is the way I would put it."

"That will be murder."

"You will certainly be dead."

Mason looked long and earnestly at the man before him. Then he shook his head. He saw a killer who had supreme confidence in himself. One of these living dead men then—one of those men who *wished* to die.

Mason bit his lips. He said to the man: "You are wasting your time with me—Mr. Strang is dead."

"No." The visitor shook his head. "Mr. Strang will never die—as long as I live."

22

TERROR

STEVE MASON WAS puzzled. This man was not mad, of course, but he was mad enough to draw a gun, and if Mason's first shot did not go right through his head, he was mad enough to brace himself against that wall and—

Mason said: "And Rudolph—who gained you admission? Where is he?"

"Rudolph is out in the hall. He stood right before that steel slot while Tiny Manning looked out. I stood very close to him. Here, I'll bring Rudolph in!"

The man half turned toward the door, swung back suddenly. There was a gun in his hand as he walked over and, with a vicious movement, knocked the automatic from beneath Steve Mason's now frozen grip. He watched it spin across the smooth surface of the desk and strike the wall before it landed on the heavy rug.

"I am sorry, Mr. Mason," he said. "But I cannot kill you yet. Under those circumstances I could not make you talk. Yes, talk. You see, four have already paid for the night that a girl died. I thought, until this moment, that there were only five to pay. You are the fifth, of course—but now I sense a sixth person behind you." He shot his face forward, "Rich men have hidden pasts, but whoever heard of a poor man being blackmailed trying to protect his good name?" And as Mason's mouth hung open—he watched that gun—the man said, "I mean Kirkman Billings, of course. Tonight I want to ask you about him—and you shall tell me."

He watched Mason closely. First surprise, then a sort of shrewd pleasure in Mason's face. And he thought: "Billings is not the man or Mason is a fine actor."

Mason thought: "This may be the man to do the job on Billings." He said: "Billings is my friend. He is an honest man. I have nothing but respect for him." Gaining confidence, since the threat of death seemed to have gone, losing it again almost as quickly as he thought that he might have a mad man to deal with: "Rudolph Weber—why not bring him in? I'd like to hear this story of your entrance from his lips."

The stranger smiled, but his eyes remained unblinking, uncompromising. He backed from the room, leaving the door open, said before he stepped into the hall:

"If your have another gun and care to use it when I return, don't hesitate on my account."

If Mason had another gun, he did not try to use it. Indeed, he might have to pound lead into the body of Rudolph Weber, for surely Weber would precede the stranger, protecting his body. Not that Steve would have minded that so much— Later, perhaps, when he had questioned Rudolph about the little business up at Tony Ricarro's and—

Then Steve Mason saw Rudolph. He was preceding the strange visitor into the room, all right, almost hiding the man's body completely.

But Mason didn't see Rudolph's eyes—his hat was

pulled well down—but he saw Rudolph's mouth down on his chest. Then he saw Rudolph's legs dragging across the floor, twisting and turning laxly. His arms that swung so limply, that—that—

For the first time in his life, Steve Mason screamed, coming to his feet behind that desk. But he didn't step back; he couldn't step back. He just stood there. Faced it—and took it.

Rudolph's head jerked up and Mason saw those blank dead eyes. After that, things happened quickly. Rudolph's body was off the floor, rushing toward him, and finally, with one great jump in the air, one mighty heave from the man who had held Rudolph erect, that body flew across the desk. It pounded against Steve Mason, sent him staggering back, tripping, falling, finally crashing under the weight of the dead man in his arms. And he saw the thing that was pinned to the dead chest.

It was that little square of cardboard that he had seen plainly, read clearly just before he screamed. Rudolph's head had gone up, and dead eyes stared at Steve Mason, but it was the cardboard with the printed letters which Steve saw.

With the Compliments of Mr. Strang!

HE WAS A fool, Mason told himself as he pushed the body away and jerked himself to a sitting position. Rudolph's dead body still lay across his knees. Of course, he should have grabbed his gun and shot it out. He might have known that things had gone wrong—terribly wrong. No other living man could act like this man; no other living man but one—Mr. Strang.

Yes, Steve Mason knew now. And Steve Mason either lost his nerve or found it again. He never could be sure which. Anyway, his right hand came up and shot beneath his left armpit where his heavy black gun snuggled in a shoulder holster.

But all he did was to reach, for Mr. Strang was beside him then. Mr. Strang's foot moved; the toe of that boot landed heavily against his chin. Steve Mason only knew that his head whirled, and that there was blackness.

Somehow he thought he heard words; words from Mr. Strang, the man who killed in the night. Then he knew that it wasn't words. The man had laughed.

Steve Mason opened his eyes, looked into running, shimmering, liquid steel. He stared straight into the dead face of Rudolph Weber, shrank back, managed to push the body from him.

Mr. Strang watched him start to his feet. Strang's right hand shot beneath his left armpit. Steve Mason cried out, felt the blow alongside of his head, toppled, fell to the floor. "What—what do you intend to do with me?" he asked thickly.

Mr. Strang snarled: "I want to know about Billings. I want to know, before you die. Is he in this? Who helps you? Whose influence frees murderers to roam the city streets? Is it Kirkman Billings?"

"Billings?" Steve Mason's mind was dull, confused. "If you thought that he was helping me, then why kill the men who went to take his life the other night?" And, as the cobwebs cleared: "Oh, I know the police and the papers didn't connect Billings up with that little affair. Just a gun-fight a short distance from his home. But you knew, Mr. Strang. You sent them."

Mr. Strang shook his head. "I did not send those men." He paused as he thought of the months he had lay hidden from this army he had assembled. "Yet they still remain faithful to me, not knowing if I was dead or alive. They were there to kill any men associated with you, Steve Mason, and from the reports in the papers, they did not make a bad job of it."

Steve Mason was fast becoming himself again. He said shrewdly: "If you kill me, then I can't tell you." Mason rested both hands flat upon the floor, looked toward the push-button beneath his desk. He saw the rising gun in Mr. Strang's hand, remained crouched. But he never lost his head. He went on:

"Be careful, Mr. Strang. You are not dealing with any common hood now. It wouldn't do to shoot Steve Mason down in his own office. Someone will be along in a minute—perhaps less." And twisting his lips, "You'd never have a chance. I've faced better men than you. Why you're nothing but a—a— Don't! Don't! Man, don't. You couldn't murder a man on his knees!"

But Mason knew differently even as he cried out the words.

Mr. Strang's gun came up, shot forward close to the kneeling man's chest. Murder, eh? And his promise to Sheila. He looked at Steve Mason now and knew that he had as much right to close a finger and snuff out this man's life as had any executioner paid by the state.

Strang stepped back a few feet, looked at the crouching man. It was dangerous to wait any longer. He said simply:

"I'm sorry, Mason, that you weren't more a man and less a rat—that you didn't take your chance when I first came in. Now—death has caught up with you. I'm going to shoot you to death."

And Strang wondered if he had waited too long. A distant door opened and closed. Mason's hand stretched out and gripped the desk, touched the lower part of it.

THE LIGHTS WENT out. A gun blazed. A human body thumped against wood—whether a dead body pounded there by heavy lead or a living body thrown there by its own sudden twisting, Mr. Strang didn't know. He saw only the yellow-blue flame of his own gun.

Now he was moving rapidly in the direction of the hall. A voice was calling; a voice that answered itself. It said:

"Oh, Steve— Steve—!" And then it said to someone else, "Steve don't answer and the trick button on his desk just threw the lights out—clean down the whole hall. It's his signal of trouble."

Was Mason dead? He did not answer the call. There was no sound in that room as Mr. Strang felt his way across it, found the open door, stepped into the hall and moved rapidly—one hand against the wall. Then in the blackness his body brushed another. A man who spoke almost timidly—then loudly:

"Is that you, Steve? Steve!"

And Steve Mason was not dead. For he answered, called out:

"Get him, boy—don't let him get away!"

At that moment, Strang struck; struck at the blotch of

whiteness which showed before him—showed in the dim light from above the alley door.

Men then—many men! A door opened and banged against the wall far down the hall; men called and Mr. Strang moved toward the partly open door to the alley and to freedom.

They found him though. Someone flashed a light just as Strang reached that outer door, stepped through and started to close it behind him. His car was there in the alley, but he couldn't use it. They'd pop out of that doorway too fast. He could hear feet before he fully shut the door, and then he heard the voice of Steve Mason—Mason, far from dead—coming down the hall. Mason shouted:

"Out the door, boys—burn him up in the alley. It's Mr. Strang!"

Mr. Strang drew his gun, prepared to sell his life dearly. A second now and they would fling open that steel door. Four—five—maybe ten against one. A minute and they'd be coming down the alley from either end and—and—

The door did not open. Mr. Strang smiled grimly as he jumped into his car and, with one mechanical movement, was shooting straight out of that alley toward the main street beyond.

As he drove up the wide street, Mr. Strang recalled brushing against the dead body of Tiny Manning, thought that those behind must have done so too. Mr. Strang knew that he owed his life to Steve Mason; Steve Mason who had cried out his name as men dashed toward the door.

Mr. Strang still meant terror in the night then. Not a shot had been fired when he left that alley. The answer to that was simple enough. The name of Mr. Strang caused fear now as it had before. None of those men wanted any part of him.

Then he frowned. He must see Sheila Barton at once. She must use all her influence with her father—make him believe the truth. For if Commissioner Barton would not make Mr. Strang a small part of the law, then Mr. Strang would make himself the whole law.

Yes, it was up to Commissioner Barton if the Legion of the Living Dead walked or not. And if they walked, men— many men—would die!

23

THE KISS OF DEATH

MR. STRANG STOPPED once in his ride to enter a drugstore and make a telephone call:

"I'll come to the side door, Sheila. I must see you alone—and no one must know I'm there. Is it safe?"

"I'll make it safe," Sheila answered. "Come."

Ten minutes later, Mr. Strang parked his car around the corner and went straight to the house of the Commissioner of Police and to the little side door. It opened before his hand reached the knob. Sheila didn't speak. She led him into a small library, locked the door behind them. She followed his eyes to the door at the other end of the room, to the tile of the floor and the dimness of glass reflected from the lights of the library.

"My laboratory," she said. "The door at the other end of it is locked. Sit down."

"There was no need to even come in." Mr. Strang remained standing. "What I have to tell you I could have told you in the hall. Resa Kent knew nothing—she was shot to death simply to further terrorize me. Not me as I am now, but as I was then. I made a mistake tonight. Steve Mason still lives. Sheila, many men are going to die."

"You are going to kill men without giving them a chance to live—is that it?" she asked.

"That is it."

"The men who killed Resa Kent?"

"No, no—they are all dead but one." He counted on his fingers, "Gunner Keen and Eddie Owen, whom you know about. Tonight there was Rudolph Weber and Tiny Manning." He paused a long time and then, "I owe a great deal to you, Sheila. Let there be no chance that you misunderstand me. This is to be a massacre. It is necessary to the future of society."

"And," she faced him squarely, "it is necessary also to your hate." She tried to be scornful, but she was surprised at his answer; the sincerity of it. He repeated her words, said simply:

"And it is necessary to my hate."

"You tell me this—yet you trust no one?"

"No one," he said.

"Then why did you come here tonight? How did you know that I would not tell Father? How do you know you can go free, that the police have not already surrounded the house—are even now closing in on you?"

Strang placed both his hands upon her shoulders.

"I *don't* know," he said. "I never think of you and the police. I never think of you in any way interfering with me."

"I see." She sighed as she tried to make those eyes blink before hers and failed miserably. "You cannot do this alone. You cannot kill alone—not so many as you plan. The whole underworld will rise up against you—the police will search you out. I tried to prevent Father from acting, but picked men are hunting for you even now. By morning, he will have given your description to the entire force. You won't live another week."

Mr. Strang looked over at the calendar. This time, Sheila thought that his smile was real. He said: "Another week will be far more than enough. I came to say good-bye, Sheila."

"Strang, Strang!" Her hands went up, hesitated, and the sudden impulse to throw both her arms about him was conquered. But she did put her hands upon his shoulders, slip them around his neck, pull his face close to hers. Long and earnestly she looked into the eyes of the man—the only man who had ever meant anything in her life.

And she had been right not to throw her arms about him. It was not there in his face. Nothing of life; nothing of that softness of a frightened child when she used to run a hand through his hair.

Mr. Strang put both his hands upon her neck, shook her head slowly from side to side. She couldn't remember when anyone had done that to her before. His eyes were different too. Oh, the fires were there, but the soft warmth of a camp fire on a cold night. And Mr. Strang said:

"I never thought of it before, Sheila. But it is nice—very nice to have one friend."

"You'll wait then—for that friend?" It wasn't often that Sheila spoke like that; spoke without thinking.

Mr. Strang moved both his hands and took hers from around his neck, pushed them down to her sides, looked straight into her eyes.

"Wait? Wait for what?"

She could have laughed then, but she didn't. Certainly, she could read things far back in his eyes and they were not pleasant and not for her. But he could not read things back in her eyes, for he would have seen in that single moment that she was a woman—a real woman—who had loved him when others called him a coward. That she loved him now—and knew it—knew it just a minute ago when she almost gave way to that impulse and plunged into his arms. But her voice was steady, when she spoke. She said: "There is nothing I can do to help you?"

"I hope there is. It depends upon your father and your influence with him. I will work again with his law—my own way. Or I will work with my own law. He has refused my help, considers me mad, has men hunting me in the streets." Strang's laugh was only in his throat, for there was no expression on his face. "Listen, Sheila, it is the end of fifty—a hundred—men, criminals, murderers. Crime will be struck a fatal blow." He leaned down and whispered close to her ear; his voice raising from an almost inaudible murmur to such a tenseness that she drew back.

WHEN HE FINISHED talking, the girl threw her arm half across her face. She felt dizzy. She clutched at a table, braced herself, knew that her face was drained of blood. She could have run from the room screaming.

Mr. Strang stood with his arms folded, looking at her. Then he stepped forward, stretched out a hand to support her.

She jerked herself free, faced him. She said:

"No brain could conceive and carry out such a plan as yours! It's a bitterness in your heart; hatred in your soul. You're not striking for others now—you're striking for yourself. The innocent with the guilty. It's true! You're going to do it."

"Yes, Sheila, I am going to do it."

"And Billings—Kirkman Billings. You have nothing against him, no proof of any kind. He is a fine, upright man."

Strang shook his head. "He is the only man big enough to aid Mason. I cannot think of another."

"You must not harm Mr. Billings. You— Wait—be sure, be certain. A little time, Strang—just a little time."

"Time! I saw Mason tonight. I tossed him the body of his chief lieutenant. The underworld will hunt me; tomorrow morning the entire police force will comb the city. Your father fears what I may do. The Senator fears it. There is no time. I dare not wait."

"If I spoke to Father—if he agreed that you were to work for him again? To destroy this parole evil, to give you an opportunity to be sure of Mr. Billings? My father dislikes Mr. Billings because Billings does not—or will not—listen to him. Yet, Father believes him innocent of all dishonesty."

"I am afraid, with your father's present attitude, there will not be time to change my plans."

"Time, time!" The girl shook his shoulders. "How much time will you give me to talk to him, tell him what you threaten?"

Strang looked at the clock. He nodded stiffly. "You have until three o'clock this morning."

The girl nodded.

Strang continued: "Then the Legion of the Living Dead will walk again. Till three o'clock—over two hours."

A month ago—no, a week ago—perhaps even an hour ago, Sheila Barton would have laughed at the whole thing as fantastic. But she did not laugh now. She was very serious, and she believed every word that Mr. Strang had whispered to her. She asked, "How will I reach you—in time?"

"You will telephone," he said, giving her the number. "Just tell me that your father is agreeable. Of course, I will expect you to—" And he stopped. There could be no agreement or real trust between them. "The phone is perfectly safe. Anyone listening on the wire will not be able to trace your call to me."

"Nevertheless," she said, "I will call you from outside. I'll give you only ten minutes' start—then I will talk to Father."

Sheila saw Mr. Strang to the door, looked up and down the block as he started down the steps. He reached the bottom step, turned quickly and mounting them again gripped both her hands.

"Good-bye, Sheila!" he said, and she thought, or at least hoped that there was a huskiness in his voice. "I know your father—and I feel that I will never see you again. Good-bye!" He leaned down and kissed her.

Funny. Sheila realized she loved this man. Yet she felt no desire to return that kiss. There was nothing of love or passion in it. It was cold and—and— She stood there until he had turned the corner. Then she went into the house. She knew then. It was the kiss of death.

24

THE LEGION OF THE LIVING DEAD

FROM NINE O'CLOCK on, that Wednesday night, men came from different directions to the old warehouse down by the river.

Some time just before three o'clock, Mr. Strang came, hat pulled down, coat flapping against the wind that blew up from the river. Once or twice he drew that coat tightly about him, for the nip from the river was sharp—and clean.

Mr. Strang tried to figure exactly how many men would meet him in that gloomy old place he had bought three years before. He couldn't guess exactly, but he would say about one hundred and fifty men— Any one of whom would gladly face the ten most desperate criminals in the city's gangland. An army of death—an army of men who preferred death; hoped for death by violence, while obeying Mr. Strang's orders, more than anything else.

Mr. Strang walked around the warehouse to a little door which was apparently boarded from the outside. He didn't use a key—only a little strength, and he was inside that dark, damp building. He didn't use his flashlight as he stepped hurriedly and assuredly through the darkness. Two steps forward, one to the left; five steps forward, three to the right until he reached the stairs—the small flight of stairs. He knew that when he mounted those steps and walked straight forward he would be standing on a platform facing many men.

He extended his hand, felt the curtain, rubbed his hand along that curtain, felt its softness, held it close to his face and breathed in to be sure there was no dirt or dust.

Mr. Strang nodded his satisfaction. The curtain was new, hung there that afternoon. He knew then that things were going according to schedule. Very slowly, and with a single step he passed between those curtains into the pitch blackness.

He called softly, stretched out both his hands almost at once. His hands touched other hands—one warm; one cold and wet—like the touch of death.

"Mr. Strang! Mr. Strang!" Two voices spoke together. One a deep strong whisper; the other wheezy, throaty.

"Right. Mr. Strang!" Strang replied, and moved forward with those moving hands toward the center of that platform. He let his hands drop, felt them touch a wooden table, stood silent.

The strong voice spoke above the soft humming sound of many voices. "You are ready?"

And Mr. Strang answered: "I am ready, Stewart."

Stewart spoke aloud then, clearly, each word carefully pronounced; each word cutting the darkness and stillness and silencing the whispering until it died entirely. The strong voice said:

"Gentlemen, you had your notice in the paper—a notice none of you could miss. THE LEGION OF THE LIVING DEAD WALKS AGAIN TONIGHT. A message which meant that Mr. Strang would be at our monthly meeting. You will now be ready to receive your instructions."

A full minute of silence by the speaker, a gasp from unseen men, and the voice again, "Mr. Strang is here!" There was a sudden flood of light over the large room where many men sat, and a single bright, green-shaded light that shone on Mr. Strang's face. There were no welcoming cheers, no clapping of hands—just grim eager faces; anxious faces; white and sickly faces which stared up at the platform and Mr. Strang.

Mr. Strang glanced out over the body of men. A hundred and fifty had he said? And he thought that he had figured safely—almost conservatively. Now he estimated the number as less than a hundred. He turned and looked at the two men beside him.

One was big and strong and the glow of health was in his face. The other was thin and gaunt and bent forward. The death pallor was in his face. Mr. Strang spoke to the stronger man.

"Tell me, Stewart," he said. "Are—are they all here? The entire Legion of the Living Dead?"

"They are all here," answered Stewart. "Not a man absent who could come—only two that are alive and did not come. I have picked five as hospital cases and they will be taken care of as soon as the meeting's over."

"So many—so many have died!" Strang's voice broke slightly.

"You picked them to die, Mr. Strang," replied Stewart. "The doctors, it would seem, are too often right." He laughed lightly. "There are myself and three others in whom the doctors guessed wrong entirely. I must run things for you alone now. Merrit—"He moved a shoulder toward the man on the other side of Strang. "I am afraid if you had called this meeting a very little later, Merrit would not be with us."

STRANG'S EYES WERE warm burning coals when he turned to Merrit, insisted the man sit down, held his hand a moment, patted his shoulder and turning back, said to Stewart:

"Have the hospital cases attended to now—at once. Yes, I know with so many, the funds must be low. But there is plenty of money. There will be little trouble about money from now on." And facing the men who were mostly seated on boards placed from barrel to barrel. "Let every man stand up."

Mr. Strang's face was hard and cold, his voice sharp. Only his heart sad; his soul a single steady pain as he leaped from the platform and went among those men. There was not a face he missed, and one or two men he could not remember he questioned from a memorandum. It was hardly possible that a spy from the police or from the underworld could get into that meeting, but Mr. Strang took no chances.

He watched the long line of standing men. Found that two must brace themselves upon chairs; one whose legs collapsed and who had to sit down, though he tried desperately to regain his feet again. These men he called to the attention of Stewart before he went back on the platform. Then, leaning over the table, he addressed that desperate, stern-faced gathering—the Legion of the Living Dead. Every man marked for death by medical science.

Mr. Strang began, as the men sat down: "When we had occasion to meet before, I came and gave you simple instructions. Tonight—or rather this morning, I am going back for a brief period over the past. It is possible that each of you may have your wish. To die, knowing that those dearest to you are safe from the poverty that you feared would follow your death.

"It was close to four years ago that my first advertisement appeared in the papers, in which I offered men of courage who had but a short time to live an opportunity to do some work before they died. I met many men; thousands were questioned. Many were useless to my cause because their time on earth was already too short. Many others faced death as they faced life—without courage or ambition. They, too, were useless to me. But you, and many like you, served my mission and society well. Gentlemen, I am here tonight with a new mission, a final mission by which you all may arrange for the safety and comfort and protection of those you must leave behind."

Mr. Strang paused there and every man sat straight and tense in his seat.

"My mission this time was not started with any motive of vengeance or hate. Or if it is a hate, it is the human hate of every good citizen— A hate against crime; a hate against those who make it possible; a hate against those who control it, and a hate against the Parole Evil of this state and this nation that feeds the great crime machine. Gentlemen, you all wish death. You will all get it—including myself—unless I hear to the contrary within the next ten minutes."

There was a hum from those men—close to a hundred men who heard that they were about to die. Although there were no shouts and no hand-clapping, it was as if they welcomed a great victory.

Mr. Strang held aloft a book.

"I call this book," he said, "the Book of Evil. In it I have the names of criminals—names many of you have gathered for me—who are terrorizing a great city and murdering its citizens. Politics prevent some of these men being brought to justice. Lack of evidence which could influence a jury freed others. Money and fear and the murdering of witnesses prevent still more of them being convicted of their crimes." A long pause and then, "I have decided that all of these men shall be shot dead on the same night. We have had the vengeance of wrong against right. On Friday night, we shall have the execution of the wrong by the right."

Mr. Strang coughed as a great murmur went through that room, and then in crisp, hard tones that these men had been used to hearing:

"Your final instructions and weapons will be dealt out to you by Mr. Stewart at once. You are less in number than I had hoped. However, we must do our best. Friday is picked because the so-called Steve Mason Athletic Club meets in the Arcadia building that night." He ran over a list of names on his desk. "I am assigning twenty of you to that job. I had hoped to use thirty men. You will all carry machine guns. Ted Bush and William Morton will lead you. You will get in easily enough and begin shooting at once. They will be armed, of course, but if there are machine guns, they will get little chance to use them. Two of Mason's lieutenants will be there. Everyone will be a criminal of some kind. Mason, of course, never attends these meetings.

"I have also picked Friday, because it is the same night that Meyers and his men meet on this side of town. Theirs is not a public affair; there will be only eleven or twelve men there. But Meyers will be with them. That is the night they divide their loot. The boat house they use is heavily guarded and machine guns will be handy. I am sending other men there, but what is left of the first raiding party must join them. Say twenty-five to Meyers' and with—well, ten of you left to join them, in an hour the job should be well done. Leave no rotten human carcass to arise and start again the cycle of crime."

FOR A GOOD five minutes more Mr. Strang talked. He spoke of others who must die, referred to his Book of Evil from time to time—even read the crimes many criminals had committed.

Mr. Strang finished with: "All your orders are written down clearly and concisely. I have the list of the dependants for whom you die. Are you all willing to kill for the good of many human beings—your last salute to a life that no longer has use for you?"

Every hand went up. Mr. Strang nodded, said:

"Very well. Mr. Stewart will collect any information you have gathered in the city. Many of you were or have become familiar with the workings of criminals."

In the next few minutes, Mr. Strang had gathered many items for his book. Merrit, there beside him, was trembling, begging to be sent on one of these missions of death.

"I know, Mr. Strang, I know," he replied when Strang assured him that his wife would be taken care of anyway.

"But I haven't much longer to live—very little longer. I could sit in one of the cars with a sub-machine gun. I used one in the war. It's just the tightening of a finger. I'm strong enough for that. Please, Mr. Strang. I'd like to go out that way."

But Mr. Strang shook his head. The information these men had brought him was shocking and horrible, yet all true. Given the time and Commissioner Barton, he could have worked the evidence up himself and handed it over to Barton. Barton— He looked at his watch. Sheila had known how important the hour was and she had not telephoned him. After three—fifteen, nearly twenty minutes after.

Someone in that audience asked:

"Mr. Strang, what of Steve Mason—the backbone of the entire criminal menace, parole?"

"Steve Mason," said Mr. Strang slowly, "I have chosen for myself. Five men took part in the slaying of Resa Kent. He was one of those five men. The four others are dead. Steve Mason is for me—alone. I am a man wanted by both the police and the criminal. But be assured that I will not be caught before Steve Mason is dead. Goodnight."

For the fifth time, Mr. Strang looked at the telephone. And this time it rang as if his burning eyes had started it.

"Just a minute!" Mr. Strang waved a hand at the moving men, walked across the platform and jerked the phone from atop a trunk.

It was Sheila Barton. He had never heard her voice so excited before. He answered her hurried question, "Am I on time?"

"I think so—if the news is pleasant."

She choked her words; he wondered if she had been crying. "Father has agreed," she said. "Come over and see me at once."

Strang dropped the phone back in its cradle.

"Gentlemen," he called. "You have heard my instructions. Well, there has been a decided—" And he stopped. Twice he started to tell them that the plans were off, and twice the words would not come. He heard himself say finally:

"If there is any change in my plans, I will notify you through the public notices. Watch your papers carefully."

Stewart gripped his arm.

"But this is Wednesday—really Thursday. Such a notice could not be sent out in time if there was any real delay."

Mr. Strang nodded, raised his hand, said to the men:

"Wait. I have an important engagement that might change all my plans at once. It is now close to half-past three. You will wait here until fifteen minutes after four. If I do not telephone by then, you will leave and carry out your orders to the letter. Mr. Merrit will attend to things here, the distribution of our hidden weapons—below."

Silently Mr. Strang watched those men who sat before him. But he was thinking of Sheila Barton. Of the joy as well as the excitement in her voice. Certainly, it could not be a joy that such vermin were not to die. Was it then, a joy that it was not going to be he who had had so many killed—or that he was to live himself?

But Stewart was talking. "I don't know if you're right, Mr. Strang. I—"

"That's right, that's right," Strang cut in on him. "You have a wife and a lovely child. You begged then for a chance to die. Now you're a well man again. There's work, there's love, there's hope. I forgot, Stewart. You will not be in with us. You are no longer of the Living Dead."

"Of course, I'm with you!" And when Strang would have turned from him, "I lied to you in the beginning—oh, not about my health, but about the money. I've got money—plenty of it. I simply wanted excitement before I died. I still want it. Look, Mr. Strang. By working carefully as you worked before—with me for your aid—we can rid the city of these criminals. I can go to the Commissioner myself and—"

"No, no!" Mr. Strang said as Stewart followed him out of the warehouse. "Things may work out that way. If they do, if they do—those poor devils who seek death; who seek to die that their loved ones may live—well—"

He turned suddenly and clutched Stewart by the hand. "You're right—right of course. We might spend our lives in my little Book of Evil and one by one wipe the city clean of its biggest criminals. It's just that we need to put some sense into Barton's head. We can accomplish little without his aid and nothing if the police hunt me in the city."

But Mr. Strang thought it was quite likely that Stewart had not heard his final words, for he was out the door and on his way to see Sheila Barton, and to find out just what arrangement she had made with her father.

25

MURDER BY TELEPHONE

IT WASN'T QUITE three o'clock, and Sheila Barton, her self-control apparently gone, paced up and down the room before her father who, seated by the fire, pretended an indifference that he did not feel.

"I tell you, Sheila," Commissioner Barton said for the tenth time, "the man's mad. And you, with your suggestion, are madder. What do you mean 'rivers of blood'? What do you mean he made me Commissioner of Police? Suppose that he did? Is that any reason why a madman should be free? He killed those two men today."

"Killed them in self defense." Sheila spoke quickly as she looked toward the clock. "He went to that place—Aaron Becker's place for his—well, for something or other."

"His book!" Barton's indifference was suddenly gone. "His book that lists criminals and their crimes! Did you see that book? Did he show it to you? Is it true that he simply telephoned you or—or—" Barton came to his feet. He fairly spat out the words. "He hid in your room that night! You let him escape! You—!"

Sheila faced him calmly now, said almost defiantly: "They would have shot him down like a dog. Shot him down in your house—your home—the home of the man he made. Yes, I've seen him, and I've talked to him. He built you up and feels that it was an inefficient job. So he's going to strike with this Legion of the Living Dead."

"And what," said the Commissioner in some sarcasm, "what exactly is the Legion of the Living Dead?"

"I don't know, exactly. It consists of men who have not much longer to live, men who want to die—for Mr. Strang."

"Yes, yes," Barton said nervously. "That is true, that is true. He had a few such men. I remember his telling me some such thing."

"He has many. Don't you see, Father? He intends to kill—to wipe out crime at one blow!"

"It's a dream, Sheila, a mad dream of a mad brain! By tomorrow, we'll have Mr. Strang. I have been patient, but now the whole department has his description and orders to pick him up. I thought, perhaps, you might induce him to return, but now—well, he'll be properly taken care of. He can't escape both the police and the underworld. I'll be doing him a real favor."

"He escaped them before—both the underworld and your department." Sheila reminded. "And he gave you the information that made you Commissioner. He can help keep you there now. I tell you he's not mad. He—"

The phone rang and the Commissioner lifted it. "No," he said, "he's not here." And after a moment's hesitation, "But he'll be here in a few minutes, Mr. Billings."

Commissioner Barton laid down the phone, said to Sheila: "Billings has been calling for him all night."

"Who? And who will be here in a few minutes?"

"Senator Bixby," Barton said gruffly. "You can tell him your story and get his advice. Remember that Mr. Strang was very close to Bixby, that the Senator counted on him in framing the Parole Bill and—"

"There won't be time. There won't be time! It's after three now—long after. Let me telephone him. Let me tell him that he may talk to you and go as he came—a free man. Let me tell him not to start this—this reign of terror."

Barton turned on her angrily; sharp words started, but never left his mouth. His eyes widened. He finally said:

"Very well, Sheila. There can be no harm in telling him that. Come, come, no more questions. Bring him here for me to talk with. There, hurry before I change my mind." And as the door bell rang, "Use your own phone upstairs if you must keep things from your father. That will be the Senator now."

Sheila Barton ran quickly up the stairs to her own private phone. Commissioner Barton opened the door to the Senator. He said as soon as they were in the library:

"I'm sorry, Senator, but Sheila was so insistent. She has seen and talked with Mr. Strang, and he speaks of his Legion of Living Dead—a massacre of criminals. Weird, fantastic—" Then, after an explanation of Strang's threat: "It bothers me, though. Can there be anything weird or fantastic about Mr. Strang? Those two dead men, you know—Gunner Keen and Eddie Owen. As hired murderers, the most desperate men in the city. Yet, they were shot to death—and hung up so—"

"Mr. Strang is coming here then? You intend to have him work with you, turn him loose in the city again?"

COMMISSIONER JAMES BARTON walked to the curtains that led to the dining room, looked through them, looked at the closed door, turned back and said to the Senator:

"Mr. Strang will be here very shortly. I told Sheila that—well, I acted a lie, if I did not actually tell her one. I intend to hold him prisoner, remove him to some safe place of detention—without a name, without a personality. I try to tell myself, Senator, that my lie is a good one, done in a good cause—that Strang is a threat to the city; a real menace, more dangerous than those he hunts. I have never lied to Sheila before."

"But it's necessary!" The Senator breathed easier. "You cannot work with him again, trust that brain of his again."

The Senator shivered slightly, but he was relieved that Mr. Strang was not to be a free man. "Besides, Barton, there is your position. If he is free, if he should resent your interference—your refusal to act with him—he may talk of the past. You more or less aided and abetted him in criminal activities. You thought then it was for the good of the city. Now—to protect yourself you must apprehend him, hold him some place—at least until he returns to normal and—"

The Commissioner cut in almost viciously: "I am not thinking of myself. I am thinking of the position I fill and the taxpayers I serve. I must hold him."

"Of course! Of course!" The Senator toyed with the thick, black ribbon that hung from his nose glasses. "Sheila, in a way, feels responsible for him, you know. It was she who had him go away. It was she who kept him sane—alive during his trying period when he seemed simply a hulk of his old self, a sniffling, frightened man. You are doing right and—"

Both men turned and looked at the desk. The phone upon it rang. The Commissioner said: "It is for you, Senator. Kirkman Billings has been calling all evening. Some politics I suppose."

The Senator lifted the instrument from its cradle, spoke into it, turned his head so that the Commissioner could not see the blood leave his face. He had no sooner given his name than Steve Mason fairly cursed the words over the wire.

"Mr. Strang!" Steve snarled. "He's back in the city again. Rudolph is dead—stabbed in the heart. I tell you, I saw this Mr. Strang. He's dynamite, actually threw Rudolph over the desk and hit me. What did you say?"

Senator Charles Philip Bixby said slowly:

"I am practically alone, Mr. Billings. Of course, the Commissioner is here but—what was that?" The Senator turned and looked at Barton, smiled, held a hand over the receiver as he said to the Commissioner, "It's Kirkman Billings. He wishes to be sure I'm alone. So don't say a word until—"

"I understand," the Commissioner said somewhat stiffly. "It will be enough for one of us to lie tonight. I'll go above and speak with Sheila. You may tell Mr. Billings that he need not be alarmed that I will hear any answers you make to his questions—"

Senator Bixby watched Barton leave the room, saw him close the door, let his lips part slightly as he noted the rather sharp click and heard Barton's feet cross the hall to the stairs.

Then he spoke rapidly: "You're a fool to keep calling here. I don't care how desperate it is. Mr. Strang will be here any minute. Barton has planned to take him into custody."

Steve Mason spoke quickly: "Kill him!" he said. "Stick a

gun in his back and kill him. Make some excuse, his trying to escape—anything—but kill him. The Commissioner, Billings, even the Governor himself is not one tenth as dangerous to our plans as this man Strang."

"But I—I can't. I— What's that? Yes, I remember Lorey, and his death. If he tries—if Mr. Strang gives me the opportunity, I am armed, of course, but the Commissioner and myself intend to hold him and—"

"And what?" Steve Mason was sarcastic, but there was fear in his voice. "Remember, Senator, we're all in the same boat now. You saw a man murdered and did nothing, said nothing. There's weak links in the chain as well as in that book of Mr. Strang's. You're part of things now, Senator."

"But we don't intend to let him go. We—"

"You—" Steve Mason's laugh was far from pleasant. "You couldn't keep him there alive. If you don't kill him why— Listen." And Steve Mason began to talk rapidly. The Senator hemmed and hawed. He had once—just that once—stood by when a murder was committed, but he didn't like discussing another murder, even listening to it over the phone. Besides, Steve Mason was not the ingratiating, servile hireling he had always pretended to be. He was giving orders now—just as he gave them to others. Senator Bixby recognized the danger in the racketeer's voice as well as in the words.

"I'll see what I can do, of course, Stephen," he said nervously as he looked toward the door. "Otherwise, I'll see that he gets out. You—you'll be there yourself, Stephen?"

"No, I got to alibi myself. And can that *Stephen* stuff from now on!"

"But I thought if you handled it yourself why—"

STEVE MASON INTERRUPTED harshly: "I'd die, eh? Well, your interest is in my life. The dead can't talk, but they can write—at least they can leave written words behind them. Understand, Senator, my life is very precious to you, that's why I'm protecting it—not for myself but for you. Remember that. When Mr. Strang leaves Barton's house tonight, he gets it."

"To be sure, to be sure!" And in a change of voice, "I'll do everything possible, Mr. Billings—the Flint boy, of course!"

He hung up the receiver just as Commissioner Barton entered the room with Sheila clinging to him, brushing her hair against his cheek, smiles flashing through her tears. "I'm sure you agree with Dad, Senator."

She went over and took both the hands the Senator held out.

"I always agree with your father in matters of police routine," the Senator smiled. "And though I don't know what it is, I must willingly agree with anything that makes you so radiantly happy. You are referring to Mr. Strang I presume?"

"Yes," the girl said. "And don't look at me like that, Senator. Such thoughts are impossible even if my career permitted me to think of it. Besides, there is no room for women in Mr. Strang's life."

"Women—well, perhaps not women." The Senator led her over to the mantel. "There is no room for women in my life either, but—" He lowered his voice, though Barton had gone back into the hall. "There is room for just one woman. Sheila, if you were—"

She chided him: "I know what you were going to say. If I were ten years older or you were ten years younger."

"I was not," contradicted the Senator, stiffly, "going to say any such thing!"

"You were going to speak about your wife then, and if—Senator, I didn't mean to hurt you, but you've been joshing me for so many years, since I was a girl."

"A girl with ideas," the Senator ran in hurriedly. "Different than others, with a mind that works alone. Don't you see, Sheila, I—?"

She laughed, but there was a puzzled look in her eyes. "You're just a faker," she told him. "But a good-natured faker—a real politician, Senator. I'm surprised people don't see through you—inside of you as I do."

"And what do you see there, inside of me—about you?"

There was an earnestness in his voice, something in his eyes that she had never seen before. But she saw it now. She was glad when her father walked into the room.

"You'd better wait in your laboratory, dear." Commissioner Barton patted the girl's head, rubbed a hand over his own forehead and was surprised to find how cold that hand was. "Mr. Strang will be right along. Isn't that what you told me?"

"Strang will come to the front door," she said proudly. "He is coming as Strang Cummings, respected in the world of art. The man who made most of his huge fortune in discovering geniuses and buying their works long before others noticed them—an authority on the old and rare paintings hardly equaled in the entire country. Why should he come like a thief in the night? You have never broken your word, Father."

Commissioner Barton coughed. He realized the unpleasant scene he must later have with his daughter.

He said: "My word, child? I didn't give my word, you know. There, there, don't be excited! Mr. Strang is perfectly safe here. I will talk to him and if I agree with your opinion—and your opinion is so often right—he may go as he came."

"That's not what you said," The girl flared. "You—you are trying to trick me—trick him. Father, you—!"

Commissioner Barton laughed, but it was not a wholesome laugh, and his already ruddy cheeks flushed.

He tried to pinch her cheek, but she drew back, her eyes dark, angry. "Surely, Sheila, you are not so terribly wrong in your opinion. The man has valuable information. I would wish to have use of it, of course."

The girl's gaze moved from her father to the Senator. She could read nothing in his eyes.

The Senator had fooled many people, including himself, for years. It was a revelation to him when he discovered how easy it was to step right into criminal graft. Even after the shooting of Lorey, it was not his conscience that bothered him or felt fear. The thing was physical more than mental—something that settled in his stomach.

But even so, the Senator only smiled and nodded at the girl and was very glad of the interruption that made his entering into the argument unnecessary. For the front door bell rang....

26

BLACKNESS

SHEILA FOLLOWED HER father to the door, stood behind him, frightened gaze on the man who entered the front door. It was Strang, of course, but not the suave Strang Cummings whom she had expected. It was Mr. Strang in all his sinister, fierce appearance. Unblinking, burning eyes; the odd downward comb to his hair; the direct forward bend to his body made his height hard to guess— yet showed clearly his breadth of shoulder, and hinted at the great strength which might be in his arms.

"Come in. Come in!" Barton felt strangely uneasy as Mr. Strang passed him and entered the library where Senator Bixby waited, rolling the end of a cigar between puckered lips, both hands plainly showing.

The Senator knew that, on the slightest provocation, this man would draw, shoot and kill. The Senator was not a man to provoke such an action. When he looked at the man, he realized that Steve Mason was right. Mr. Strang had to die.

The Commissioner did not like the confident way Strang turned his back. It was either assurance in himself or assurance in Barton—in the word of Barton—which Sheila had given him over the phone. Barton held his hand in his jacket pocket and clutched the trigger of the gun that he had placed there when he spoke: "Sit down. Sit down. I understand that you wish to talk to me?"

Broad shoulders moved. Mr. Strang said: "Not necessarily. I don't need you, Barton. I don't need the Senator. I can get along nicely without either one of you."

"Miss Sheila—" the Commissioner placed great emphasis on the *Miss,* "informed me that you wanted to see me."

Mr. Strang ignored the seat Barton pointed out and remained standing.

"Sheila was right." Mr. Strang plunged into the discussion. "I am not at all sure you can get along without me. I made you, Barton. There are no two ways about that. You had everything that a good Commissioner needed—except one thing. You had honesty. A dogged determination to do right. A hate for criminals that was almost as great an obsession as mine." All the time Mr. Strang talked, his gaze was fixed on Barton's right-hand pocket. "Yes, you had everything that a good—even a great—Commissioner needed. Everything but brains. I could supply those."

"Well?" Barton grinned rather unpleasantly. "Certainly that is an auspicious beginning for a man who seeks clemency!"

Mr. Strang's expression never changed, but there was a queer sound in his throat that might have been a laugh.

"I seek nothing from you—but offer something. As for brains—I did not mean that in a literal sense. You have plenty of brains. It is simply that your brains have been trained to see things only from the law's viewpoint. I do not seek the law. I demand to kill criminals. And take that hand from your pocket—empty—or I'll be obliged to put a bullet in your chest."

Commissioner Barton's hand jerked from his pocket, fell to his side. He said thickly: "I might have killed you in the doorway."

"I doubt it," Mr. Strang said.

"Strang!" The Commissioner tried hard to control the rising anger in his voice; anger at himself and the ridiculous position he was in. "I worked with you before—we trusted each other. Why, when you were invited here, do you distrust me now?"

"Sheila," Mr. Strang explained simply. "A moment ago I looked into her eyes. There was fear there. If she does not trust her own father, why should I?" With a grim sort of smile, without turning his head, he said: "I hope, Senator, that your motive in slipping behind me is simply an innocent one."

Senator Bixby jumped back from behind Mr. Strang. His face was crimson; his legs shook as he leaned upon the table. He was glad that the gun he had half drawn from his inner jacket pocket was in a position to drop back again. His hands twitched so that he could not have held it. He said: "Dear me! Dear me, Mr. Strang!"

Strang said: "I have no intention of harming either one of you. I had plans of tramping through the night and paying my debt to society, making amends for the time an eminent surgeon made me a trembling counterfeit of a man. Oh no, Commissioner! I don't doubt your ability to get me finally. But I think my mission will be accomplished—and I will be dead."

"If you have made such plans," said the Commissioner, "then why did you come here? Why the threats to us—or the lack of trust or fear of us—? Or even the lack of trust in Sheila?"

MR. STRANG LOOKED toward Sheila. She came forward and took his left hand; took it as she had so often taken it in those days when he crouched at her feet in fear—in a deadly terror of his own life. She had kept him from going mad then. Now he said, "Sheila wished it that way."

"And what," said Barton, "is her way? The working with me again? Well, that is simple. You have a book that, in my hands, will convict many men. Yet you will not give it to me. Why?"

Mr. Strang said: "Because of the Parole Racket. Steve Mason seems to profit most by it. And I can, perhaps, prove his part in it—through my book."

"Then why hesitate?"

"Because there must be someone behind Steve Mason. Someone far bigger; someone respected and well thought of. Someone who through a greed we cannot understand or through a blackmail that we do not know, must serve Mason. You can guess whom I mean, Barton."

"Billings! Kirkman Billings?" Barton rasped out the name. "I dislike the man. I detest him. The feeling, I believe, is mutual. But it is his judgment, not his honesty I question. The Senator here has advised me to stay clear of him for a bit."

"Many of the men he releases work for Mason. The Senator should know that."

"Damn it!" Barton puffed. "These men are given jobs by Billings—at least they obtain positions through his influence. And they make good."

"Could there," said Mr. Strang, "be any possible connection between Billings and Mason?"

"Ridiculous," said Barton.

Senator Bixby pulled at his chin. "Mr. Strang may not be aware," he said, "that I frequent Mason's Black Knight Club quite often. Sometimes I smoke a cigar with Mason in his room. Quite frankly, I do not believe that there is any connection between the men. But, Barton, Mr. Strang's suspicions may not be entirely without foundation. Steve Mason and his kind are not free talkers. But he has dropped a word at times—a hint with bitterness in it—that many of his men are freed through Billings and somehow find their way to the—er—this outfit called—the Meyers gang, I believe. I myself have seen Meyers coming from Mr. Billings' house. At least, a man who was pointed out to me as Meyers." And throwing out his chest with an air of importance which it was not hard for the Senator to assume: "So you see, in my small way, I have played the detective rather to advantage while at Mason's place."

The last remark was pointed straight at Barton. Inside himself, Senator Bixby felt a certain elation. Mr. Strang had pointed the finger of suspicion directly at Kirkman Billings. Bixby had, to a certain extent, encouraged that suspicion. It would smoulder in the Commissioner's head, blaze into a certainty when Kirkman Billings died violently with every clue leading to the Meyers crowd.

No one could interfere with the thought put in Barton's head now. No one but Mr. Strang, who would never find out he was wrong. Not unless he made that discovery within the next thirty minutes—perhaps less than twenty minutes. For he would be dead. Very dead indeed. The Senator was quite sure of that.

The Senator's pleasant thoughts of soon being Governor of the State were broken into by Mr. Strang's voice. In a dull way, the Senator had heard some of what had been said, but Mr. Strang was finishing with:

"So you see, Barton, Kirkman Billings, to a certain extent, is virtual czar over the Parole Board. It may have been planned that way. It may have been just that Billings was really the man for it and the power it gave him turned his head. Or it may be just possible that he is simply being blackmailed."

Barton looked at Strang a long time. He recalled the days when Mr. Strang had thrust him forward. Then he shook his head. After all, he was Commissioner of Police. He did have a sworn duty to the citizens. He said:

"We'll make a deal, Strang." His voice was friendly. "You give me that book, then go as you came. I can't see my way clear to work with you, but I feel—and I am sure the Senator will feel also—that the service you do the city in giving me that book will—"

"Will put you back on your feet as Commissioner of Police?"

"No, Strang, no!" The Commissioner was not angry, but very serious. "I believe that we will do right in forgetting those killings, taking your statement that it was in self-defense." And leaning forward, glaring his lie as he might have brow-beaten any ordinary criminal, "This place is surrounded by police. A threatening move on your part and they will enter. I am afraid, Mr. Strang, that the District Attorney and a jury of twelve men, not knowing your mental quirk and the flare for striking terror into the underworld, would not understand those two dead men hanging by their heels so that their dead faces struck together."

"We cannot use the book until after I am sure of Billings. I must work fast because—"

Hands empty at his sides, Commissioner James Barton strode toward Mr. Strang. As he saw the burning light in the man's eyes and the slowly moving right hand going toward his left armpit, he raised both his hands high, opening them—showing they contained no weapon.

Barton said: "The police—what will you do about them?"

For a moment Mr. Strang gazed at Sheila. He smiled.

"Sheila would have known of that and not permitted it, or warned me before or as soon as I came in. Still it would not matter, Barton. Not to me; only to you. You know my quickness with a gun. You know I would not hesitate to—"

Strang's left hand shot to his right armpit. He did not exactly recognize the danger; the real danger. He only knew that Barton stood close to him and that both his hands were still raised.

Mr. Strang's gun fell easily into his hand. But he did not shoot. He simply held it close to his body and started to speak when the blow came. Something pounded down hard upon his head. Then a sudden blackness as he sank slowly, half into the seat of the chair behind him.

27

MEN MUST DIE

THE SENATOR SAID: "Barton, he would have killed you. What—? Oh!" He was looking at the leather-covered blackjack in Barton's hand, at the strap that was still twisted about his wrist.

Barton said: "I was a plain cop for many years. I learned how to carry a persuader—how to use it quickly in an emergency. I had that tucked up my sleeve tonight. A gun in my hand when Strang entered would have meant his death or mine. I know him, and he would not have stayed here alive unless—" He looked down at the man slumped against the back of the chair.

Barton raised his foot, kicked the gun from Mr. Strang's hand so that it skidded across the room. Then he leaned forward and thrust a hand into Strang's pocket. His breath whistled in his throat. The book was there. Barton had it! He also removed another gun from Strang's shoulder holster, gave it to the Senator, said, "Keep that against Mr. Strang's head. If he attempts to escape, shoot."

Mr. Strang's eyes were bright now. He pushed himself up, said in a faraway voice:

"I could have shot you, Barton."

Barton answered, and although the elation was still in his voice, the hardness had gone:

"Come, come, Strang. What I did and will do is for your own good. We are going to take care of you for a bit. I could have shot—killed you." Mr. Strang's head nodded vaguely. "But I couldn't kill Sheila's father."

"I say now—"

Barton started and stopped. Sheila had swung him around, was talking to him, pleading; begging, telling him that Strang had been promised protection.

And Senator Bixby? Here was his chance; his great opportunity to rid the world—his world—from its greatest menace. He had his orders right from the Commissioner of Police. It would be easy for him to say Mr. Strang started to draw a third weapon, jumped at him. The Senator could say that he was nervous, that he knew little about guns. Here was a thirty-eight caliber revolver, held tightly in his hand, put there by the Commissioner. And the nose of it was hard against the side of Strang's head.

The Senator knew enough about guns to know that the bullet would probably blow the top of Strang's head off. That there was no chance that he would miss. No strength needed either.

Just the pressure of his finger and Mr. Strang would be dead. Mr. Strang, who had been killing off Mason's followers, and so the Senator's followers, one right after the other. Mr. Strang who stood in the way of his being Governor of the State. Mr. Strang who might already have evidence to convict Steve Mason of murder, and Mason who might turn against the Senator himself to save his own life.

Yes, it might be all there in the little book. And Senator Charles Philip Bixby tightened his finger, half shut his eyes. And—his eyes opened wide again; his finger loosened on that trigger; great beads of perspiration formed on his forehead.

His thoughts had been right, but his conclusions, if he had really drawn any conclusions, had been wrong—terribly wrong. And he had nearly shot a man to death; a man whose death at that moment would put the Senator in the electric chair. For it suddenly struck the Senator with tremendous force that Mr. Strang no longer had the book. It was in the hands of James Barton—Commissioner of Police.

Queer that! Very queer, the Senator thought, that something so small, so insignificant to the Senator himself, could roll up such great force—a little black book that stood between him and the Governor's mansion.

The Senator's eyes narrowed; his fingers steadied again. He had never killed a man in his life and now—a single shot and Strang would be dead. Another one before Barton realized the truth and Barton himself would be dead. After that the girl—and power!

Barton was turning toward him. Senator Bixby tightened his fingers on the trigger and loosened it at once. The thing was impossible. Others were in that house, and outside on the street were men—picked men who would not only shoot Mr. Strang to death, but would take the book from his dead body—if the book was in the pocket of that dead body. And Senator Bixby would see that it was in that pocket. He stepped between the Commissioner and Strang, said in his buff, honest election voice:

"Come, come, Commissioner. We can't do anything

like this. Sheila's promise was your promise—and even my promise. After all, I too have known Mr. Strang in his bad and his good periods. At your suggestion, he was to help me with a new parole bill. Give him back his book and let him go. We have our honor to consider."

Barton glared at the Senator; the gun half raised in his hand.

"We have," he countered, "the people of the entire city to consider. Mr. Strang is now a danger to the community. I intend him no harm. He will be well taken care of. I will disclose none of his past—and later, if his maniacal tendency to wipe out—er—half the city, has passed, then— Come, Senator, stand aside."

The Senator grew a little panicky, but he tried to make his voice steady; his words forcible.

"Am I to understand that you wish to break permanently with me, Commissioner?" He held his dignity fairly well, and as the rugged face of Barton seemed to tighten, "I—I—"

He stopped, dropped the gun.

MR. STRANG WAS standing directly behind him. He was speaking softly over the Senator's shoulder, stretching a hand beneath the Senator's arm and looking down, the Senator saw that that hand held a small gun. Mr. Strang said:

"You're not the only man who can use a sleeve, Commissioner James Barton. There, I don't have to tell you now that I am not looking on you as Sheila's father, but as just one man in the way of my plans. It's a small gun as you see. It would be necessary to shoot you right between the eyes."

And as Barton hesitated, Strang's voice rasped out, "I don't want to kill you. Drop that gun, you fool!"

Barton looked at Senator Bixby and the gun in Mr. Strang's hand. He could not see Mr. Strang behind that huge body. But he didn't need to see him. Barton did not know fear. Barton had never been bluffed. Now—he simply cursed once and dropped his gun to the floor.

"You idiot," he addressed the Senator. "You—"

"He saved your life," Mr. Strang cut in. "My gun was entirely too small to attempt to wound you. But I thank you just the same, Senator." And with a twisted grimace. "You saved your own life also, for you had a gun held tightly against my head— I was about to fire straight up at you. Okay, Barton—throw the book over. Now!"

Barton was a brave man, but he tossed the book over by Strang's feet. He had known Mr. Strang for a long time— several years. He knew that any hesitancy upon his part meant death—quick and certain. There were no two ways about that.

Strang said: "And I thank you again, Senator, because you did not know that I make it a business to enter traps fully prepared."

"There is no thanks needed, Mr. Strang." Senator Bixby was very friendly, very calm, too, in a severe sort of way, as he watched Strang lift up the book and regain his two guns. "I think I may speak for the Commissioner when I say you must leave the city within the next twelve hours— the country within the next few days. I will help you obtain a passport under your correct name—er—Strang Cummings?"

"Is there anything expected of me in return?" Mr. Strang's eyes widened, but they were unblinking.

"Nothing in return. Let us say that what I do is done for Sheila. And let us say that you will keep silent about your former association with the Commissioner for Sheila's sake."

"You heard the Senator," Barton said through set teeth. "I don't need your help—you and your damned book! Get out of the country, or every police officer in the city—the country even—will be hunting you for the murders of Keen and Owen."

Strang grinned.

"Things have changed, Commissioner. There are some other murders for which you might hold me. Murders that you called simply police killings at the time, and took the credit for with the newspapers and the people." And suddenly before Barton could cut in, "Do you think I like to kill? Do you class me with those who serve me? Living dead men who seek only their own death. I wanted to live before that operation. I wanted to live after it—hiding in dark corners. Then, perhaps I had no right to live. Now—"

Mr. Strang paused for a long moment; his eyes finally rested on Sheila though he spoke to her father.

"Now—you refuse my aid, Barton—will prevent my work. So I strike but once, and in that single blow rid the city of many criminals, leave the Parole Racket, perhaps the machinery of crime in the entire city so crippled that—that—yes, that even you should be able to control it. What if a few innocent people die with the guilty? All the Legion of the Living Dead are innocent men, and all are willing to die—glad to die. It is right that I should die with them. I want to live. But I am glad to die."

"And why," said Barton, "do you want to live?"

"Because I am a man—with a man's human weakness." He raised a finger and pointed it at Sheila Barton. "I want to live for her."

Then he strode across the room toward the door. Barton stretched a hand toward him. He was wondering if it might not be better to keep him—work with him. The months swept back, even the years.

But the Senator held his arm and shook his head as Sheila followed Strang to the front door.

Sheila tried to say many things, but she didn't try very hard. She saw only one thing now; one thing as she stood in that doorway—the man she loved was going to die. She said: "Can't you act—and live?"

And when he shook his head, "With the others it is different. They must die anyway!"

"I cannot live. Dead, I will be a martyr to a great cause. Alive, a murderer ready for the chair. I know, Sheila. I wish with you that it could be some other way. I wish that your father and I were as close as we once were. Good-bye, Sheila. You have not created a Frankenstein, but a machine that will dispense a justice that the laws of our city cannot dispense. You are my friend—my only friend. Goodbye."

"You can't! You won't! You mustn't!" she told him as she threw her arms about his neck.

HE DIDN'T SPEAK and she didn't speak when she dropped back on her heels. She wanted to say that she loved him, but she didn't. She couldn't. And she had no need to. For a full minute, those eyes held hers; fires growing brighter until they finally blazed. His whole being seemed to change—inside and out. His shoulders bent forward. An arm stretched out and swept her aside—gently and yet firmly, Then his huge body moved, apparently without effort, slid out onto the stone steps and disappeared into the night....

Sheila Barton didn't move as she heard the door close with a soft swish, heard the latch click with a sharp metallic sound.

Inside, Senator Bixby heard that sharp click too. He straightened his glasses, smothered a smile behind his hand. So Mr. Strang wanted death, eh? He would get it much sooner than he expected. Mason's boys were waiting on that block. Machine-guns were already trained upon Mr. Strang's bent figure. As Resa Kent had died—so, too, would Mr. Strang die, a dancing, twirling marionette with the strings crossed just before he crashed to the pavement.

Sheila was standing before him.

"I want to thank you, Senator," she said very seriously. "Oh, not for saving Strang, for he didn't need that. But for saving me, saving that bit of honor that my father always taught me to have."

And when Barton simply coughed, the Senator said: "Nothing, child. It was nothing. Mr. Strang was quite capable of saving himself."

He wanted to say more. But he didn't. He was listening. Surely, doors or no doors, the crash of a machine-gun would be heard plainly. All was silence. Fear struck at the Senator. Mason had had time—and Mason had failed.

But Steve Mason had not failed. The two men and the girl jerked erect. They turned toward the front door and stood like living statues. Only Senator Bixby knew and understood the truth; understood at the first blast. The distant *ping* of a machine-gun, and then no longer distant and sharp, but a steady, confused roar. The Senator nodded. Steve Mason always did a good job. He could picture several men with machine-guns all pounding lead into the writhing body of Mr. Strang.

Just a second of that confused roar. Then clearly, but distantly the staccato notes of a single machine-gun. Senator Bixby's lips parted; his glasses settled back easily on his nose. He could plainly visualize Mr. Strang upon the sidewalk and the single gunner above him crashing bullets into his helpless body. That was Steve Mason's way. Men didn't come around later in the hospital and talk about attempts on their lives.

Sheila screamed and ran toward the front door, pulled it open. Barton had started too. The Senator grabbed at his arm, pointed toward the phone and said:

"Too bad, Barton. Mr. Strang is dead, of course. Perhaps it is better so."

Commissioner James Barton looked blankly at Senator Bixby. Somehow he couldn't understand clearly just what the Senator meant, except that he, Barton, had sent a man—a—yes, a friend, now he thought, directly to his death.

28

MACHINE GUNS ROAR

MR. STRANG WALKED leisurely down the front steps of the Commissioner's home. His head didn't pain so much now. Peculiar that. The blow that should have hurt seemed instead to dull the steady pain that was forever in his head.

To Sheila's embrace he gave little thought. It was pleasant, a nice memory, as if a child had clung to him. As for Barton—well Barton had acted as he was built to act. The new house, the better surroundings, the title of Commissioner had not changed him any. He was still the same as Mr. Strang had first found him; still an honest, straightforward cop; still the sergeant he would have always been.

Mr. Strang grinned as he thought of the blow on the head, and the dexterity with which Barton had drawn the blackjack from his sleeve. Yes, Barton was still the sergeant who could be counted on to obey orders—if he got those orders.

The Senator? Mr. Strang could not understand him. Never had understood him. Big and blustering and self-important, and thinking only of himself, he had wanted Mr. Strang to push him up the ladder. Strang smiled too as he thought of the Senator playing the detective to get information from Steve Mason; Steve Mason the wisest boy who had climbed his own particular ladder; climbed it quickly and did not intend to loiter on any step but the top one.

Yet—Senator Bixby had been Mr. Strang's friend that night. He had saved a particular ugly scene. He had forced Barton into letting him go free, had even seen that the Book of Evil was returned to him.

Strang crossed the street from the Commissioner's house and walked slowly toward the corner, saw the sedan across the street and noted that the windows were tightly closed and that no driver sat behind the wheel. He shrugged his shoulders and started thinking again.

Senator Bixby was important and pompous and—

Mr. Strang stopped thinking, shot his right hand beneath his left armpit. A car was gliding along the street behind him. It was an open touring with the curtains drawn.

The car slowed. The driver leaned toward him, both his hands gripping the wheel and evidently, Strang thought, saw the position of Strang's right hand and stepped on the gas again.

Mr. Strang smiled, started to drop his hand to his side, then knew the truth. The boys who wanted his life had been clever, very clever. The black touring no longer blocked his vision from the sedan across the street. Nor from the figures who stood before that sedan. Three figures. One almost directly before the car. Another perhaps twenty feet down and almost in the middle of the street—and still a third another twenty feet up the block.

They had jumped from that big sedan—or had come from behind it. But where they came from did not matter to Mr. Strang. It was that they were there—that and the things they held in their hands. Each one was holding a sub-machine-gun, and each one was raising his gun to level it on the body of Mr. Strang.

The man in the center spoke. "Show us some of that famous gun-play of yours, Mr. Strang. Steve said you were to know before you took the dose, it's with the compliments of Rudolph."

The years swept back over Mr. Strang in a split second. He had faced death many times before, faced it with blazing guns in his hands. And now—yes, Mr. Strang felt that he would have at least a chance of sweeping a hand across his chest and bringing sudden death to that speaker before enough bullets pounded into his body to kill him.

Yes, Mr. Strang knew how quick he was. But Mason knew also—thus the three men and the message of death. The three. He knew them all; all three of them were in that book, that book which would be riddled with bullets; all three of them murderers many times over.

Hard-faced, soft-named, Angelo Fario, who had left a knife sticking in a young girl's chest. Grim, thick-lipped Dutch Swart, and just plain Hard Luck Charlie whose last name no one seemed to know—perhaps not even Charlie himself. But all gunners—all trained gunners—the best that money could buy.

It was death, of course. Mr. Strang had no doubt of that. He wasn't afraid; would have been even indifferent if it weren't for Steve Mason remaining alive. And he had not yet discovered if Billings was behind Mason. He had looked over the paper, the information that the Living Dead Men had brought him. There was suspicion of Billings and—

Like a drowning man, these whirling thoughts, but cut as clear as fine small camera prints shot through his mind. A full second, a split second—just the—the—

Angelo had left the knife in a dead girl's chest, and—Mr. Strang's right hand flashed to his left armpit, lead spat from his gun as he threw himself down on the pavement.

Machine guns roared above his head, against stone, bounced off the pavement, pinged against the house. His single shot had started them firing wildly anyway, without lowering their guns—that is without lowering them accurately in that first sudden wild volley.

There was no escape, no chance to live. It was just a hope with Mr. Strang that one man might also die—the one who'd left the knife and—

The bullets would be pounding into his body now. It was hard work not to lower his head. Yet he did keep his head up. He'd take that withering, raking lead—facing it!

29

MIRACLE

THE BULLETS WEREN'T hitting his body—or if they were, he didn't feel them. Strang couldn't understand that. The sound of firing was still audible, yet no one seemed to be shooting at him.

Angelo Fario lay sprawled very still in the street. The other two killers had turned slightly, taking on queer positions—writhing, convulsive movements. Certainly only one machine gun was in action now. The sharp notes of it were clear, distinct, rapid, controlled by the fingers of a single man.

For the first time in his career as Mr. Strang, he was confused. He lifted his gun, but there were no dancing figures to shoot at—just three men lying limply there in the street. Then a fourth suddenly stuck his head from the sedan window, lifted a tommygun, curved it toward Mr. Strang. But he never fired.

Mr. Strang hooked his trigger finger once. The white face disappeared from the window, the heavy gun crashed upon the pavement and Mr. Strang sprang erect.

Feet beat upon the pavement behind him; a voice called: "This way, Mr. Strang—through this alley, the fence. My car is there. Hurry! *Hurry!*"

"Funny thing," Madox grated. "You okayed my parole and I was sprung just to bump you off!"

Mr. Strang did hurry; his footbeats in rhythm with those of the man beside him; his agile body vaulting the fence with his rescuer; his feet again keeping time down the bleak alley. Then he was in a car, heard rather than saw the machine gun his companion tossed into the back of the car, and they were off.

Strang gasped: "You saved my life, Stewart! I've been nicked on the arm once, nothing more. Hardly a scratch. It was a miracle they didn't fill me with lead."

"It was a miracle they hit you at all," Stewart countered indignantly as he rounded a corner, ran down one block and cut off the main thoroughfare. "Why, I opened up just as soon as you fell to the sidewalk. Before they even started to shoot. If my position had been just a bit better, they never would have closed a finger on their guns. You're a wonder, Mr. Strang, to kill that man in the car under such circumstances. I didn't even know he was there."

Strang gripped the man's arm, noted the steadiness of it, lack of nerves as they swung another corner. He said: "You followed me, of course, Stewart. You, of all those men! You who no longer are condemned to die, except that you work for me."

"With you," corrected Stewart.

"With me?" Strang shook his head as he told Stewart to drive to that building on the block behind Strang Cummings' shop. He could hide there in safety. For it was there that Sheila used to telephone him—and more often he'd telephone her.

"Yes, with you until the Legion of the Living Dead strikes its last blow." Stewart continued, "There is a chance that you and I may both come through—maybe only one of us."

Mr. Strang shook his head again. "I am like the others now. I may only live to die. The Commissioner of Police knows of my threat—the one big strike at the criminals. He was my friend—his daughter is still my friend—until you came tonight, I thought my only friend. No, it will be too horrible for that girl. I would only live to die by the law. I must spare her that."

And putting his hand on Stewart's arm: "You are sure about Fiester and Henderson? I mean, they are up for parole?" And when Stewart nodded, "Mason cannot be working this alone, Stewart. There must be someone, big, behind him."

"I sent men to protect Billings the other night," Stewart said. "Yet he could so easily be the one."

Strang answered simply: "I must see Kirkman Billings tomorrow night before the big knock-over. If Billings is the man behind this racket, it is essential we know it, that he is not left alive to start things all over again. Remember, if every big crook in the city were to die—if every criminal connected with this Parole Evil were to die—and Billings did head it—then, the Parole Evil would be only temporarily halted, to spring to life again—and I would be too dead to prevent it."

"But if Billings is simply an honest man, unfamiliar with crime, trying to make of parole a good, not an evil? What then?"

"Then we must know that, too. Tell me again of these doubts you have of Billings."

The car turned left and Stewart talked. Mr. Strang nodded occasionally, and frequently snapped his teeth together with a dull click. Some of the story was decidedly interesting. Especially about the visit of Kirkman Billings' most trusted secretary, Mortimer Jackson, to Steve Mason—and the intended parole of Marty Henderson.

30

"THE FIRST MURDER"

KIRKMAN BILLINGS WAS not a young man. But he drove himself as few young men could do. Tonight he was working at a furious pace, going over report after report, examining carefully the many papers on the desk before him, comparing them with other papers. Though it was quite early, Mortimer Jackson, his secretary, was asleep in the room at the end of the library so that, early in the morning, the memos Billings had made would be neatly typed and placed with many of his other "findings" which would someday startle the city, and "revolutionize the entire Parole System."

Kirkman Billings arranged the papers neatly, half rose from his chair as his eyes drifted to the safe, to the clock upon the mantel, then to the mirror beside that clock. He replaced the papers carefully on his desk, covered them with other documents, glanced toward the door at the end of the room, drummed his fingers upon the flat surface of the desk, then let the fingers of his right hand drift nearer to the pushbutton on the end of his desk.

His fingers stopped, though not frozen to the desk by the voice behind him, for he had half-expected that voice any moment. At least he had expected the owner of that voice, whom he now saw plainly in the mirror, to walk straight into the room.

The voice said: "Don't press that button, Mr. Billings. Don't cry out; don't even raise your voice—or I shall find it necessary to shoot you to death."

Kirkman Billings took his hands from the desk, half swung in his chair, said: "Shall I turn and face you or will you enter the room and face me? Surely you are one to face people directly, Mr. Strang."

Mr. Strang hesitated only a moment in his stride. Then, coming directly to Billings, he ran his hands over him, opened two drawers, shut another one that was partly open and, walking in front of Billings, directed his gun almost straight at the man's forehead.

"So you know me, Mr. Billings? It will then not only be advisable to kill you but perhaps necessary."

The little man leaned far back in his chair, unblinking black eyes staring at unblinking ones of fire. Billings said: "I am not a young man, Mr. Strang, and I am not afraid to die. But it will be a pity for those I would help."

"You mean Mason, and men like him—perhaps yourself?"

"Certainly myself." And leaning forward. "You cannot intimidate me, Mr. Strang. I have never carried a gun. I found that it was too late in life for me to take up seriously the use of firearms. You have come to me for information, I presume?"

"You know a lot about me," Mr. Strang said. "At least you know who I am, yet you never saw me before."

"Yes, I know a lot about you. I have never seen you, but I have had you described to me. I think the burning eyes would have been quite sufficient. They, of course, are natural—that is the intensity of some hate. I consider the peculiar cut of your hair as entirely theatrical. I might say the same thing about your mouth, the curl to it. It gives your face an evil twist which I believe it does not naturally have, but will soon be a habit with you." And after a pause in which Mr. Strang stood staring at the man's apparent indifference to his presence. "It may become a habit which you may find difficulty in breaking—and a great desire to break."

Mr. Strang said: "You are well informed, Mr. Billings. Too well informed. I shall not live long enough to change my habits, even the habit of taking the lives of the enemies of—of the people."

"You might," said Kirkman Billings, "mean me by that threat. I understand your desire to avenge a young lady's death, and destroy a terrible disease called parole which is gnawing at the heart of society. I have far less time to live than you have—"

"Perhaps far less than you think, Mr. Billings."

"Yes, yes, I understand that." Mr. Billings seemed simply impatient. "But I am comparing our normal span of life, and not taking into consideration the death by violence you plan not only for others, but for yourself. If you know so much of the working of parole, and the racketeers you think control it, what good will your death do if the same evil arises again, the leader, perhaps, lives on?"

"That's why I'm here, to be certain that the leader does not live on. You say you are not armed, that you do not fear death. It may change your attitude, Mr. Billings, when you understand I may be here for the purpose of killing you. I won't call it murder, for contrary to the opinions of others, I have never taken a life except in protecting my own or the lives of others."

"If that information," said Mr. Billings, "was passed along to certain other people, they would sleep better tonight. No, I must disappoint you, Mr. Strang. I am one of the few people who do not fear you."

"You compliment me, Mr. Billings." Mr. Strang bowed mockingly. "When I look at you, now, I wonder why you would head such an organization. To be honest, I am quite alone in my opinion of you."

Kirkman Billings smiled. "I wonder, Mr. Strang," he said, "if I am quite alone in my opinion of you."

MR. STRANG'S FACE twisted slightly. For a moment he thought that he rather liked the old man. But his smile and his thought went at once. He had no emotions left for liking people. He said: "Probably your opinion is shared by most people who know me. At least by the people you turn out from prison. No honest man would act as you have acted. You are practically the czar of the Parole Board, appointed by the Governor himself, a position that Senator Bixby would have had if I had not—not—"

"Become sick—mentally sick?" Billings studied Mr. Strang from half closed lids.

"No, if I had not failed him." And with a little gulp, "Failed Commissioner Barton."

"Barton. Barton!" Billings chuckled. "Now there is a man with no tact, no diplomacy, no respect for politics and certainly can hardly be accused of being ingratiating to people who might aid him." And after a pause, while somber, cold, steel-colored eyes looked into hot steel ones,

"I sometimes wonder if it was the Senator who put him up to coming into my house and talking me down—yes, hammering me down."

"Barton," Mr. Strang was surprised to find himself defending the Commissioner, "is straight and honest! He likes to walk a direct line; he cannot step around obstacles, but must trample them down." He leaned forward. "Things are happening in the city, Mr. Billings. I am soon to die. I must be convinced about you tonight—one way or another. Big business men have often been notoriously stupid in civic, state or political positions. Parole has become a public scandal. The Governor might have appointed you to save his face. No one could nor should question your honesty. You have plenty of money. Your reputation is spotless, but someplace, hidden in your past, there may be something that someone has discovered; something that forces you to act as you do. It may come directly from Steve Mason or it may come from someone above Mason. I want to know."

"And if it is not blackmail—then what?"

"Then," said Mr. Strang, "I cannot put it down to stupidity on your part. I will find out the truth about you and—" Mr. Strang spoke very slowly. "You will be my first murder, Mr. Billings."

"So you'd go that far for your cause." Billings head bobbed up and down. "No, I doubt that you could, Mr. Strang. I doubt it very much." He came to his feet. "But I am glad to have met you. Delighted to know that we have one citizen with the courage of his convictions to come here and threaten—yes, threaten to murder me. But since you are not going to do it now," and Billings kept his eyes on that gun by Mr. Strang's side, "I will bid you good night.

I do not believe your visit and your threat worth mentioning to the police. I have far greater dangers hanging over my head."

Mr. Strang bit his lip, but he did not move.

"It's going to be hard—very hard," he said and there was a faraway note in his voice that made Billings cock up his head like a bird and listen attentively. "Somehow, I have the impression that you are honest, Mr. Billings. Yet I cannot believe in your stupidity." And almost in desperation as his hand tightened upon his gun, "I am a man condemned to die, Mr. Billings. I've got to know—now!"

Kirkman Billings said: "Just what do you want to know?"

"I want to know," said Strang, "if you are going to parole Marty Henderson."

"Yes," said Billings, "I am."

"And you know his past record?"

"I most certainly do."

"And where did you get this information?"

"I got it as I get all my records—from my secretary, Mr. Jackson, who can give me a finer and more detailed report than the police. Of course, he starts with the police records."

"Will you show me these records?"

"Certainly," said Mr. Billings. "If you will permit me to ring for my secretary. They are all kept on file—there." He pointed to a long row of filing cabinets. When Mr. Strang hesitated, "Are you afraid? He is not a very awe-inspiring figure, I assure you."

"Very well," Mr. Strang said. "Bring him in—alone."

"And the gun?" Kirkman Billings placed his hand upon the desk button. "Jackson is a rather timid man, and though extremely clever and invaluable, has a deathly terror of firearms."

Mr. Strang started a word of warning, decided that it was unnecessary and slipped his gun and his right hand into his jacket pocket. He wondered if Mr. Billings would be surprised when he learned the truth about Marty Henderson. When he learned also that his secretary caught in a financial jam, had tied himself up with Steve Mason, and was making reports to Billings that were entirely false. He wondered, too, if Billings did not know that these reports were false. Was he saving his face by having them come through his secretary? Or was Billings, after all, simply trusting a man who had been in his employ for years. This secretary who—

The secretary was entering from the far door, pausing, tightening his dressing robe. When he saw Mr. Strang he drew back, said: "I'm sorry, Mr. Billings, I didn't know you had company. If you will permit me—"

"Not at all, Jackson." Billings beckoned the man in. "This is Mr. Strang of whom we talked quite a little. Will you please get me the report on Henderson, the man we are freeing on parole—fine, high-minded chap, should have been out long ago." Billings smiled grimly.

"There, Mr. Strang." A minute later Billings had opened the folder, laid it upon the desk. "Our notes are quite heavy on Marty Henderson. Perhaps a reading of the first page will suffice. A sort of table of contents."

MR. STRANG NODDED, glanced down that first page expecting to see a list of fine things in this desperate and vicious criminal's life. Then his eyes bulged. It wasn't often that Mr. Strang was surprised, but here was a complete list of vicious crimes, many marked "suspected, proof lacking," and far more complete than Mr. Strang himself possessed on the deeds of this hardened criminal.

Strang said: "You have read this report yourself, Mr. Billings? I—mean—are you sure this is the report your secretary, Mr. Jackson, brought to you?"

"Certainly." Billings nodded. "You can't connect this Henderson up in any way with Steve Mason—yet Steve Mason wishes him paroled. A fine lad, Mason. It would be a pity not to oblige him. That is all, Jackson. I won't want you again."

"Stop!" There was a sharp metallic ring to Mr. Strang's voice that was strange even to him. Billings seemed to be mocking him. Was it possible that Billings was far shrewder than he thought? Was it possible that he, Mr. Strang, was expected to die there tonight? But he finished what he started as the secretary stopped in the doorway. He said: "Are you aware, Mr. Billings, that your secretary, Mr. Jackson, has visited Steve Mason, that he accepted money from him, that he has bought a small car and—"

"And is saving up to build a house in the country. Yes, I am quite aware of all that. It would hardly be decent of me, Mr. Strang, not to oblige Mr. Mason in such a small matter as paroling this man when he has been so kind to my secretary. I was quite surprised when I first heard of it and encouraged Jackson in this beautiful friendship with Steve Mason. You may go, Jackson." And when the secretary had gone and closed the door behind him, "I never took you for a fool, Mr. Strang. I do not like your taking me for one."

"I do not understand," was the best Mr. Strang could

return. He had always, as Mr. Strang, dominated the situation; now he was lost in it, uncertain, doubtful. Was Billings a clever man, too deep, too brilliant, perhaps, for even Mr. Strang to understand? Was he a crook who felt big enough to defy the man whom all criminals feared? But Mr. Kirkman Billings was talking, and in his words, the erectness of his small stature, Strang saw the force that had made those millions, perhaps had made him the czar of the Parole Board.

"I am bidding you good night, Mr. Strang. You have taken the law into your own hands, which is fundamentally wrong. No man is bigger than the state he serves. Parole in itself is not an evil. It is the administration of parole that is evil. Prohibition taught us that we must not condemn the many for the faults of a few. We must cure the evil in parole, preserve the good. You should know better than any man that it is not an easy task."

Kirkman Billings stepped to the curtains through which Mr. Strang had come. "I have had few failures in life, Mr. Strang—very few. I know the Governor well. I asked for this job, and I will see it through."

Mr. Strang waited in the center of that room. He did not move toward the curtains. He recognized in Billings a strong man, very strong indeed, but he did not know if that strength was for good or evil.

"Mr. Billings," Mr. Strang had difficulty in speaking, "I said when I came here tonight my intention was to kill. I do not know if that intention has changed."

Billings looked at Strang for a long time. "Well," he shrugged his narrow bent shoulders, "that is, of course, for you to decide. I am unarmed—and quite defenseless."

Strang looked into those cold eyes, but read nothing there. Nothing of fear, certainly. And he saw no trembling of the arm which stretched toward the curtains nor no trembling of the fingers that held them back. Finally he moved forward. Kirkman Billings said:

"I imagine I am the first man to read your mind, Mr. Strang. Oh, I don't mean the first one to see death in your eyes. You feel that you are making a mistake in leaving me alive, wondering if you can rectify that mistake later, but you cannot kill me now."

Strang turned at the curtain, said thickly: "You are a very brave man, Mr. Billings—a very brave man."

"Only pretending to be brave," Billings told him. "You see, I had a trump card up my sleeve—a single name that I would have given you if I felt that death was coming. Go as you came. No one will bother you." And as Mr. Strang threw a foot over the window sill in the dining room, "I have enjoyed your visit immensely. You must come and see me again—soon."

Mr. Strang dropped into the alley, looked up and down it. Just before Kirkman Billings closed that window he put out his head and whispered:

"The single name that would have saved me was the name of a woman." And seeing those glaring balls of molten steel in the blackness, "And the name of that woman would have been Sheila Barton!"

31

LIVING BAIT

STEVE MASON PACED up and down the room and glared at Senator Bixby. His questions were fast, so fast that he could not have expected answers.

"Why didn't you tell me his name was Strang Cummings? I might have killed him then. Why didn't you tell me he wasn't dead as soon as you found it out? And then you with a gun against his head—and the Commissioner of Police himself wanting the man—why didn't you pull the trigger?"

The Senator gulped, straightened on his chair, leaned heavily upon his gold-headed cane. He looked at the third man in that room. A big brute who slouched against the wall and let a badly rolled cigarette hang from his lower lip. But the Senator finally did speak: "You were to have men waiting outside to—to— I thought it better to—"

"Don't mind Chris." Mason jerked a thumb toward the man with the cigarette. "And don't mind that cigarette nor the sneer on his puss. He's been seeing too many pictures. What you mean is that you sent Mr. Strang out for the boys to shoot down, kill him—murder him, isn't that it?"

"My dear Stephen!" The Senator hammered the floor with his cane. "You must be careful of your language. I won't have it. I—" The Senator came to his feet, stared angrily at Steve Mason. He saw Mason's open hand come out. It came slowly until it was almost against the Senator's face. Then it stopped, dropped to the Senator's shoulder. Mason looked toward the ceiling. No, he thought, it wasn't the time for "mush pushing" then. Mason jerked his hands apart, said:

"Forget it. No hard feelings. We need each other." And turning, "On your way, Chris. Just as I outlined it. Remember, he's a cocky bird, no guard, no gun, nothing." And as he put an arm around Chris and led him to the door, "Put them all right smack in his stomach. Close range, understand? Make it hurt like hell." And at the door, "Don't forget, Chris, this is Senator Bixby, the big boss—" And with a grin and a pat on the back, "—next to me."

The door closed, Steve spun the key and slapped the Senator on the back.

"You're hot stuff, Senator. There's no getting away from that. And you've got the finest front the Avenue has ever seen. I'm just jealous of it, I guess. But don't forget that we stood in on a killing together."

"A killing—a murder you mean!"

"What's the difference so long as the guy's dead?" Steve shrugged.

"Difference! But I didn't want to be there."

"None of us wanted to be there," Mason said easily. "There isn't much pleasure in knocking off a guy like Lorey, but you *were* there, and you didn't talk afterward. Now, I'm not threatening. I just want to let you know how we stand. I'm going to push you up, Senator, not drag you down. Don't look so glum."

"And this man tonight—this man who is to be killed by Chris. It's not Mr. Strang?"

"No." Steve Mason set his lips tightly. "It's not Mr. Strang. But about this Mr. Strang. You didn't have the nerve for it, Senator. You could have killed him."

THE SENATOR COUGHED, looked about the room. He never liked to talk straight out, but now he had to. "Mr. Strang was a prisoner there in the Commissioner's house. He had that book with him. The book that holds evidence against so many—er—criminals. Maybe you, too, Stephen, or someone close to you. Don't you see? Commissioner Barton would have taken the book from his dead body as he very nearly did from his live one. You had told me that you were prepared for Mr. Strang; prepared to kill him if he left that house. You can't put your failure on me." The Senator got the last line off with some of his old-time importance.

"Failure!" Steve Mason snarled. "What do you mean 'failure'?"

"We heard the shots, of course, Sheila, the Commissioner and myself. Also the officer down the street. When we reached the—er—place—" The Senator ran his hand over his eyes. "It was horrible! Three men with machine-guns lay dead in the street. A fourth was dead behind the wheel of a car across the street. You should have managed it better."

"Managed it better?" Steve Mason gasped. "Three experts with tommy-guns, a lad in the car for the get-away. I never paid any guy that much respect before. Mr. Strang shot them all to death. You let him walk out of the Commissioner's house toting a machine-gun!"

"Ridiculous," countered the Senator. "He carried two guns—heavy revolvers. I think one was a thirty-eight. I'm not up on firearms, but a machinegun—impossible!"

"They were all dead—riddled to death." Steve thought a moment. "Three of the best gunners I ever had. And I've got it straight from the morgue, a machine-gun did the trick. You don't think the girl gave Mr. Strang the machine-gun in the doorway?"

"You must be out of your mind." The Senator looked straight at Steve Mason. "I only pretended I let Mr. Strang go because of the girl. It was really because of the book. The girl, Sheila, is young, charming, highly-educated. We have things in common. You would hardly understand my interest in her."

"Oh, wouldn't I?" Mason sneered. "She'd do a lot for Mr. Strang, eh? And maybe a lot for you—now."

"She would do a great deal for me—and perhaps for Mr. Strang. She blames herself a good deal for his—latest actions."

"He's bad—" growled Steve, "—damn bad. I sent Rudolph uptown to do a job, and somehow Mr. Strang finds him. Then he walked into my office and hurled the dead body of Rudolph—my closest friend, understand?—hurled it across the desk right on top of me."

"He's mad." The Senator nodded vigorously. "No sane man would do that."

"Mad—hell, no! He chucked Rudolph onto my chest for a purpose—to strike terror. Yes, strike terror to me, to Steve Mason who fears neither man nor devil." Steve Mason turned white, then a pasty yellow as he banged his hand upon the desk. "Not me, Senator. Not me!" He fairly shrieked the words. "No man can do that—not to Steve Mason."

The Senator watched the blotches of yellow on that rough-skinned face thin themselves out and slowly disappear. He had known fear himself—even terror that night when Lorey was murdered.

Steve Mason noticed the expression on the Senator's face, walked over to a little cupboard, took out a bottle and two glasses and filling them tossed one off himself. He filled his glass again and brought the other drink to the Senator.

Mason said: "Tell me again about this—this killing that Mr. Strang has planned, this general wipe-out of my boys—other boys."

The Senator laid his glass down on the wide arm of his chair, lifted it again, sipped it slowly, refilled it and said: "It's just what he told Sheila—Miss Barton—and what she told her father. He is to wipe you all out tomorrow night."

"With this Legion of the Living Dead, eh?" Steve Mason's sneer was not very real. And then, "I believe he is going to try for a big knock-over. The Steve Mason Athletic Club is meeting tomorrow night. Just a free-and-easy bit of drinking and games. No trouble expected. So that's it!" And with a laugh that was real this time, "It's a long narrow flight of stairs, Senator. A few men at the top with tommy-guns should do the trick. Mr. Strang wants a slaughter, does he? And these living dead men long to die? Hell, they'll all get their wish."

"But you, Steve. I understand he will kill you himself."

"Yeah? We'll attend to that right now. He's a sucker for this girl, Sheila, just as you are, Senator. The boys will wipe out the Legion of the Living Dead. I'll do for Strang myself. We'll get Sheila to—"

"Sheila must and will be left out of it." Senator Bixby meant what he said—or thought he did.

"Listen," Mason gripped Bixby by the lapels of his jacket, "you'll ask Sheila to meet you—now, at once. Then you'll take her to my place—that little bungalow over the bridge at Washington Beach." And with a wink, "You've used it before. She owes something to you. She thinks she owes more to Mr. Strang. Don't you see, Senator? You'll tell her you're helping Mr. Strang, that her father must not know you're meeting her. Simple, eh? She's the bait that traps Mr. Strang."

"But afterwards? The girl, her father. Why—?"

"THAT'S IT," SAID Mason. "We'll use the same set-up to trap her into your arms." He poked the Senator in the ribs. "You know the stuff you got. You can keep her father in his position. You're going to be head of the Parole Board next week."

"Head of it—how? Billings is already beginning to— well, not exactly to criticize my suggestions, but he questions me rather closely."

"Billings," prophesied Mason, "will be dead."

"Dead? Why he seemed in the best of health! I know he's on in years—"

"Can the chatter," barked Mason. "You and me are not going to talk around things anymore. You know Chris just went out to kill him. Easy stuff. He's reporting straight to Billings to tell him how well he's doing since his parole. Get in touch with Sheila Barton at once. Chris was over to the bungalow this afternoon. I'm using him now in place of Rudolph. Not so polished maybe, but he knows how to kill and keep his mouth shut."

"I see, I see!" Senator Bixby straightened in his chair, took another drink of brandy. "But Billings? You told this Chris to shoot him in the stomach. Why?"

"Because it hurts in the stomach. The papers will play that up. He'll be a mess to look at. Don't you see? None of the others will fancy his job, thinking of their wives and families—that sort of hooey. But you'll take his place, want to go on where a great man left off. Die as he died if necessary—a protection to the citizens. Hell, you know that line. None better at it."

"But if I turn loose some—?"

"You won't at first. We'll have stories of you fighting tooth and nail to keep lads with political friends in—that is, the wrong kind of political friends for you. When you're Governor, you'll turn boys out for the right people, the people who put you in. Our Parole Board, our—"

"Our?"

"Our is right!" Mason snapped. "Don't get too important, Bixby. They'd roast a Governor as quick as anyone else." And as the Senator puffed out his chest and picked up the phone: "Don't forget. When you talk to this Sheila Barton, warn her that Mr. Strang's life depends on her secrecy—that no one is to know she meets you. But, hell, you know the woman."

"Right," said the Senator. "Right." He was wondering if Sheila, with her dignity and assurance, charm and knowledge, would not after all make a good friend. Certainly, a very good friend to a future Governor. A Governor who would hold her father's position in the palm of his hand—

his very life—for that matter. Sheila loved her father, was very loyal and—and—she wouldn't be in a position to argue then. The Senator liked women—and Sheila—she was different. He liked her enough to shower every luxury on her.

"This big kill," said Mason. "Mr. Strang might call it off?"

The Senator shook his head. "That," he said, "would be impossible. He communicates with these living dead men through the public notices of the morning papers. There won't be time for that. He suspects nothing and tomorrow night will be quickly upon us. He—he may not live much longer?"

"He won't," said Mason grimly. "You can count on that."

The Senator lifted the receiver and called Sheila Barton's number. He did not know if it was a relief to hear her voice or not. But she said: "Mr. Strang?"

"No," answered the Senator softly. "But I speak for him. He needs you, Sheila—needs you terribly. I must see you at once."

There was more, but when the Senator dropped the instrument back in its cradle, he turned to Mason, straightened his collar, jerked down his vest and said: "Things are quite satisfactory, Stephen. I will meet her in fifteen minutes."

"Fine!" agreed Steve Mason. Mr. Strang would come for Sheila and Mason would throw her dead body to him just as Mr. Strang had thrown the dead body of Rudolph to him.

Sheila Barton, eh? Yes, Strang would see her. Mason's

lips set tightly. She would die slowly and horribly. He looked at the Senator, shrugged.

The Senator could have his pick of any girl in the floor show—any one the Senator wanted. Steve thought he knew the Senator pretty well. As for his being Governor... Steve looked at him again; his erect carriage, the stick he had tucked under his arm. Yes, Senator Bixby looked more like a Governor than any Governor Mason had ever seen.

32

"THEY DO NOT ANSWER"

MR. STRANG LEFT the taxi a block and a half from his art gallery, the gallery of Strang Cummings. Unless the police were desperately after him, he felt sure he was safe there. His manager had been handling his business as best he could since Strang's "illness." But Sheila Barton had actually been running the business.

Years before, Strang had placed his little entrance on the court behind, and his private room hidden by a famous master's work. There he had always been safe both from the police and the underworld, would be now unless they tore the place apart.

Tonight, just after leaving Billings, he had gone there to rest. Not to think, yet he did think. He thought of Sheila Barton, and his thoughts were not the thoughts for a man who expected to die, but of a man who hoped to live. He shook his head. Less than twenty-four hours now and the Legion of the Living Dead would walk for the last time.

He had put his house in order. His will read simply enough. Everything went to Sheila Barton. In his safety deposit box was a list of the dependents of his living dead men. Sheila was to see that the families of these men who died, received his money. It wasn't hard to ask Sheila to do that. It wasn't hard to ask Sheila anything. Sheila was much in his mind, and he felt an urge to talk with her. The hour was still fairly early. But if it had been four o'clock in the morning he would have called her just the same. She was never tired, never irritable, always glad to hear his voice, always glad to do what he wished.

Several times Strang said "Yes" to the operator's, "They do not answer. Shall I continue ringing the party?"

It merely annoyed Strang at first, then it began to bother him. He hung up. Sheila should be home. She hadn't heard from since the attempt upon his life. She should be there by her private phone—certainly at this time of night.

He clicked the phone several times and called Commissioner Barton's number. That would be the downstairs phone in the same house. The answer was quick, abrupt. It was Barton speaking:

Strang said: "Mr. Strang calling. I wish to speak to Sheila."

"She hasn't met you yet?" There was uncertainty, a sort of gnawing doubt in Barton's voice, and he added: "What do you intend to do with her? I'm not saying I'm right, Strang. I am saying I'm dead wrong about last night. You're not threatening her harm. You couldn't do that. Not after—"

"Where is Sheila?" Strang cut in sharply.

"She left a note." Barton's voice broke slightly. "Wait, I'll read it." A moment of silence and then, " 'Strang needs me and, of course, I have gone to him. Sheila.' "

"Did you say, 'of course'?" Strang heard himself speak, though he did not mean the words. It was a trick, a plant, a trap of some kind for him. Where did it originate? He cursed Barton, and was surprised at Barton's reaction.

There was no anger in Barton's voice. He just wished to get his own words in; his own anxious questions. "Didn't she meet you? Didn't you send for her? Didn't—?"

Strang wasn't listening now, nor talking either. Who? Who? Who could have fooled her like this? Steve Mason. But he would hardly know that Strang even knew the girl. Of course, he knew that Strang visited the Commissioner's house. He had always known that. He—he—

Strang had it. He jammed down the phone and came to his feet. He recalled Kirkman Billings' words of that very night. Billings had said, "The single name that would have saved me was the name of a woman. And the name of that woman would have been Sheila Barton."

So that was it, Mr. Strang thought as he picked up his hat and coat. That was what? He didn't know. Just something that Kirkman Billings must have held over Sheila's head, over her father's head, maybe even over Mr. Strang's head. But Sheila could have saved Billings. How? Why? And the answers to those two questions could only come from Kirkman Billings himself.

So Billings was in it after all. In it up to his neck. He had invited Strang to call again. Mr. Strang *would* call.

KIRKMAN BILLINGS STILL sat behind his desk. He turned paper after paper examining the carefully planned report that Steve Mason had given his secretary and comparing it rather grimly with the actual report from the police and other records.

Then Kirkman Billings cocked his head to one side and listened. He guessed he didn't hear anything except perhaps the moving of the curtains which led to the dining room and so to the window beyond—the window by which Mr. Strang had entered.

A strange man, Mr. Strang, but certainly not mad. Billings wondered what made him think as he did. And Billings' head jarred again.

Yes, the curtains were moving. So Mr. Strang had accepted his invitation to return; accepted it very quickly. He had hardly been gone over an hour—well, two at the most.

Kirkman Billings didn't turn his head. He spoke without even looking up. "Come in, Mr. Strang. Come in!"

Feet crossed the floor. A voice spoke. It was deep, guttural, and certainly not the voice of Mr. Strang. The voice said: "So you've been playing around with Mr. Strang? I'm about on time then."

Kirkman Billings started to swing when that voice spoke. But there was no use of swinging now. The man was in front of him, huge shoulders, a flat face, slouch hat pushed back on his forehead. Mean, rat-like eyes regarded Billings; thick lips parted. His hands were large too—at least the left one which he laid upon the desk. The right was raised; black filled the whiteness of that hand. Fingers tightening about that black showed a duller white along the knuckles.

Kirkman Billings raised his eyes from the nose of that heavy black revolver to the face of the man again. He said slowly: "High forehead, thick sandy hair, muddy brown eyes, hard protruding chin, flat nose and—certainly Christopher Madox. Yes, I remember now. I had you paroled." And in a deep commanding voice, "Put down that gun, and let me straighten out your troubles."

"So you want to talk me back into the Big House?" The flat-faced man let his lips part. "Yep, Chris Madox is right. You had me paroled. Funny that. I was sprung to do this kill on you. You're getting a little too easy, a little too soft. Guys get to wondering if there isn't some jack going into your pocket or suspicion going into your mind."

"And just what do you intend to do with that gun?" Kirkman Billings' voice never shook. It held that note of command it had always held, that people had always obeyed. But now as he looked at that hard, set, cruel face, heard the words sneered out from twisted lips, he knew the truth. You can't talk down a gun. Chris said: "I'm going to empty it into you, Mr. Billings."

And as Chris bent further over the desk and shoved the gun forward, Billings cried out: "Why? Why?" It was perhaps the first time in his life that he was not sure of himself. He would have liked to have told this man of the chair, of the mistake he was making, of the uncertainty of his being caught and punished. But he couldn't. The words stuck in his throat; he saw death—death sure and violent. There was no mistaking what was in that man's eyes.

Chris Madox laughed, a whistling sound through his teeth.

"Why?" he said. "Well, you're making things too easy for the criminal. We're all going soft. So we thought we'd get someone else to head the Parole System." And leaning more forward, "I ain't a guy to be talked out of it. A gun-full right in the tum-tum." And Chris Madox's hatred for all law coming to the surface, "You never seen a guy take it that way, eh, Billings? Well, they don't twist at first, but on the second—" And thrusting his gun straight across that desk and against the body of Billings, his finger tightened upon the trigger.

A shot crashed out. Billings jerked back, though he felt no pain. Another shot, and Billings jarred erect. The gun wasn't there before him any longer. It was lying on his desk. And Chris—Chris was staggering back, grasping at his chest, staring to the left of Billings; staring at the curtains. Billings turned his head. He saw the man there with the gun in his hand, the molten steel in his eyes, the easy, almost pleasant curl to his lips.

But it was Chris who cried out his name: "Strang—Mr. Strang! Not again! It will mean death for the dame—a horrible death for the dame!"

BILLINGS SAT FROZEN in his chair. Not with fear now—just fascination as that bent figure of Mr. Strang moved slowly forward toward the man who had come to murder him. He saw Mr. Strang reach Chris; saw the gun in Chris' hand start up and Mr. Strang tear it from his hand as if he grasped something from a small child.

Mr. Strang threw the gun across the room, watched the man's hand, moved toward his left side, saw the knife, then struck. Chris' knees might have given from the force of that blow. But Kirkman Billings did not see them bend. It was as if the feet of the man went straight through the floor so suddenly did he go down. But his feet were there now—spread out grotesquely beneath him, and by his side was a knife.

Mr. Strang leaned over and picked up the knife. Then he stood looking down at the figure upon the floor, watched his feet straighten, his eyes roll, his whole body stretch itself out on the floor. Then when those eyes ceased to roll, Strang said:

"Where is the girl—Miss Barton?" And when there was no answer, Strang ran a finger along that razor-like blade, said half to himself, half to the man upon the floor, "Steve Mason's boys go in for knives. Rudolph used one to kill his own brother; another one I found in his chest. He was quite dead, Chris—quite dead. Where is Miss Barton?"

"She's in a house at—"

Mr. Strang looked at the man in the dressing gown who stood in the doorway at the end of the room. It was the second time that night that Mr. Strang had seen Mortimer Jackson, the secretary of Mr. Billings. He looked now at the gun in that trembling hand, said to Billings:

"Send him back. If there are servants in the house, have him warn them to keep quiet, say that they heard nothing. This man knows the whereabouts of Sheila Barton—and is going to tell me."

But this time, Chris would not talk. He held his tongue, despite the glaring burning eyes, the threats of Mr. Strang. Mr. Strang finally said: "You know who I am. You know I do not bluff." And bringing the knife down close to the now twisted face, "It isn't going to be a pleasant way to die, Christopher Madox."

"No." Billings was across the room. "You can't do that, Mr. Strang. The man has made an attempt on my life; you saved me and I am grateful, of course. But the law must take its course. If what he says about the disappearance of the girl is true, the police will—"

"The police," said Mr. Strang, "will put him in a hospital. The doctors will operate and pull my bullets out of his chest. Then the head surgeon will issue orders that he cannot be questioned for several days and—" Strang knelt beside the man, put the edge of the knife close against his throat, said, "I know how to twist it, Chris. Each time you do not answer, you—but then you understand a knife. Where is Miss Barton?"

Chris held his lips tight, tried to pull his chest away, though he was flat upon the floor, and the knife started down.

Kirkman Billings clutched Mr. Strang's arm, jerked it back started to issue a crisp order when he was hurled half across the room. Mr. Strang was on his feet following him. Billings tried to hold his ground, found that it was impossible. He had never seen such eyes before; hate, burning, vicious hate that was a living, blazing thing. Mr. Strang only said: "Back—back! Stand back."

And Kirkman Billings did stand back, petrified with horror more than fear. Somehow he knew that Mr. Strang was not bluffing, not giving any police third degree. Mr. Strang simply swung, knelt down close to Chris, held the knife in both his hands and said quite calmly:

"Chris, Rudolph dragged a knife across his brother's throat. I want to know where Sheila Barton is. There is no time to force it from you. Tell me—or I'll drag this knife across your throat—just once—only once."

"You wouldn't dare!" Feebly, Chris raised a hand and let it flop toward Billings. "Not with him here you wouldn't."

Strang leaned forward; the knife was in his right hand now. He looked for a long time into the eyes of Chris Madox. At length he said: "Look at me, Chris. You have exactly ten seconds to look into my eyes. I won't threaten after that. I'll know that you know the truth, and that you are willing to take it. Look!"

Kirkman Billings tried to look too. But he couldn't see those eyes. Yet he knew. He tried to cry out, but no words came. It must have been ten seconds. It must have been— and— That knife was raising, sweeping down again, when Chris Madox cried out:

"I'll tell, I'll tell!" There was a break in Chris' voice, a break that turned into a gurgle as the knife stopped, held, and Mr. Strang rose to his feet.

"The man is dead," he announced slowly. "If it were not for you, Billings, he might have talked in time. Murder, eh? Perhaps you stand there now as the murderer of Sheila Barton—whose life you took when you grasped my arm."

33

THE CALL

MR. STRANG SAT straight and stiff in the little room back of his art shop until long after dawn. Once he telephoned Barton and snapped down the phone after he had given his curt message:

"Get hold of Kirkman Billings, Barton. There was an attempt on his life tonight. I think it might be better if, for a while, it was kept secret that the attempt failed and that Chris Madox was killed."

He made no mention of the threat against Sheila's life. He felt that it was better that he didn't. He didn't know why he felt that way.

After that, Mr. Strang sat in silence staring at his phone; his private phone that Sheila knew and which number she would call if she needed him—and was able to call, alive to call.

Mr. Strang's fingers closed tightly. In what way could Sheila's abduction help this Parole Racket, and Steve Mason? Steve Mason knew about his book, and Steve Mason might very easily hold Sheila for that book—for Strang's life even.

He laughed a little at that thought. What would make Steve Mason believe that Strang would sacrifice his life or even his book for the life of Barton's daughter? Of course it was possible that Mason knew of their friendship, of the girl risking her life on that dangerous cliff that Mr. Strang might live.

The telephone on his desk rang.

Mr. Strang stretched out a hand and lifted the phone. The quick eager words snapped from his lips. "Sheila, Sheila," he said. "Are you all right?"

"Sheila," answered a man's voice which Strang thought that he recognized, or at least feared he recognized, "Sheila is quite well for the moment. Remember Rudolph, Mr. Strang? You tossed his body into the arms of his friend, Steve Mason. Well, Steve got a break. He was able to recognize his friend—dead or not dead. You won't recognize the girl as Steve recognized his friend, Rudolph, by looking into her dead eyes."

"No—!" Mr. Strang hardly knew that he whispered the word.

"No, because she won't have any eyes for you to recognize. I'm just ringing up to tell you she's going out tough—tougher than hell."

"So you'd like to leave me here in the city with that thought of you, Steve Mason?"

"Any thought you wish," said Steve easily. "You like the girl, eh? She'll be a mess."

Strang bit his lip, said harshly: "You just rang me up to tell me this? How did you get my number?"

"The dame gave me the number. I asked her for it. She hollered a bit. You know how dames are. I'm not going to libel her, Mr. Strang. It wasn't the smack in the face or the sock that knocked her down that made her give me your number. It was the kick in her face that— Did you say something?"

"Why do you call me up? Is there something you wish me to do?" And then, hardening his voice and trying desperately to keep the passion and the hate out of it: "You certainly wouldn't expect any interest from me."

"No, no, of course not!" Steve Mason seemed to stifle a yawn. "I just wanted to let you know how soon and how— well, just how I paid my debts." A silence for a moment and then, "It isn't like me to go into this private vengeance, Mr. Strang." Steve, like all the others, never dropped the Mr. in addressing Mr. Strang. "Hell, I'm a business man. Cutting up the girl would be entirely pleasure. You bring me that book of yours and you and the dame can go free."

"Your word on that I suppose?"

"My word?" Steve Mason laughed. "Why you don't need my word. If I had the book, what interest would I have in you? That's all you've got."

"And I'll meet you armed?"

Steve Mason's laugh was pleasant.

"Imagine us meeting like that, armed! Why one of us would turn up dead!"

"And you don't want to be that one?"

"That's right," Steve said easily. "I don't want to be that one. Think it over, Mr. Strang. I can put the girl on the wire later and make her do a radio scream for you if you're set on the melodramatic. Or I can send you parts of her anatomy bit by bit if you're of a sentimental nature. But me—I like to do things right. You pay the whole price—the book— and you get the whole girl. I'll send a lad in to see you, a fast worker, but he won't know you're Mr. Strang. Meet him as Strang Cummings. He's reliable, doesn't know a thing. Can't harm my plans if you cut him to ribbons to make him talk."

Mr. Strang had a mental picture of events. The book in the hands of Steve Mason, the girl killed—tortured to death before his eyes.

After a long silence, Steve said good-naturedly: "There's no hurry. Think it over. But stay at your gallery or shop or whatever the hell you call it until my messenger arrives to arrange your visit. Bye-bye, Mr. Strang. That baby of yours is kicking up a fuss and needs another kick in the mouth."

Strang gripped the hand-piece of his phone, held the words that came to his lips and as a gentle click came over the wire dropped his own phone back in the cradle.

There was no doubt that Steve Mason intended to murder both Sheila and himself—horribly. His face was hard and grim as he looked upon the blank wall before him.

He was not afraid to die. There was a possibility that Steve Mason might not kill Sheila, that Sheila did not even know who her abductors were. There could be no question that Steve Mason intended to kill him. Now—did Mr. Strang have the right to give his life for that girl when it meant that, despite his planned clean-up of all criminals, Steve Mason would live on? He had picked Steve Mason for himself. What did he owe to Sheila? Was it more than he owed to the entire city? To Sheila he owed his life—but did that life belong to him to give?

34

GREED AND FEAR

NINE O'CLOCK FOUND not Mr. Strang, but Strang Cummings, expert on works of art, sitting outside that small room in his large comfortable office. As Strang Cummings he gave his arriving manager quite a surprise.

"I am just looking over the books, Mr. Cochrane," he said. And in answer to his manager's question, "Yes, my health is much improved, thank you. I wish to sit here alone today. Just one visitor later—probably much later."

It was much later and Mr. Strang stood facing the door to his outer gallery when his expected visitor was admitted. The man was tall and thin. His clothes in good taste and of the most expensive material.

"Mr. Strang Cummings, eh?" The man looked directly at him. "I've come from a lady—you understand?"

"Sit down, sit down." Mr. Strang almost without visible movement slipped a gun back into its holster. "Well, Mr.—er—I didn't catch the name."

The visitor said abruptly: "My name doesn't matter."

Mr. Strang shook his head, but he didn't speak. The man was right but the man didn't know it. His name didn't matter, for Mr. Strang already knew his name. Johnny Waring, the slick, smooth criminal who had never taken a rap, beaten them all. The lone worker who never made a mistake—except just one, but no one knew of that mistake; no one knew that it was murder. That is, no one but Mr. Strang knew it. For Johnny Waring was in his little book; his Book of Evil. There was a full page given to Johnny, and so minute were the details, that a jury would hardly take more than five minutes to convict Waring of murder in the first degree.

The man spoke rapidly. He said: "I don't suppose it will be necessary for me to go into details. I am simply preparing for the trip. A short time from now I shall call for you, search you to be sure you are not armed, then escort you to a certain car. I do not know who has sent me. I do not know why you are wanted, but I do know that you are to bring something with you, a book which you shall wrap in paper before me. To me—" he looked at Strang Cummings for a long time as if he wondered why he had been paid for this particularly simple job—"there seems nothing dangerous in the proceedings. But I am to tell you that I have no idea where you are to go." His lips parted, even, white teeth showed. He said as if enjoying a joke, "I am to advise you that I could give you no information of any kind—even if you were to cut me to ribbons."

"And you find that part of your instructions rather amusing?"

"I must admit that I do, but I have a reputation for following instructions implicitly. I will return then in—" he consulted his wrist watch—"say twenty minutes, after informing the men by the car that you are ready to make the trip."

"Come here." Mr. Strang turned to the side wall, pushed

back a heavy canvass and invited his visitor into the little room beyond. When the man hesitated, he said, "Surely you are not afraid, and I wish to show you the book I am to bring with me."

"I am not afraid." The man followed him and watched the door slide back. "But I am not interested in the contents of that book, and if you have foolish ideas, I am armed, of course."

Strang Cummings did not speak. He leaned down beside the desk, opened a small safe and lifted out the book. He tossed it on the desk beside Johnny Waring, said:

"You should be interested in that book, Mr. Waring, and you should be interested in me, the owner of it. Together, that book and I, may mean your life, parted we will certainly mean your death. Come, look at me."

Johnny Waring had been watching Mr. Strang's hands; his empty hands. He looked up now, almost casually, then stepped back as if a gigantic unseen hand had pressed itself flat against his chest. His eyes popped to enormous proportions; his mouth hung open, but his right hand started across his chest.

"Don't do that!" Mr. Strang spoke very slowly; molten steel in his eyes bored into the bulging ones before him. "Before you could ever lay a hand upon it, I would have shot you dead. Ah, that's better. You know me, eh?"

Johnny Waring continued to stare, but he could back no further. He was flat against the wall now.

"I never saw you before in my life," he finally said.

"No, Johnny Waring. You have never seen me before. But you know me. Look. Look!" Mr. Strang's feet moved; his body bent forward, terrifying eyes burnt into Johnny

Waring's. "But you know me," Mr. Strang said. "Yes, you've heard about me, had me described. Answer me—you know me?"

Johnny Waring wet his lips, cursed Steve Mason beneath his breath. But he said: "Yes, I know you. You are Mr. Strang."

"Mr. Strang is quite correct. I am flattered. And I have found at once your two weaknesses which shall become my strength—your strength tonight. It was greed that brought you here, and it is fear that makes you stand there not daring to draw a gun. So Steve Mason didn't tell you whom you were going to meet."

Johnny Waring cried out: "I didn't say it was Mason. I didn't— Mr. Strang, I know nothing at all, not even if it's a snatch—just that the car is waiting, that they will search you even after I do. I could not permit you to reach that car armed." And trying to look Strang straight in the eyes, "You wouldn't—kill me, anyway?"

AND MR. STRANG laughed. There was no threat in his voice. It was soft and low, but he laughed again before he spoke. And it was the laugh that bothered Waring. He had never heard anything quite like it, certainly nothing human like it.

"Tonight," said Mr. Strang, "many men are to die. Your death would hardly interest me except that it suggests itself at the moment. If I decide to play the knight who rides to a lady's supposed rescue, then I will have you killed, of course."

Mr. Strang turned sideways and dropped into the chair by the flat desk. He lifted the book in both his hands, turned and looked at Johnny Waring, shook his head.

"Your gun, Johnny, is only for someone's back. I'm not saying you haven't the misguided courage to use it, but you lack the skill, and recognizing that lack of skill, you hire others to do your shooting for you. A lone wolf—the man who plays it safe. But you killed just once, Johnny—and weren't alone. Come nearer—look here."

Johnny Waring advanced like a man in a dream and looking down read the finely written words upon the page of the open book. Though the handwriting was very small, and hard for Johnny to read at first, it finally stood out like gigantic letters upon a billboard.

"So you see, Johnny." Mr. Strang talked as Johnny Waring reread that fine writing for the third time. "If Mr. Steve Mason had that book, he would have you. If the police had that book, they would burn you." And turning suddenly and looking up at the trembling man, he tore the page neatly from the book and said, "But if you had this single page from the book, neither Steve Mason nor the police could harm you."

Johnny Waring gasped and stared at the jumping letters.

"Simple matter," said Mr. Strang. "I will entrust this page to a friend who will give it back to me if I live. Mason intends to kill me, of course. And Johnny—if Mr. Steve Mason should die in the attempt upon my life, I will present that page to you in the center of ten thousand dollars worth of government currency. You see, I appeal to both your fear and your greed."

"I couldn't. I couldn't. There is no way—and Steve would kill me."

"Perhaps," said Mr. Strang. "I can show you a way, and

if that way is the correct way, why Steve Mason will not be alive to kill you."

Mr. Strang came slowly to his feet and put both his hands on Johnny Waring's shoulders.

"It's the lone wolf, Johnny; the game you always played. That murder you committed is not even important to me. But it is to the law, Johnny; the law that demands a dead body for a dead body. Rather barbarian, to be sure." Strang laughed lightly. "You burn them down and they burn you up, and the smell of your own burning flesh sickens those who watch you fry."

Johnny Waring half collapsed, half fell into the chair. Mr. Strang's hands still rested upon his shoulders, and his burning eyes—eyes that reminded Johnny of burning flesh—bit deep inside of him. But his voice was steady, and when Mr. Strang finished talking, Johnny Waring said:

"It wouldn't work. It's mad—it's—!"

"It's the madness of mankind that causes death," Mr. Strang said. "Your madness or Steve Mason's madness or my madness. If I die, you must die also."

Johnny Waring staggered from the chair, leaned against the wall. His whole body was cold, even the great beads of sweat that formed upon his forehead and ran down his face.

"Sit down," said Mr. Strang. "A drink, Johnny, just one. You must appear upon the street your own debonair, cocksure self." He tucked the folded page from the book into his pocket. "While you are gone, I will make arrangements about this page—arrangements that will mean your life or death."

There was another drink, and another ten minutes' wait before Johnny Waring left that room. Mr. Strang watched him and nodded his approval. Johnny Waring was himself again.

Mr. Strang smiled—at least his lips slipped up and his teeth showed.

He didn't mind heavy odds against him. Was it a hundred-to-one that he wouldn't come through safely? Perhaps for another man, but not him. Ten-to-one. He shook his head. That would depend upon—well, he might never have a chance, but he liked to think that he did—a good chance.

35

THE HOUSE AT
WASHINGTON BEACH

WASHINGTON BEACH WAS just across the bay from
the city itself. It was a lovely section with many small
single-storied bungalows and a few more pretentious ones
several miles down by the grove of trees. It was an attractive
and busy little summer colony, but this was early November
and the summer resort was deserted.

In one of the more pretentious of the two-story houses
Sheila Barton paced the floor of a second story room. She
turned sharply when Senator Charles Philip Bixby spoke
to her. "Why must the curtains be drawn?" she demanded.
"And why must we stay here, Senator Bixby?"

"Charles, dear." The Senator put an arm about her
shoulders. "Why, whatever is the matter with you!"

"I don't know." Her eyes blazed as she faced him, but
she didn't voice the thought that was in her mind. She had
known the Senator for a long time.

"It's for Mr. Strang. I've told you that a dozen times.
He's your friend. He's my friend. He'll come—he told
me to bring you here. It's harder on me than—than—"
He touched her arm and added, "Be more pleasant to me,
Sheila."

She jerked away. She read things in the Senator's eyes now—things she had always seen there, she guessed, but never could believe. She couldn't believe them now. She tried not to let her voice crack when she spoke.

"But this man who walks around, who telephones in the next room. Why can't I see him, see his face? Sometimes I think that he listens at the door. Why?" And suddenly, "How do I know this isn't some plan of Father's to force Strang into a position where he would have to—"

"So you believe Strang thinks that much of you?" This time the Senator placed both his fat hands upon her shoulders and held them there. "You think he'd even come to his—well, his death for you?"

"You don't like him." The girl tired without success to shake herself free from those hands that gripped her shoulders. "Why did you want the number—his telephone number from me? You're not his friend."

"Of course I am! Didn't I protect him from your father last night? Didn't I keep him from being put away in jail? Didn't I send him from the house when—?"

The Senator paused, stopped dead. He tried to shake the girl's shoulders. He couldn't. His hands wouldn't move. It was her eyes that bothered him, not the opening of her mouth and the sound of breath as if she tried to cry out. But her eyes were full of suspicion, then hate and loathing. The cry came:

"You sent him out—you sent him out of our house because you thought he was going to his death. They didn't kill him then. He killed instead. Now, I am the bait. This is the trap—for his death."

"Sheila, Sheila," the Senator said over and over in sudden panic. "You don't know what you mean!"

"Don't I? Don't I?" she cried out. "I should have suspected. Mr. Billings gave me hints enough. He said the truth was all going to be a shock to me and—it is."

"Stop! Stop!" The Senator thrust a hand over her mouth. "You don't know what you're saying."

But his warning, if warning it was, came too late. The door opened. Steve Mason walked into the room. There was a smirk to the corner of his lips. He said: "She knows what she's saying all right. And so do I. Hell, Senator, she's been working for Billings—just how, I don't know."

Sheila Barton said defiantly: "I'll tell you just how. I went to Mr. Billings when Strang was too ill to go. He didn't take me seriously at first. Then he did. But he never fully trusted me. He never told me his suspicions of you, Senator Bixby. He asked me about you, your conversations with Father, but—"

"So," Steve Mason cut in, "you played the game even against your old man?"

"It was parole." The girl held her head high. "I played it only for one person—for Mr. Strang!"

"Well, he's playing it for you now. He's coming here to save you, bringing that book to save you. Coming with two of my best men—unarmed and alone—for you."

"For me. For me!" Sheila clutched at her chest, but her eyes were no longer filled with hate; they were bright. "He'd do that for me!"

"None of that!" The girl had rushed for the door. Steve Mason stepped before her, struck once, a short-armed jolting punch.

Sheila Barton jarred back, blood showing on her lips. She rocked for a moment on her heels, then crashed to the floor.

Senator Bixby said: "Dear me, Stephen, dear me! We can't have this."

"Don't squawk," Steve said. "Things ain't so bad if Mr. Strang is half a man and comes. We'll get rid of both of them today. Don't look at her like that. And don't beef. I know a hundred girls with better looks, better bodies—and a damned sight less knowledge in their heads. Help me carry her into the other room."

"But I loved her so much!" The Senator took out his handkerchief and rubbed at his eyes. "She is very intellectual, very lovely."

"Nuts," replied Steve Mason. "I'll show you a doll that will make you forget this one before she's stiff enough to bury. Come on. Take her feet." The two men carried the frail young girl to the large bedroom that faced directly on the bay.

THE SMALL RADIO in the room hummed and occasionally gave forth a blast as Steve Mason was busy tying up the girl. He turned and listened:

"Calling Car 16. Calling Car 16! Go to East and Seventh. Drunk lying in the gutter. Go to East and—"

The Senator said: "Why do you keep those police calls on?"

"Because of Barton." Steve Mason knocked the girl's head hard back in the chair as he adjusted her unconscious body. "Suppose a general order has gone out for Mr. Strang's arrest? It's a hundred to one that he won't be discovered in our car, but I'm a guy who never takes chances."

"You needn't worry about Barton. I talked him out of any such order for a day or two. But these killings that are to happen tonight. I wish we knew more about—"

"Mr. Strang will be dead and won't give any orders."

"I don't think his orders are necessary, Stephen. About Sheila—"

"What about her?" Steve looked up from strapping her ankles. "She's been trying to play you for a sucker. Taking orders from Billings. Hell, you got a lucky break!"

"I suppose so," the Senator mused. "But if Billings suspected, has any proof why—!"

Steve slammed in: "Billings was shot to death last night. You know Chris did the job. You're safe all around. I was telephoned that things went through like clockwork. Mr. Strang got into the car, the boys went through him again, took a look-see that nothing was in the package but the book, then drove off. None of my boys were even seen with him. Only Johnny Waring handled that, and he couldn't prove I sent him if he wanted to."

The Senator nodded, wiped his eyes, blew his nose, said: "I'm sorry about Sheila, Stephen—terribly sorry." And as he looked at the reviving girl, "Who—well, I was just wondering, Stephen, who this girl was you had in mind. I've done a lot for you, Stephen."

"Okay," Steve nodded. "Name your woman. I'll make good."

"Stephen." The Senator straightened. "You have a peculiar sense of the unfitness of things. Lydia Kemp is very attractive."

Steve Mason stood up, put both his hands on his hips, laughed, said: "No lying, Senator, you were born for trouble with women." Steve was really amused. "Big Pete Murphy's girl. You want to start guns popping all over town and—and by thunder, you'll have her! But this one—" He smacked a hand against Sheila's face, "—is mine!"

"She betrayed my trust in her. I wash my hands of her." The Senator took on a hurt air. "It's Lydia, understand?"

"Sure, sure, but remember, I'm going to cut this dame to pieces before Mr. Strang's eyes. You—" And Steve Mason stopped talking. The Senator had parted the curtains slightly and looking out over the railing of the balcony, pretended that he did not hear.

Steve Mason shook his head, bit his lips. The Senator had even fooled him. Outside he was as smooth as glass, but inside—Steve shuddered slightly—the Senator must have swallowed some of that glass and ground it up in his stomach.

"Now—look." Steve began to fix things in the room. "Joe and Haley will prod Mr. Strang up the stairs—two of my best boys, and thanks to Mr. Strang, my best boys have been dying off fast. They'll tie him over there. That will put the girl under the lamp. They say you can't break him, that he don't feel pain. I'm going to break him, Senator, and the sooner he breaks, the better it will be for the girl. I'm going to break him if— Listen!"

The radio again:

"Car 43. Car 39. Go to Beach Road and Washington Street. Left turn over the bridge. Two men dead on street. Look like ride victims. One identified as Joe Parelo, gangster. Other with face blown clean away. Cars 43 and 39. Ambulance on way. Disperse crowd."

"Say!" cried Steve. "It's Mr. Strang! He put up a fight! Somehow Joe got killed and—Strang had his head blown off. That would be Haley who killed him. Joe was driving. Nothing about the car—and did Haley get that damned book?"

The radio: "Cars 43 and 39...."

The Senator, red of face, Steve Mason, tight-lipped and face drawn had to listen to the same message again.

Then came further information: "Black sedan, believed death car, turned left toward Washington Beach making terrific speed."

Steve Mason looked at the Senator. The Senator looked back. There was more confusion in his eyes than fear. He didn't understand; didn't know what to do.

Mason said and his voice didn't shake: "Haley's a fool. They'll search every house here. Lucky our car is grey— light grey. We got to get going, Senator—just a bullet in the girl's head. She gets a break."

Mason turned, pushed a gun close against the girl's head. Her eyes opened—clear—crystal clear. They looked straight past that gun and into the eyes of the Senator. He turned his head, leaned back against the window sill and said to Steve Mason:

"That's right, Steve. She gets a break. If we get far enough away, things will be all right. I'm pretty well known and a cop or so will easily forget seeing me. I get around privately a bit, you know."

And as Steve grinned at him: "All right, Stephen."

The Senator bowed his head slightly. Mason's lips curled, and his finger tightened upon the trigger.

36

THE TURN IN THE ROAD

MR. STRANG SAT straight and stiff in the front seat of the speeding black sedan. He knew the man beside him was Joe Parelo, and he knew the man in the seat behind him was Fred Haley. His lips split and parted to a thin line of white teeth. He could not, he thought, have chosen two more vicious murderers. But neither one of them was in his book. They worked close to Mason and only for Mason, and their protection had always been good.

The windows were not covered nor was Strang tied and put upon the floor of the car. Neither was he blindfolded. He knew that ride for what it was meant to be. Mr. Strang was not going to tell where he had been—for he was not coming back.

Twice, a motorcycle policeman passed them when they were well along on the road toward the bridge. Each time the cop passed, Haley in the back seat spoke to Mr. Strang.

"If them cops stop us, take that awful puss off. They're looking for you, brother, and we don't want to turn the heat on the cops."

"Steve wants to see me that bad, eh?" Mr. Strang questioned.

"We all liked Rudolph." Haley, in the back seat held a

gun in his right hand and a small knife in his left as he did the talking. "Steve missed him. It's going to be rough on you. Steve will carve you up—like that."

Mr. Strang jerked forward, straightened again. There was a sharp pain in the back of his head; he felt something warm running down his neck, heard the laugh behind him.

"Knife—see?" Haley said as he thrust it forward and wiped the back of it across Mr. Strang's face. Blood showed. Mr. Strang saw it clearly in the mirror above the dash.

"Cut it out!" Joe, the driver, spoke for the first time.

"Wise crack, eh?" Haley laughed as he scraped the knife down the raw surface of Strang's neck. "He don't like it," Haley went on. "Better slow down as you cross the bridge, Joe."

Joe's answer was gruff. "Better sit back and keep quiet. A guy with blood running down his neck won't look so good."

Haley sat back and talked as they slowed down on the mile bridge. His conversation was not pleasant, but Mr. Strang looked neither to right nor left. His hands were by his sides, but the right moved swiftly back, seemed to sink into the crack of the seat behind him as if he stiffened himself against pain.

Pain? Well, yes, but not the pain that Haley caused him. Another—a new kind of pain. He wondered if Johnny Waring had made good—had wanted to make good. His study of the criminal told Mr. Strang that Johnny Waring would think only of one person when the showdown came. And that person would be Johnny Waring himself. This was the showdown.

Even if Johnny Waring had made good, Strang had no idea as yet where the car was taking him. It might drive directly into a garage full of gunmen, but the crossing of the bridge gave him hope that it wouldn't.

Once Strang jarred forward and the blood curled around his neck. The knife had gone deeper. Haley said in answer to Joe's complaint as they reached the end of the bridge:

"I'm in charge of this party, boy. You're only the driver and ain't expected to have any fun. Turn left here, you fool. The house is at the end of Washington Beach. The two-story one by the trees. You know where—"

"Keep your mouth closed," Joe returned almost viciously.

"Hell," laughed Haley. "It's no secret from Mr. Strang. There's a lovely room with twin beds in it overlooking the water. After that—the morgue. Who's to take care of the bodies? What's the matter? The great Mr. Strang done a faint at the sight of blood?"

Something was the matter. Mr. Strang had dropped down in the front seat; his head toward Joe Parelo. He had spoken too, and his words were too low for Haley to understand.

Mr. Strang had whispered: "There's a gun in your side, Joe—a forty-five. Not a word to Haley, and don't stop the car."

Joe Parelo started to say something about not "kidding him." Then he looked down, shot a hand to his coat pocket and stepped hard on the brakes. The car swerved and skidded. The tires shrieked. It sounded to Haley in the back like the sudden explosion of twin bullets.

The car was still in motion when Haley, a gun in his right hand, leaned over the front seat.

For one single moment Haley looked into the burning eyes of the twisted malignant face of Mr. Strang. In that moment, he knew that Joe was dead, and in that one moment, as he brought his gun down and started to close a finger upon the trigger, he saw something else. He was also looking into the barrel of a long black-nosed gun. Looking into it—why it was hard against his face!

Fred Haley cried out in terror as he drove down the muzzle of his gun.

Just that one single cry. Then Mr. Strang's finger closed once upon the trigger of a forty-five. Just once. There was no need to fire again. The face that had been Haley's had disappeared; disappeared forever, and the body had crashed back against one of the rear doors. Either the door was loose or Fred Haley's dead fingers gripped the handle. Anyway Fred Haley rolled out onto the street.

Mr. Strang acted quickly after that. He closed the back door, leaned over Joe Parelo and opened the front one. A moment later another body crashed to the pavement and Mr. Strang was behind the wheel of a car that was speeding madly down the road to Washington Beach, and the two-story house at the end of it.

Yes, Johnny Waring had thought only of Johnny Waring and had planted Mr. Strang's own gun back of that front seat. Fred Haley, by his directions as to just where they were going, had given Mr. Strang the cue to use it.

Mr. Strang held the wheel tightly, occasionally rubbing a hand at the back of his bleeding neck. Unconsciously he ran that hand across his face. He wasn't thinking of blood then nor the deep cuts on his neck. Nor was he thinking of the two dead men in the road—one without a face. He was not thinking of death. He was thinking of life—the life of Sheila Barton.

37

VOICES FROM BELOW

BACK IN THAT room of the pretentious two-story bunga-low at the far end of Washington Beach, the picture had not changed. The girl still sat bound in the chair. The Senator, his head turning to and from the muzzle of the gun Steve Mason held against her head, stood leaning against the window sill. Through that window could be seen the shimmering waters of the bay. Could be seen, but weren't, because before that locked window the shade was tightly drawn.

Steve Mason hesitated, his gun still pressed against the girl's head. He liked the look of fear in Sheila Barton's eyes and was surprised at the apparent indifference shown by the Senator. Apparent indifference—well, perhaps real indifference. For when the big moment came, the Senator was like other criminals—other murderers. He knew that upon the girl's death stood his whole career; his position in private life. Most of all, his position in public life. Money, power, the greatest honor a state could give, the guberna-torial nomination—which amounted to the same thing as the governorship itself.

He was impatient with Steve now, scraped his foot, said: "Well, Stephen—well!"

Steve Mason jarred out of it. He had been thinking of Mr. Strang, of the personal vengeance he had planned, of tossing that mutilated girl's dead body into the arms of Mr. Strang. But Mr. Strang was dead now, and Haley, the fool, was coming straight toward that cottage. Would be there in a minute if—if—

"Here goes, Senator," he said and shoved his gun straight into Sheila Barton's ear. But like many of his kind he had to get his joke in, show how little a murder meant to him. It would be a good thing for the Senator to remember too if they crossed later.

The radio still hummed dully; Steve Mason said: "When you hear the sound of the gun, Senator, it will be exactly eternity for—"

The words died on his lips. His finger almost mechanically closed upon that trigger. Almost, but not quite. Things happened quickly. There was a terrific crash in that room. The breaking of glass, the shattering of wood as the French windows were torn from their hinges.

Sheila Barton screamed. The Senator half stepped, half fell forward. Steve Mason swung his gun; swung his gun directly toward the Senator. The Senator regained his balance and staggered back; staggered back against a tall bent figure, a figure whose face was covered with blood— blood and hate.

Mason cried out as he saw that face. He cried out first in warning for the Senator to step aside, then in fear, and at last in terror. His voice was high pitched as he raised his gun in a trembling hand.

"On your knees, Senator," he cried then, "It's him—he's alive. It's Mr. Strang!"

Mr. Strang didn't stop to think, to question the peculiar set-up and his sudden discovery that Senator Bixby was the man who backed Steve Mason. He simply saw the back of the Senator's head, the ample protection those broad shoulders gave him, and hope—yes, almost worship in Sheila Barton's eyes.

In the eyes of Steve Mason—the fearful Steve Mason—he read just one thing—terror—abject terror. Mr. Strang showed no gun when he spoke. He said simply:

"You're a rat, eh, Steve? Well, all the rats—your rats are taking the dose tonight. My men won't fail me. I won't fail them." And with a shake of his head, "It's to be my first murder—at least my first shooting of a man in cold blood. Somehow, Steve, I don't think I'm going to mind it, I—"

Steve Mason screamed once, jerked up his gun and fired. The man he had to kill was behind the Senator, behind his friend. But that didn't matter then. It was the Senator's life or Steve's. No thought necessary there. Steve Mason simply shot the Senator through the head.

Steve saw the hole in his forehead before the Senator pitched forward on his face. The Senator was no longer between Steve and Mr. Strang.

They stood facing each other—man to man as Steve might have thought, if he thought at all. But man to rat would have been the way to put it. An infuriated rat now—a rat that was cornered and was going to die unless—unless—

Sheila saw Strang slowly stretch his right hand across his chest and slip it just as slowly beneath his left armpit. She cried out a warning as Steve Mason jumped toward her as he fired at Mr. Strang. She saw Strang go back, clutch at the window sill and pull himself erect.

Mr. Strang laughed. Laughed as Steve Mason started to sink behind Sheila's chair. Mr. Strang laughed and fired, and Steve Mason cried out in pain, staggered into the open of the room, steadied himself on his feet, cursed viciously and flashed up his gun.

For a minute, far less than a minute, hardly more than a few seconds, Sheila sat there in silence. She tried desperately to close her eyes, but couldn't. She tried desperately to speak, but couldn't. She was looking into the eyes of Mr. Strang, listening to the words of Mr. Strang—a different, more terrible Mr. Strang than she had ever heard. It was about her Strang talked as he fired. "Cut her to pieces, eh, Steve, and send me parts of her body?"

AS MR. STRANG mumbled on he fired slowly, carefully, deliberately, throwing Steve Mason off balance with each shot, twisting his body that was turned to face him—gun lifted to kill him.

Finally Sheila did cry out:

"Strang—Strang! Don't! Don't!" The final roar came. Mercifully Sheila Barton's brain sent a swift message to the muscles of her eyelids. Her eyes closed; closed for a single moment; a single moment while she heard the crash. When she opened them again, Steve Mason was no longer staggering about the room. He was not crouched ready to jerk his gun. He was lying there on his back beside a bed, his arms stretched far out on either side of him.

"Strang—oh, Strang!" Sheila was sobbing while he tore the ropes from her. "You're not—it's not—? It's over now!"

"It's over," said Mr. Strang. "They are both dead."

"I don't mean about them." The girl came to her feet. "I mean about you. The Frankenstein monster you said that I created. It was true then—true for those few seconds. True until—"

"Until you called to me." He nodded. "I don't understand it, Sheila. It's a terrible hate, a terrible lust—a lust to kill-just as the criminals have the lust to kill. It—it's hard to believe. I mean about the Senator."

And she told him. About the Senator—about Billings. "He was a very bright man—a brilliant man, this Kirkman Billings. I tried to help him—for you. Yes, he knew of you, who you were. Any time he wished he could have had you arrested—in those days when you were sick. But he didn't. It was the book. He knew about that book. I told him that someday the law could use that book. He could use that book. He suspected the Senator. He let desperate criminals go free because they led him to Mason, and Mason led him to the Senator."

"You knew—about the Senator?" Strang gasped.

"No. Mr. Billings told me lately that I must be ready for a great shock, and a great shock to my father. I thought it was you. I feared it was about you." She was clinging to him now. He stood there straight and stiff. It was as if she clung to a pole. "I telephoned Mr. Billings when you went to visit him last night. I was afraid harm might come to you—or to him through you. I told him to simply mention my name, have you call me if he could not handle you."

"So that was it!" Strang stroked his chin.

"And now—now Kirkman Billings is dead. A man called Chris—"

Strang laughed and the girl looked at him. The laugh

was different. It was real—not that scraping of finger-nails along a wall. Strang said: "Mr. Billings is still alive. Chris met with an accident; a fatal accident."

"Strang, you—!" she started and stopped, again looked at his face. No hate; no madness, and there was something different in his eyes. They were still brilliant, but it was not hot lead. She drew his head down, pushed her soft hair against his face. Yes, he was different—so different. There was a smile on his face and his arms went up and rested on her shoulders.

"I've conquered for the time being, Sheila. Maybe now your father will take me and the book."

"The Living Dead—they walk tonight. You'll stop them?"

He drew his arms from her shoulders, the mask came over his face. Muscles did not move. Just his lips moved as if controlled by a ventriloquist's wires. He said:

"For the moment I wanted to live again—a free man. But now—even if I wished, I could not stop them. It must go through."

"But you might wish if you thought that Father would—Why, Strang, you've been hurt!" She took her handkerchief, tore open his coat, dabbed at the blood upon his shirt. "You're white, deathly white. You've—you've been shot."

"A scratch—a scratch, nothing more," Strang told her. "I don't think it was that I underrated Steve Mason. I would hate to believe that. I like to think that he simply had luck."

"Strang," she said again. "This Living Dead—walking tonight. If you gave them orders not to walk, then they'd obey, wouldn't they?"

"I have no way of giving them orders."

"But you must—you *must!* Not for society—not for me, but for them—these men—these helpless men. A trap has been set for them. I heard Mason discussing it with the Senator when they thought I was unconscious. You can tell Father where these deaths are to take place and he—"

She stopped talking, dropped her hands. Her feet stuck to the floor. Mr. Strang moved across the room. The front door had closed below. The girl said: "It was the radio—police calls—a car coming this way. Mason thought—"

Strang raised his fingers to his lips, softly opened the door, then taking the girl's hand led her out into the hall, close to the head of the stairs.

A voice came plainly from below. It said: "This is the house all right. Didn't I spend all day finding that man of mine who had traced the Senator here before when he held little parties? Now—I thought I heard something above. Man, you're not going up there alone!"

A second voice spoke as feet hit the bottom step.

"I'm going up alone. You shouldn't have let my daughter trust Senator Bixby suspecting—actually knowing what you did. What if you did think I wouldn't believe it. I'm going to kill—just as Mr. Strang kills if—"

Strang was too late to stop the girl. She had passed him, reached the head of the stairs. She was talking as she stumbled down those steps into the speaker's arms.

"Father—Father!" was all that she said as she clung to him.

38

FRONT PAGE

MR. STRANG STILL held his gun in his hand as Kirkman Billings and Commissioner James Barton looked down at the two bodies. The Commissioner knelt by the side of the Senator, stretched a hand toward him.

"Don't touch him," said Mr. Strang. "I must talk to you below."

Kirkman Billings paced that living-room below and talked to Barton.

"We never hit it off, Barton. My way was not your way. I may have sacrificed a few for the sake of the many. But I had trusted men about the city. My secretary was actually in the employ of Steve Mason. Sheila watched, perhaps unknowingly to you— Oh, yes, Commissioner, there was a time when I even suspected you.

"Now, I think Mr. Strang is right about this evening. It is growing dark and the police have not found this house. I think we should let them find the two bodies so that both you and I may be surprised at their discovery. I think it is a good idea to whitewash the Senator. To leave the impression that he was killed defending a cause—the evil of parole. Oh, it will stand up. My life was attempted only last night. Come, come, Barton. We can't be following regulations all the time. I am not thinking of the Senator's wife and family—though one might very easily think of them. I am thinking of parole, and the scandal it will create, the investigation the truth will cause. All that I have built up will fall down. Besides, there's your daughter. We can't go halfway in the matter." And when Barton looked at him, "At least I won't."

"The scum!" Barton was thinking of the Senator. "And to give him a decent burial—an honored one."

"They give that burial to noted gangsters," Billings said with some irony. "Surely the Senator is entitled to that." And when Barton spread his hands far apart, Billings continued, "And if I may make a suggestion of my own. I think that you and I and Mr. Strang and his little book should all work together. You agree—and I'm sure Mr. Strang—"

Billings stopped, turned toward the window where Mr. Strang had stood. He didn't see Strang at first, and then he did as Sheila rushed across the room. Mr. Strang was lying on the floor below that window.

Sheila was no longer a frightened girl. She sent the men to the kitchen for water, tore Strang's shirt open, found the wound, stopped the heavy flow of blood.

"We'll have a lot to explain if we're seen with him," Barton said as they lifted the limp body of Mr. Strang from the floor and carried it toward the door. Where's Sheila?"

Sheila was there. She was coming down the stairs from the floor above. Both men looked the question.

She answered it.

"I wanted a towel—a big one in the bathroom." And

when they looked at her empty hands Sheila added, "There was none there."

After that no one spoke until they were in the car, the still unconscious Mr. Strang held between Mr. Billings and Sheila. Then Barton said from behind the wheel:

"About the book. He didn't have it on him, I suppose?"

"You suppose?" There was no doubt of the question in Sheila's voice.

"I—well, I didn't feel it." Barton did not exactly admit that he had searched the man, and he believed Sheila when she said:

"He hasn't got it with him." Sheila did not exactly lie as she pressed the book close against her warm little body beneath her dress.

Twice they met patrol cars, and twice the men saluted the Commissioner and passed on without a glance in the back of that car. Once Sheila had her father stop the car at a drugstore.

Kirkman Billings said when she returned: "You have nothing to fear, Sheila—nothing at all for his life. He'll come around all right without those drugs."

Sheila only answered: "I wasn't thinking of him. I was thinking for him, wondering what thought he'll have if he comes to and finds that men—his men—dying men— are to be mowed down by the gangsters he intended they should kill."

BARTON SAID TO the doctor for the tenth time: "I don't care about his later condition. I want to know if you can't jazz him up—just a minute so that he can talk."

"If I could," The doctor looked down at Mr. Strang, so

still and white upon the bed, "it would have a bad effect on him. Give him an hour more—perhaps two."

Barton turned to Billings.

"If he could talk only for a minute, could tell us where these men are to be. I could put a hundred police on the block—five hundred, for that matter. But there he lies and he can't talk and he knows and—" He grabbed the doctor's arm again. "You've got to, Doc. Damn it, it's nearly time now! You've got to jazz him up if it's only for a minute."

"Impossible," said the doctor. "The bullet wound outside of the loss of blood amounts to nothing. It's the shock. Yes, yes, I don't care what sort of man he is. I've seen heavy weight champions of the world suffering from shock. He'll wake up himself and be—" The doctor picked up his bag. "I'm not a police surgeon you know, Jim, and I don't have to murder patients so they can tell you where they hid a stolen watch."

"A watch!" gasped the Commissioner. "His talking means saving of nearly a hundred lives."

"It wouldn't matter if it were a million," Doctor Simons said indifferently. "But I'll wait around a few hours if you wish. Then perhaps I can do something."

Sheila Barton sat beside that bed and said nothing.

It was two hours later when the doctor said to Commissioner Barton as they stood by the bedside: "He's coming around now—and quite all right too. There, you can talk to him. He'll understand."

"It's too late," said the Commissioner as the telephone rang in the hall. "The massacre has already taken place. No, Sheila—I'll answer it."

At that moment a servant ran up the rear stairs and handed a folded newspaper to Sheila Barton.

Barton simply glanced back, but both the doctor and Kirkman Billings, yes, and Mr. Strang, too, turned their heads and looked at the girl.

They were all silent, for they felt that she prayed. It was Strang who spoke first.

"Sheila!" he cried. "The time—the time?" His dull eyes wandered about the room, saw the clock upon the mantel. His voice raised. The doctor tried to push him back on the pillows. Mr. Strang cried out, "It's too late—five minutes too late and—!"

"No, no." Sheila came to her feet, had hard work steadying herself. "Strang, Strang! They got it. The message! Got it as they got it once before from you." She thrust the paper before his face. "Look, in blazing letters!"

The message across the top read:

THE LEGION OF THE LIVING DEAD WILL NOT
WALK TONIGHT!

And after Strang's gasp of surprise, Sheila asked: "They'll understand that, won't they? It will reach them, won't it? The paper's been on the street an hour almost."

"Yes," said Strang. "It will reach them, if the paper has been on the street."

"We'll hear now," said Kirkman Billings, "just what message Barton received."

Commissioner James Barton stormed into the room.

"The bodies of the Senator and Mason have been found. By that damned newspaperman, Halerhan. And there was a card on Mason's chest, a card that read— It's there in the paper! Just like that fool Halerhan told me to read it." And suddenly, "But there was no card on the body of Mason."

Kirkman Billings looked shrewdly at Sheila Barton, but he spoke to the Commissioner. "Was there any other message?"

"No, no." Barton had his face screwed up in a little knot. "Some kidding that Halerhan wouldn't ride the department, and that he sent his love to Sheila, and she could have her picture over the whole front page the day she married—or some such damn fool thing. Now I wonder who got in the house and—"

Kirkman Billings smiled. "I think the message upon Mason's chest may have had something to do with Sheila's unfortunate search in the bathroom above for a towel."

"I'll be—" Barton stopped and then, "There will be no— no killings in the city tonight?"

"No," said Mr. Strang in such a powerful voice that Doctor Simons jerked back. "The Legion of the Living Dead will not walk tonight."

The doctor picked up his bag. There was a smile in his eyes when he said: "If this patient dies, why call in the city medical examiner and see if you can get him to swear that the death was from natural causes? But really, he should be alone with— Well, he'll do nicely with just Miss Barton to watch him."

MR. STRANG WAS alone with Sheila for nearly an hour before he spoke. Then he said: "No telephone call. The Legion of the Living Dead did not walk tonight. You remembered, then my telling you how I first brought my men back to me. That first headline in the papers."

"Yes." She nodded. "I remembered. I had to give my name to Halerhan to make sure the story would go in—as I wished.

"He kept his word about headlining the wording on the card I wrote and left there."

"His word?" sniffed Strang. "Why it was a big scoop!" He was silent again so long that Sheila would have thought he slept except that his eyes stared so steadily upward. "Sheila!" he said at length.

"Yes, Strang?"

"What was it this Halerhan said about putting your picture all over the front page?"

Sheila didn't hesitate. "He said I could have my picture all over the front page the day I was married."

Strang sighed. His eyes closed. His fingers tightened on the girl's hand. He murmured:

"Yes, Sheila. That's what I thought he said."